Tom Benjamin grew up in the suburbs of north London and began his working life as a journalist before becoming a spokesman for Scotland Yard. He later moved into public health, where he developed Britain's first national campaign against alcohol abuse, and led drugs-awareness programme FRANK. He now lives in Bologna.

Find Tom on Instagram, Twitter and Facebook @tombenjaminsays

Also by Tom Benjamin

A Quiet Death in Italy
The Hunting Season
Requiem in La Rossa
Italian Rules
Last Testament in Bologna

The Bologna Vendetta

Tom Benjamin

CONSTABLE

First published in Great Britain in 2024 by Constable

Chapter opening images from iStock

Quote from *The Red Tenda of Bologna* by John Berger, Penguin Classics; 1st edition (2018)
'Bologna' by Nicola Muschitiello taken from *Lo Strazio* (Poesie 1980–1986), Calamaro Edizioni, Bologna (2024)

1 3 5 7 9 10 8 6 4 2

A CIP catalogue record for this book is available from the British Library.

ISBN: 978-1-40871-552-9

Typeset in Garamond by Initial Typesetting Services, Edinburgh
Printed and bound in Great Britain by Clays Ltd, Elcograf S.p.A.

Papers used by Constable are from well-managed forests and other responsible sources.

Constable
An imprint of
Little, Brown Book Group
Carmelite House
50 Victoria Embankment
London EC4Y 0DZ

An Hachette UK Company
www.hachette.co.uk

www.littlebrown.co.uk

To Shirley Lodge, and those summer outings
in her Morris Minor. Onwards!
To spiky grass and rain-swept seafronts,
Roman ruins, fish and chips.

The Bologna Vendetta

'My brother masons swear by blood that they are ready to sacrifice everything for their neighbour, but they do not give a rouble each to the collection for the poor . . .'

War and Peace, Leo Tolstoy

'It's an improbable city, Bologna – like one you might walk through after you have died'

The Red Tenda of Bologna, John Berger

I

It was the evening before the end, and our usual Sunday night at the Circolo San Mamolo, a social centre just outside the walls.

During the day, you would find the old people of the quarter playing Scopa or Briscola or sharing newspapers and complaining about the ruling Partito Democratico, which everyone agreed was a pale reflection of the communists who used to run Bologna. There was a bar, and a kitchen that served the local staples like *tagliatelle al ragù* and *tortelloni*, plus, on nights like this in the depths of winter, *tortellini in brodo.*

Many evenings the dance floor would fill to *liscio Romagnolo*, a local mash-up of polka and the waltz, which certainly kept the old folk in shape, along with line dancing. Reflected in the snow-darkened windows, the pensioners turned with the precision of starlings at the appropriate beat, performing impressive hand and footwork to contemporary Italian pop, although anyone familiar with the San Remo-infused genre would appreciate there was very little contemporaneous about the music to trouble them.

And at weekends, the families of members were welcome to join their *nonni* and take advantage of the cheap food and excellent Sangiovese or Pignoletto served in litre jugs.

'What's up?' my wife asked in English.

'I'm just distracted.' We watched our daughter on the dance floor with her grandfather, the old boy nimbly walking our ten-year-old through the dance steps.

Lucia gave me a sympathetic look. 'Our eccentric Signor Lambertini?'

'It's got its hooks in me,' I admitted.

'It was certainly an adventure.' Her dark eyebrows arched. 'But, hell, that's Italy. What's that expression of yours? Out of the saucepan . . . ?'

'The frying pan.'

'Into the fire.'

'What have you gotten me into?' I asked.

She prodded me teasingly: 'As usual, *amore*, you got yourself into it. Even in Italy, you can't seem to keep out of trouble.'

The song had finished and they were returning to the table, Rose brimming with excitement, while Giovanni Faidate, or 'the Comandante' as everyone, including his family, called him, chuckled along. I bet the old boy couldn't believe his luck – he had been facing a widower's life banging about the Residence, as his old *palazzo*-cum-stronghold down the road was called. Now here was his daughter, his granddaughter, oh, and that awkward English husband in tow.

'Come on.' Lucia grabbed my hand.

'I've told you . . .'

'You have to learn!'

She dragged me to the dance floor where we joined the back row. In front of us were multiple generations who knew all the moves. Lucia imitated them with aplomb, me, more like a plum. Let's just say I was glad when it was over.

My wife assessed me, hands on hips: 'Hopeless!'

'I tried to tell you.'

She pulled me close, gave me an interrogatory look. 'You know, we always *can* go back.'

I appreciated the sentiment, but neither of us could have thought it would be that simple.

'Actually,' I said. 'I'm beginning to think it was what I needed all along.'

'You're saying you're really okay in this damn country?'

I nodded. She glanced over my shoulder at Giovanni and Rose, then kissed me fiercely. 'I'm so happy,' she whispered.

I hope you were, Lucia. I truly hope you were.

II

The heat-scoured expanse of Piazza Verdi. It is mid-morning and the air has already swollen to stifle sound itself. Only the cicadas performing their castanet symphony from nearby Giardino del Guasto cut through, and soon even they will be silenced. It beats down from above, it radiates from the old stone *palazzi*, exuding the rusty whiff of the medieval kiln. The florid perfumes of June and July have burnt off. It is August in Bologna and we remaining locals usually emerge only at dusk, like vampires.

Hence, I keep to the shade. I had actually been surprised to discover Freud's bar open, but I suppose like everywhere else it is seeking to exploit the burgeoning tourist trade, although the only other people sat outside – a German couple, blinking nervously – have plainly understood that this time of year Bologna is more like a trap and are consulting their guide-book as if discussing routes of escape.

I know how they feel – with the exception of my partner, Dolores, the rest of Faidate Investigations has already fled: the Comandante and his niece Alba and her daughter to the beach house in Cesenatico. His son Jacopo and fiancée Celeste south to her home in Naples, and thence, apparently, Capri. Eighteen-year-old Rose, who is not strictly-speaking an employee but certainly a beneficiary of the company's largesse, to her boyfriend's family's place in the Dolomites. So it is just me and Dolores holding the fort, and she's due off soon – to London, of all places. 'Home of Punk!' she exclaimed. 'You'll be lucky,' I replied.

But misery doesn't go on vacation, and that is our business.

The opera house is closed for the season, yet a woman emerges from the side *biglietteria* door. Even from across the square, it is plain she is a lady of quality. While I am in my regulation polo shirt and chinos, which are already beginning to cling, and the Germans in short shorts and baggy T-shirts, the stout, late-middle-aged woman is wearing a colourful Dolce & Gabbana dress and smart white shoes. An expensively curated silver-blonde bob floats above her pale, not unattractive oval face, while a cream handbag hangs from a gold chain over her shoulder. I'm surprised she's on foot – she's not the sort of person one ordinarily sees anywhere outside frescoed receptions and gallery openings. There should have been a black limo sat outside, a suited driver ready to jump out and open the door. Instead, she puts on a pair of Jackie-O sunglasses, and heads directly towards me.

I am not overly concerned. Signora Bonelli can't have any idea I'm on her case, although I do wonder as she approaches whether she is about to ask me directions – the only other half-respectable-looking person in the *piazza*. Instead, she passes by and, to the evident surprise of a pair of drug dealers stationed on the corner, heads purposefully up Via Petroni.

The pushers brazenly size me up as I go after her, clearly presuming I am some kind of bodyguard instructed to keep a distance. They give me a wary nod as if to indicate that they're in on it, which I guess in a way they now are. I wonder – is this signora Nancy Bonelli's dirty secret? She's a drug fiend?

I had been given the assignment the previous week by a similarly-outfitted lady at one of our regular lunches, although this time the Contessa di Castiglione had suggested we meet at Lemongrass, an upmarket Thai restaurant which was currently all the rage, but certainly not one of our usuals – Ginevra habitually loathed anything rage-worthy and, despite being rake thin, always ordered the local, a meat-heavy pasta *primo*, a *secondo*, and more often than not, a *dolce*. 'My secret,' she liked to say, 'is only eating out.' Our relationship, although officially professional, was mostly social. She had had our company on a retainer more or less since its foundation, and we had looked into a thing or two for her – the background of her daughters' fiancés (now spouses), sniffing out a couple of paintings that had 'wandered out' of her Venice residence (without involving the police), and setting up a state-of-the-art security system at her country villa – but, as she liked to point out, the relationship between the Castiglione and Faidate went back centuries, and she had taken a particular interest in my well-being when I had lost my wife, as she had lost her husband, young (he had a weak heart) and only the widowed truly understood the burden of *dolore d'amore* or 'love-grief' (which may or may not have been true).

'Chopsticks,' she said sourly.

'What did you expect?'

'I know how to use them, of course.' She expertly raised them between her long, manicured fingers. 'But it's the rice that's so . . . inelegant.' She set them down and looked around. 'Well, this is different.'

'It is. I didn't realise you liked Thai.' She laughed with straight, capped white teeth. She was in her mid-sixties but, like the lady I would later be following, had avoided over-exposure to the sun and obvious plastic surgery to age as gracefully as top-class beauty treatment and solid genes would permit.

'Didn't someone say that one should try everything once? How silly. There are plenty of things I wouldn't ever want to try. Honestly, I think curiosity is over-rated.'

'You're not alone – many Italians feel the same.'

'But I *was* curious about this place. Virginia kept going on about it.'

'Your daughter has no end of enthusiasms.'

'Is she still banging her yoga teacher?'

'I couldn't say she's not. You only asked us to confirm that she was.'

'As long as she doesn't give too much money away. Do you know how much setting him up in that studio cost?'

'Several hundred thousand, I would imagine. But I believe she hung on to the lease?'

'I should certainly hope so – my daughter may like her exercise, but I wouldn't want to think I had raised a fool.'

The waiter came to take our orders. I had a chicken curry and salad. The Contessa, who hadn't examined her menu, had 'what he's having'.

'Were you genuinely interested in this restaurant, Ginevra, or did you choose it because you wanted to meet somewhere out of the way?'

'What do you think?'

'That you don't like spilling rice.'

'You mean, I prefer to "speel the bins"?' She said the last part in English.

'Very good. Is there an equivalent in Italian?'

'Many. So,' she lowered her voice, 'there's a certain signora in whom I have taken an interest.' She picked up her phone, pursing her lips as she scrolled. She apparently found what she was looking for and mine buzzed. She had sent me a WhatsApp containing a photograph.

'Problem?'

'I'm having trouble opening the photo.'

'Probably my fault, my phone's, I mean. My daughter was telling me my settings were too high or something, too many pixies, apparently.'

I laughed. 'Pixels. Damn pixies, they get into everything. Oh, here we go.' A photo appeared of Nancy Bonelli stood in a group in a frescoed ballroom.

'From an IWF trip,' said the Contessa. 'That's the International Women's Forum. I took a photo of the photo, if you know what I mean.'

'And what do you want to know?'

She frowned. 'It's sensitive.'

'Naturally.'

'Well, it's actually on behalf of a friend. I mean, she doesn't know we're meeting, but, in short, she believes this woman is having an affair with her husband, and I would like you to monitor her.'

'And who's the husband?'

'You know I trust you, Daniel,' she rested a hand on mine, 'but I would prefer not to say.'

'I only ask,' I said, 'because in these situations, it is usually the man that takes the initiative, books the hotel and so on.'

'Be that as it may,' she smiled sadly, 'I would prefer we did it this way.'

'Very well.' Had the Contessa not been widowed, I would have presumed the gentleman in question was her spouse. Instead, I wondered if he was her lover.

She arranged her chopsticks in a pyramid to face me. 'I would like a report on her activities.'

'You will have one.'

The waiter reappeared with some pickles. The Contessa scooped up her sticks. 'I'm not really sure what I'm still doing here, I'm usually in the mountains.' She plucked up a pickle and popped it in her mouth. 'They're hot!' The Contessa clacked her sticks at me. 'Try one.'

Signora Nancy Bonelli continued along the low-beamed portico of Via Petroni past its kebab stores and grocers, the only establishments not shuttered.

Bologna becomes a city of dark-skinned migrants and pale-skinned tourists this time of year and we weave between them, both exceptions in our own ways. But signora Bonelli doesn't enter through one of those graffiti-riddled, syrup-brown doors, or dip down a dingy corridor. She continues on to the corner of Via San Vitale, where the height of the portico rises along with the calibre of establishment.

She lingers beneath a green pharmacy sign, the thermometer reading 39°C, waiting for the lights to change. Across the road, Piazza Aldrovandi opens like a lung among the ribs of porticoes. Through the polarised lenses of my sunglasses the sky broods opal.

I hang back, pretending to examine the pages of the communist-supporting *Il Manifesto* on a noticeboard while, despite the absence of traffic, the signora continues to wait. Bourgeois Bolognese are as punctilious as Germans, even in this heat.

She finally crosses San Vitale, passing the crowded tables outside a bar before ducking back beneath the portico running south up to Strada Maggiore. The eateries are setting up for lunch, while almost everything else – from the Italian-run grocers and bakers to the posh furniture stores and interior decorators – is closed.

The signora arrives at Maggiore, or 'main street', turning the corner where a pair of massive, weary-looking mountain nymphs support the entrance of Palazzo Bargellini. Opposite, ancient porticoes wrap around the Basilica di Santa Maria dei Servi. Within five minutes, we have gone from the rookeries of Petroni to the *palazzi* of Maggiore. Bologna remains a medieval city to her core.

I follow the signora past the *palazzo* and along the portico running parallel to dei Servi, mostly antiquarian stores and *palazzi* parcelled into offices and apartments. She presses a buzzer and waits for a huge set of oak doors to open. Once she has gone inside, I hurry up to slip through before they close. There is another pair of spiked iron gates beyond, but these are even slower to shut behind the signora, who is already halfway along the road that runs beside a garden square.

She steps into a side entrance and I follow closely behind.

I am at the base of an elegant, curved stairwell in time to hear the signora being greeted by another woman on the floor above. By the time the door closes, I've climbed high enough to see which one.

I step softly on to a landing.

Fresh pink carnations are set in a blue-and-white-painted porcelain vase in the centre of an alcove seat beneath the open window – a decoration, and a disincentive to loiter. On one side, the smart oak door of a lawyer's office. Opposite, outside the apartment signora Bonelli entered, the discreet bronze plaque:

Associazione Studi Culturali Mazzini

Association for Cultural Studies Mazzini. I take a photograph and make my way back down the stairs.

On the surface, a wealthy lady's trip from the opera house to a cultural club would hardly set alarm bells ringing, but Nancy Bonelli's seemingly innocuous destination has given me pause for thought. I will need to talk with the Comandante over the phone this evening.

I walk back up the road, keeping to the shade of the building, and press the brass button marked *Tiro* set in the wall. While the gates and doors open, I put my sunglasses back on.

I leave the *palazzo* and turn down Maggiore, heading for home.

I stop dead.

I remove my sunglasses. Despite the heat, a chill runs through me. Sweat drips down my flanks. I feel my shirt flat against my back and chest.

My heart is beating fast.

I turn, and walk slowly back to the *palazzo*.

Beneath the arch of the portico, opposite the door and chained to a pole beside the road, is a bicycle. It is bottle green with racing handlebars, old-fashioned, as well it should be – it was second-hand when we bought it in London, its distinctive gold Raleigh heron quite a novelty in Bologna.

It is definitely hers – Lucia's. The bike she was riding on the day she died. The bike that only days or weeks – or was it months? – later I, we, one of the family, realised we had never seen again. She had been sent flying as she jumped some lights, according to the reports, and we had presumed it had been taken in evidence, but when we had contacted the police, they had no record of it. It had just disappeared.

Yet here it is, chained to this pole.

I try the chain. It is firmly locked. I look around. The portico is deserted.

I run my fingertips over the saddle, the handlebars. Clasp them as Lucia must have done, as if to absorb some kinetic memory. I let out a noise, which may be a whimper, and squat by the machine. An onlooker might presume there is a problem with the chain or wheel, but I am simply clinging to this relic of her.

Perspiration splashes off me, darkens the pavement like

rain, or blood. But I cannot leave it. I cannot leave her. I will buy the bike – or take it – from whomever has left it here, whatever the price.

It must be over forty degrees by now, but the shade isn't making it easier – the heat collects beneath the portico like poison gas. I can feel it in my pores, the back of my throat. I need to do something.

I can start by sitting down.

I cross the road and lower myself upon the wall that separates the portico of the basilica from the street. The age-pitted marble slab, smoothed by centuries of wear, is comfortable enough.

I still can't quite believe the bike is Lucia's, but there's no doubt about it. It had been mine before we moved to Bologna and hers was stolen soon after. I'd said we should get another, but, as I was walking to work, she said she would use the Raleigh, despite the crossbar. She lowered the seat and her toes just about managed to touch the floor. Now, I note, the seat has been raised. A bloke, then, most likely. That makes it easier – a woman might not want to part with it, whatever I offered, and then what could I do? A guy, if he turned down the money, I'd just grab it from him and to hell with the consequences.

I lean back against the Romanesque column and, after it becomes clear no one is coming straight away, lift my feet up and stretch my legs along the slab.

There was a time when it would have been completely deserted in this part of the city, but these days there's enough money flushing about to maintain a low buzz of traffic, both on foot and behind the wheel. Along the portico, pedestrians plod past, while on the other side, cars and trolley-buses rumble by.

Was the bike already there when I followed the signora in? I was focusing on Nancy, the opening and closing doors. I probably wouldn't have noticed it, although my inner inquisitor is already demanding how that could be possible, to miss something so iconic?

Look – I saw it in the end, didn't I? My unconscious registered the thing even while my conscious was looking forward to getting back to some air-conditioning. And there it now stands, as if it was waiting for me all along, as if it had been waiting for me ever since the accident; roaming these streets in search of its owner like a dog separated from its master.

Speaking of which – there is a cold nose against the back of my hand. I look down, into the all-too-human eyes of my Lagotto Romagnolo, Rufus, his woolly chocolate-brown fur freshly shorn for summer.

'What are you doing here?' I ask him. 'Shouldn't you be at the beach with the Comandante?' He gazes back up at me, panting. I reach out to tickle beneath his muzzle but, curiously, feel nothing. He has disappeared.

A bus trundles past.

I rouse, blinking.

Sit up, refocus on the doorway. But there's something missing.

The bike is missing.

I jump to my feet. Look wildly up and down the road. Nothing. I begin to walk towards the doorway. The blare of a horn. I stumble back and let the SUV pass.

Then I notice movement beneath the portico.

I make it across. A guy is wrapping the chain around the seat post. He looks at me, and I at him. He is, to my eyes, a strange confection – moustachioed with a curly mullet dyed lime green and wearing a tight pink woman's T-shirt, artistically slashed, and short shorts that show off a pert bottom and smooth legs.

'Hey,' I say, coming toward him. 'Excuse me, but—' He jumps on the bike. 'Look, I only want—' He begins to move off along the portico, raised above the saddle to achieve maximum propulsion. 'Hey!' I call. He glances over his shoulder. 'Stop!' He puts more into it.

He's speeding up, he's getting away.

I begin to run.

III

Despite being an immigrant, I initially treated Italy like a tourist, as a sort of theme park of the senses. The food, architecture, countryside, weather. I had certainly never let my lack of Italian bother me before, be it accompanying Lucia on visits from London or ping-ponging between work in the UK and nappies in Italy after she had given birth to Rose at Bologna's Ospedale Maggiore. If I had considered the language at all, I may have presumed I would somehow acquire it by osmosis.

Even when Lucia's supposedly temporary stay to help care for her ailing mother dragged on, the Italian primer remained a permanent fixture at the bottom of my travel bag. It was only when she was offered the job at the housing charity in Bologna and that temporary move became permanent that I began seriously thinking about it, but armed with a modest advance to pen a paperback on London's criminal underworld,

I was not overly concerned about my subsequent failure to acquire more than a handful of phrases. After publishing my bestseller, I told myself, I would surely be contracted to write another 'true crime', so I would only need enough Italian to get by, especially as I would have Lucia or Rose by my side.

Not precisely a tourist, then, but arguably more 'expat' than immigrant.

However, as the advance dwindled and I discovered that writing a hundred-thousand-word book was nowhere near as easy as knocking out a thousand-word article, I began to notice the concessions the English-speaking side of my family had made for me had begun to melt away, and I was passing my days in a linguistic bubble, or babble.

I dug out my old travel bag and there it still was – the depressingly pristine-looking language course.

I managed to master enough basic vocabulary and grammar to navigate most simple tasks, from buying a bus ticket to ordering at a restaurant, but soon came to appreciate that this was far removed from being able to understand, let alone participate in, the ebb and flow of conversation. Like many non-linguists, I had assumed that if a book said 'learn Italian in three months', it meant just that. In reality, for all my memorisation and practice, I remained essentially deaf and dumb.

I enrolled at a language school, and although my grasp of Italian marginally improved (I could chat lucidly with Turkish and German teenagers about the best way to get to the swimming pool) as soon as I stepped on to the street and had to ask a local something, I was stumped.

But if I couldn't grasp Italian, and couldn't finish the book, what *could* I do? I would sit in my 'office' – in fact a space with a desk along the corridor – once they had left for the day, endlessly scrolling the forty-thousand words or so of the book I had completed, my mind, like the following page, a blank.

Then one evening, the Comandante announced they needed someone at a canteen for down-and-outs and he had 'taken the liberty' of putting my name forward. At first, I was vaguely offended – it was far removed from the café lifestyle I'd envisaged, although I suppose it did involve table service – but I could see his point: it would place me in an Italian-speaking environment and, providing I made an effort, I might actually learn something. I could 'absorb' Italian in the mornings and write in the afternoons. It seemed like the perfect compromise.

At least that was what I kept telling myself.

The entrance to the canteen was in the courtyard of a former monastery.

The snow was falling hard that morning, settling upon the iron cover of the ancient well like icing sugar. Porticoes lined the cloister, sheltering the mostly hooded crowd huddled before me, but these weren't holy men.

I scanned the mob, my mood not helped by a hangover. Things hadn't exactly gone to plan, writing-wise, at least. The 'true crime' book I had managed to eventually squeeze out, under word count and overdue, had been rejected by my publisher as 'in no way resembling your outline and utterly failing to meet our expectations. In short, we're really disappointed, Dan.' They had been kind enough to 'invite' me 'to resubmit when/if you feel you have fulfilled the obligations of your advance', which I think may have been a polite way to ask for it back – thank God for British publishers! – but I had yet to do so, as I didn't believe I was ready to fulfil those obligations. In fact, I hadn't yet felt ready to even try. Perhaps, I had decided, fiction would provide the inspiration I required – I had begun three or four crime novels which had kicked-off promisingly enough with a murder, explosion or missing person, but had failed to progress beyond the third chapter. I had hopefully sent off the outlines of a couple of TV scripts to production companies, with predictable results.

And somewhere along the line, I had taken to imbibing 'a wee dram', as I'd jokily put it to Lucia, of an evening to help me sleep, although truth was I'd been downing rather more than a wee one once she and Rose had preceded me to bed.

'You.' I pulled in a tiny guy up from the south who had spent the night sleeping at the bus station. 'You.' A small-time drug dealer I owed for helping me disarm a guy with a shank. 'And . . .' I scanned the faces of the crowd with the neutral half-gaze I had perfected. By now most of them – the poor, the drunks, the illegals – I had become familiar with, but there were only so many free spaces and just one more would be eating today.

'*Daniel*,' said a shivering Nigerian. What was his name? I remember he had been relieved to find someone who could speak English. He didn't stand a chance in this country, but here he still was, turned clay-grey. Flu? Pneumonia? I looked at the others – who wasn't sick? Still, I'd buy him one more day.

I reached through the bodies and pulled him inside.

'Sorry, that's it,' I filled the doorway, 'no more places.'

A general sigh went up.

'What do you mean no more places?'

'Why are you choosing these foreigners? What about the Italians?'

'I've been waiting longer than him.'

'I'm sorry,' I knew not to argue, 'stand back please.' I stepped forward.

The unlucky ones gathered in front of the rust-spotted sign that read MEALS FOR THE POOR miraculously, as ever, made way.

I reached behind the metal door and unhooked it from the wall. The crowd looked resentfully on as I closed up for another day.

I shepherded the three down the steps and into the canteen where lunch was already well underway, the windows closed because of the cold and opaque with the condensation of damp clothes. A ripe funk filled the air.

The canteen sat eighty. Most places were occupied by card-holders already registered with the welfare office. The crowd outside had consisted of the cardless, for whatever reason – you were on the waiting list; passing through or paperless; wished to stay off the radar of the authorities (we were required to send all the details to the Questura, the police HQ); or just too mentally ill or drink-addled to have got around to it.

I steered the lucky three to their places, and Luca, who ran the shelter, served them food from the trolley. I stood behind the low wall that separated the corridor from the canteen, casting an eye across the room. Although it was true that the *utenti*, or 'users', as we called them, were mostly placid, the drunks would sometimes cause problems and I'd find myself having to get between them like a referee (*basta* was one of the first new Italian words I had learned) or remind a junkie that this was not a shooting gallery.

'I swear,' Alfonso said in English as he filled his pipe, 'they eat better than I do.' He had materialised that morning, unremarked upon by Luca or the other staff, almost like an apparition from another century: a tubby fellow in a grass-green cape and deerstalker that he removed to reveal tweeds and a curly frizz of grey-speckled hair to go with his neat, cavalier-style beard. He might have been a character Samuel Pickwick encountered had he embarked upon his own *Travels in Italy*.

I couldn't help glancing at the girth straining beneath his buttoned, tartan waistcoat.

'Quality, not quantity.' He cheerfully patted his belly. 'I wanted to check,' he said, 'that the ingredients are of the finest quality, which is more than I can say for some of the dinners I am obliged to attend.' He placed the pipe, unlit – he respected the rules – in the corner of his mouth and, being on the short side, squinted up at me.

'You're not happy,' he said diagnostically.

I raised an eyebrow. 'It's not a comedy club.'

'What I mean is – you're not happy here, in Italy.'

I felt affronted, and possibly slightly alarmed. 'Your glasses,' I said. 'Maybe you can't see so well – I'm actually grinning.'

'Ah, my glasses. They cloudy.'

'Steam up,' I corrected him.

'Ah, "steam". Like steam *engine*, *vero*?'

'That's it.'

'You can help me improve my English.'

'I'm actually here to improve my Italian.'

'I know,' he waved the stem of his pipe at me.

'How do you know?'

'Because it was me who got you the job.'

It had always struck me as a little odd that the Comandante had been able to pull Luca's particular string – as a committed leftist, complete with a 'Che' beard, he seemed a strange contact for a former Comandante of the Carabinieri, although he had accepted me with the same equanimity he did the rest of Bologna's waifs and strays. Now Alfonso explained he had been only too happy to put in a word for me after 'all the help the Comandante gave to us'.

'The shelter, you mean?' Alfonso frowned.

'He didn't mention it, then?'

'Mention what?'

Signor Lambertini, it transpired, was an enthusiastic freemason. 'Signor Monza is aware, naturally,' he said, meaning Luca, 'but he's too discreet to mention it. He would actually make a rather good member himself, were he not a communist.'

'You were saying that your . . . *lodge* supplies all the food for the kitchen?'

'That's right – I mean, we pay for it. That's why I'm here – quality control.'

'And the comune knows?' The shelter was actually council-run.

'Yes, and no. They do and do not. Our legal identity is *Circolo sociale di Bologna Centro, Garibaldi* – Social Circle Central Bologna, Garibaldi – from whom they are happy to receive a generous contribution. But if anyone were to ask,

I would be happy to inform them that we are the Mixed Lodge of Italy's Right and Acknowledged Masons, Bologna branch.

'Garibaldi himself was a freemason,' he continued. 'As were many of the founders of Italy – Cavour, Carducci, Mazzini – and in America, Franklin, Washington, Hancock, then there is your own Kipling, Churchill, Prince Philip . . .'

'So why the artifice?'

Alfonso gave me a quizzical look, then patted me on the shoulder: 'You have a great deal to learn, young man.'

'You never mentioned anything about masons,' I said at dinner that evening. 'I feel as if I'm in *The Da Vinci Code*.'

Myself, the Comandante and Rose were sat at our kitchen table, while Lucia was helping Alba at the stove.

'According to me,' the Comandante translated the Italian literally into English, 'they are more like that novel by Eco, *Il Pendolo di Foucault*.'

'Foucault's Pendulum,' said Rose, without looking up from her plate of gnocchi. As a child, she had a head start on the rest of us, being served a pasta *primo*, but would also join in for the forthcoming lamb and baked potatoes. The Comandante continued in Italian, and Rose automatically translated: 'Folk who replace religion with esoterica. What's esoterica, Dad?'

'Obscure . . . lore.'

'Law?'

'Weird stuff, like magic.'

'Magic!'

'The boring bits. For a secret society,' I observed, 'it's not very secret.'

'Secret societies are illegal under the constitution,' called out Lucia.

'*Tecnicamente*, no secret,' said the Comandante in English. 'They're . . . how you say? *Discrete*.'

'Discreet,' said Rose.

'You meet Signor Lambertini, I am guessing.'

'You're not one, then,' I said. Giovanni looked scornfully back at me. 'So how come you have links with them?'

'Is my business. Like is my business,' he held his wrists out as if they were bound, and said something in Italian. His hands broke symbolically free as a plate was laid before him. Rose, uncannily imitating her grandfather's voice and demeanour, said: 'to remain free.' The Comandante smiled appreciatively and the pair – granddaughter and grandfather – exchanged a collaborative nod. Not for the first time, I felt as if I could be easily dispensed with.

'He said you had given them help . . .'

'Not so much,' he said in English. 'Maybe little. Long time ago.'

'Didn't you help them during P2?' said Lucia as she came to sit down.

'P2?' I asked.

She began to dole the best cuts of lamb on to Rose's plate like a blackbird with its hatchling. 'It was a big scandal in the eighties. The police were arresting lots of masons up and down the country and publishing their membership lists. People were losing their jobs, being abused in the street and so on, but Papa refused to release the names to the media. Even after they accused him of being one, too.'

'Why was that?'

'Why must I?' he asked. Now he spoke quickly in Italian.

'I arrested the guilty,' translated Lucia, 'but I was not going to persecute the innocent. I don't participate in witch hunts.'

'Even when they claimed you were a mason?' The Comandante mumbled something.

'Papá,' said Lucia. Rose giggled.

Lucia began to place the second-best cuts on my plate. Speaking of blackbirds, there was a definite pecking order at our table, with Granddad coming next and Mum receiving the final scraps, although if I wasn't quick enough, she would help herself to mine. Lucia seemed so at home in this old apartment in this old city, it seemed almost impossible to picture her anywhere else now, and even when I had first set eyes on her stood behind the London coffee shop counter wearing an amused smile as I arrived for my first day of work, I immediately thought: Italian, *irrepressibly* Italian. Only later would I come to appreciate it was her irrepressibility that amplified her identity, rather than the other way around.

Lucia's short, wild black hair nested at the top of her pale neck with the fringe cut high across her forehead as if to impose order upon a natural recalcitrance that was otherwise impervious to styling. It was perhaps this that added to the impression that she had thrown on the first thing that had come to hand that morning, yet still somehow managed to look fantastic. An occasional dash of bold blue eye shadow and absinthe-green nail varnish were her sole concessions to cosmetics. In the UK, I had sometimes caught English women checking her out as if to intuit her secret, but it was all in the genes: she might have modelled for the statue of the female partisan at Porta Lame stood in baggy fatigues and big boots with an ammunition belt flung across her shoulder, or in waterproofs and a lifejacket fishing migrants from the sea in the video her pal had shown me of her spell with *SOS Mediterraneo*.

Since she had become a mum, she had removed the nose ring and refrained from adding to the dove tattoo on her shoulder blade, but otherwise remained capable of stepping from the shower into a Decathalon tracksuit or designer dress and making it out of the door in equal time.

She passed me my plate. 'We were thinking, you could help us.'

'Oh? I didn't realise *Bologna dei Popoli* was looking for a bouncer.'

'Silly. As an investigator – it's what you do, no?' It was as much of a challenge as a question. Although she had long-since stopped asking about my literary endeavours, she had changed tack and kept coming up with ideas about what I could do 'once you've properly learned the language'. True: within a year of working at that coffee place she had been sufficiently adept to begin an MSc (in urban planning – a choice that had perplexed me until she had landed the job at *Bologna dei Popoli*, or Bologna for the People, which campaigned for a 'liveable' city) but she had studied English from childhood and was good at that kind of thing.

'So,' she continued, 'a resident's association from San Donato has approached us – they live in a newly built condominium, well, it was put up about a dozen years back, on ex-military land. In fact, it had been used to store munitions. Now they're claiming a lot of them are getting sick – there have been cancers, immune-deficiency illnesses, children born,' she shuddered, glancing at Rose, 'with defects.'

'And they believe this is something to do with the land?' I asked. 'Chemicals, and so on?'

'That's it. Through the comune we were able to access the records of the survey. Soil samples were taken at the time, and they were fine.'

'The residents know their homes were built on potentially dangerous land?' She nodded. 'If people get ill,' I said, 'there may be a tendency to blame it on that. Statistically, however, the incidents may not be abnormal. I would begin by speaking to a health statistician.'

'Hold on.' She went over to the counter and grabbed a pad and pencil.

'Who carried out the sample analysis? The company?'

She shook her head. 'Surveyors for the comune.'

'Could someone have corrupted an official?'

'It wouldn't be the first time.'

'It's not normal, though, is it? I thought that was more the kind of thing that happened south of Rome. You always talk about Bologna, the north, as being relatively clean.'

'In the past,' the Comandante pitched in, 'the communists were, how you say?' He glanced at his daughter. '*Incorruttibili*.'

'Incorruptible,' she said.

'They *believed*. Today,' he waggled a hand, '*niente*.'

'I thought you hated the communists, Giovanni,' I said. I preferred to call him by his forename back then – calling him the Comandante struck me as somewhat absurd, and using 'Giovanni' also seemed to wind him up.

Now he spoke quickly in Italian. Lucia said: 'He respected them. There's a difference.'

'Well,' I said to Lucia, 'before you begin making accusations, or asking your dad to begin digging into people's financial affairs, it might be easier to commission a soil sample yourself. Is there available ground?'

'Yes, there's a park right in the middle of the development. In fact, they don't let their kids play out there any more because they're afraid.'

'Isteria di massa,' said the Comandante without looking up from his plate.

'Mass hysteria,' translated Rose. 'Dad?'

'It means a sort of fear that is infectious.'

'You mean you can catch it, like a cold?'

'Precisely that. Well,' I turned to my wife, 'your father has supplied us with what you can expect to be the official line.'

'It is certainly how the comune has responded so far,' she agreed.

'My daughter always begin by think the state is wrong,' said the Comandante. 'I don't know why.' He gave her a thin smile.

'Why?' Rose asked her mother.

'Your *nonno* as usual thinks it's all about him – *L'État, c'est moi*.'

'What?'

'Something General de Gaulle said – "I am the state" – although he *was* President of France at the time.' Rose shrugged, plainly never having heard of de Gaulle.

'Actually,' said the Comandante with a smirk. 'It was Louis XIV.'

'But we are really not so different,' she continued. 'We both like to battle, even if it does mean challenging authority.'

She gave him an affectionate look. The Comandante harrumphed. Giovanni had been obliged to resign from the Carabinieri having exposed a conspiracy which not only brought the perpetrators to justice, but also made it impossible for him to remain unless he wanted to sit out the rest of his career behind a desk in a one-horse town in Calabria. 'Anyway,' Lucia continued, 'thanks, *amore*, that makes sense. You see,' she added to her father, 'Daniel knows his stuff – you should take him on.'

'He must be fluent,' replied the Comandante. 'Maybe then – we'll see.'

I looked between them. Apparently, I didn't have a say.

IV

I'm not as young as I used to be. Once I would have probably caught the little bastard, but by the time I'd reached the end of Maggiore, where the old stone gate stands limbless on the corner of the ring road, I'm gasping. Granted, the swollen air can't help, or running in sweat-leaden street clothes, but this is no time for excuses – he's across the Viale and got up a good speed while I'm bent double watching him go and passers-by are slowing, ready to call 118 in case I keel over.

Then I spot the rank of bikes for hire. I lumber over and pull out my phone. I've never actually used the app, but Rose set it up for me. Fortunately, she had me fill in all my credit card details, 'because I know if I don't make you now, you never will,' and unlocking the bike is only a click away.

Magically, it works.

I roll the bike back and climb on. It certainly feels heavier than any I've ridden before, but as I cross the junction during a break in the traffic, I realise it is propelled by some kind of electric motor and I'm soon belting along the Roman-straight road with the minimum of effort. In the distance, I spot the guy's lime mullet. He has to believe he's got away by now, and seems to be taking it easy. Even youth must be feeling this heat.

We're outside the old city walls, but Maggiore's portico continues on my right while the left is a hotchpotch of terracotta and yolk-yellow apartment buildings, broken by the odd Liberty *palazzo* and gated park. It's an upmarket area, the tree-lined streets off the main drag consisting of the tranquil, gardened properties of the middle classes. The hairdressers, gelaterias and restaurants I zip past reflect the quality of their clientele.

But the lad doesn't turn off here. As he continues along the road, swerving precariously around parked and parking cars, the road finally shrugs off its portico and becomes an evermore mundane strip of low-rise office and apartment blocks, petrol stations, furniture stores, pizza restaurants, kebab shops, and supermarkets. We are deep in the suburbs now, and only the fact that he finally turns in to Viale Ilic Uljanov Lenin indicates we are still in Bologna.

It's an ordinary residential area, largely free of graffiti. He takes another turn, then another. Say what you like about the old communists, they cared about urban planning, and the modest four- or five-storey salmon-coloured apartment blocks are set among ample gardens. Cicadas are sawing deafeningly in the trees, providing a kind of aural cover.

But the kid doesn't enter one of the blocks – there's an older house on a corner. He pulls up outside and dismounts, opens the garden gate and wheels the bike inside.

From the shade of a neighbouring garden, I survey the

place. It's an Italian version of a semi-detached – two houses within one which share a main entrance and probably divide the garden down the middle.

I cross the road and peer through the chain-link fence. Obscured by foliage, I can see perhaps half a dozen bicycles in various states of repair, listing together at the rear like a drunken chorus line. A single chain has been threaded through their frames to keep them in place.

There are another four bikes properly secured to an iron loop set in a concrete block beneath a ragged pine tree; among them, Lucia's.

I cross back over the street and call Dolores. 'I need you to bring the bolt cutters.'

'Dan,' it sounds as if she's eating, 'what have you gotten yourself into?'

'Nothing,' I say irritably. 'Just get here, quick.'

It must be some kind of student accommodation. If the house was a squat, they would not, no doubt, be shy about it – there would be a banner advertising their cause hung from the balcony or strung between a pair of windows. In any case, I'm not going to knock and ask politely, that time has passed. Once my partner arrives, I'll go into the garden and take the bike, and if anyone tries to stop me, well, the bolt cutters can double as a useful deterrent.

My phone buzzes. I've picked it up thinking it's Dolores when I realise it's the Contessa.

'Daniel,' she says. 'Where are you? It's very loud.'

'Piazza Aldrovandi,' I lie. 'Having a cool drink.'

'Is it terribly hot there? I'm in Val Gardena.' She means the Dolomites.

'The usual for August.'

'I'm sorry – I'm keeping you from your holidays.'

'No problem.'

'I'll be seeing that . . . *friend* I mentioned soon. Apparently, her husband also has to stay in the city for business, or so he says. It's just like that film, *The Seven Year Itch*.'

'I'm sorry?' Despite the shade, I feel as if my body is beginning to shut down.

'With Jack Lemon and Marilyn Monroe.'

'Ah, yes. That one.'

'And I was wondering if you had anything to report.'

I need to focus. Despite Ginevra's playful tone, she's paying top dollar.

'We've been on signora Bonelli's tail for three days, following her from her home to various health and beauty appointments. She has also met a couple of friends, at least I presume they're friends . . .'

'Women, you mean. Like her.'

'That's it, in the sort of places where one might expect them to go – I will send you a detailed list of locations when I'm back in the office, but I haven't seen her with any man.' Then I remember. 'There is one thing . . .'

'Yes?' she says quickly.

'It's just a suspicion, I'll have to check when I get back to the office.'

'What's that?'

'It's a bit . . .' I sigh. 'Look, there's no easy way to put this: you wouldn't happen to know whether Nancy Bonelli is a freemason, would you?' A crackle at the other end. 'Ginevra?'

'It's actually a bit chilly here,' she says. 'Breeze.'

'What I wouldn't give for a breeze now.'

'I'm sorry, what did you say?' I repeat the question.

'But Daniel,' she says with a hint of condescension, 'women can't be masons.'

'That's a common misconception. If they follow the British rite, then that's the case, but if, like many European lodges, they follow Paris, then they admit both sexes.'

'So women *can* be masons? Well, I've learned something today. How do you know all this?' She gasps: 'You're not one, are you?'

'Against company policy. Just someone I used to know.'

'But why do you ask?'

'I believe I saw her visiting a lodge today. However, I will have to check – it may *actually* be a cultural organisation.'

'Nancy Bonelli, a *mason* . . .'

'*Whoa!* Let's not get ahead of ourselves.' I had visions of Ginevra gossiping with the rest of 'Bologna Bene' as they hiked the hillsides of the Gardena. 'I'll really need to check first.'

'Of course. But – no man.'

'No. No man.'

'As yet.'

'As yet. Does this mean you would like us to continue? You know it would be a lot easier, like I said, if . . .'

'Give it a few more days, then you are excused. In fact, if you fancy a spell in the mountains, I have some young – well, youngish – friends, divorcées, who were complaining the other evening they never get to meet anyone.'

'That's very kind . . .'

'And I'm sure that none of them are masons. Well, now

you mention it, you never know, do you? I might be surrounded by them! I'm beginning to feel quite upset no one has ever asked me.'

'Wasn't your late husband also a count of the Catholic church? And the church is the most implacable foe of *massoneria*.'

A throaty laugh: 'Oh my goodness, this is getting very cloak and dagger! I suppose it's because all those old men want to keep the best dresses for themselves. That's obviously why they never approached me, they were afraid I would have the Inquisition on them. Really, Daniel, you're either turning properly native with all this talk of secret societies, or perhaps the heat's getting to you?'

'Could be.'

'I'll let you go. And stay out of the sun!'

Dolores pulls up on her pushbike, a rucksack strapped to her back. She had a severe crop at the beginning of the summer which makes her seem younger than her twenty-eight years. In her perspiration-tight black T-shirt and brown cargo shorts, she doesn't look much different to when we met six years ago. She probably doesn't look very different to the kids occupying the house, and I stifle the urge to ask her to go in and do the deed on my behalf.

'Do you have any water?' She pulls out a litre bottle. While I chug it down, she produces the bolt cutters.

'You didn't say which ones,' she says, 'so I brought the heavy duty. I thought someone might have chained you up.'

I lower the bottle. 'You thought that?'

She shrugs. 'You never know.' I raise the bottle again and

splash some over my face. 'Are you all right?'

'A little hot.' I swap the bottle for the bolt cutters. 'You stay here.'

'What are you going to do?'

'Steal a bike.'

'Dan.' She grins. 'Really?'

'Just get ready to make a getaway.'

'You're kidding,' she calls after me.

Taking a final glance around before opening the garden gate, I notice a white and dark-blue Polizia Municipale car turn into the road. It's too late to back away without appearing suspicious, so I enter the garden anyway, but instead of heading straight to the rear, I move around the side to stand at the front corner, screened from the road by bushes, while I wait for the car to pass.

Only it doesn't. It stops directly outside the house. I back into the bushes as the gate opens and a hatless municipal police officer marches up the path. He unlocks the front door and enters. Through the bushes, I can see his car is empty – there's no partner. Could he be sharing the house with these kids? Does he live next door? Although armed, Bologna's municipal police are local hires occupied with the lowest rung of policing – traffic stops, parking tickets, zoning violations and residence checks. Maybe this is one?

A tremendous bang.

Shit. I shrink back into the foliage. Has he shot someone? If he's gone postal, I don't want him to plug me on his way out.

Now – coughing. Brown smoke billowing out of the open entrance door. A shape emerging on its hands and knees – the cop. He slips and tumbles down the three entrance steps on to the ground. I ditch the bolt cutters and run over.

'What happened?' I ask. He blinks up at me with a soot-blackened face. 'Dolores!' I call.

She bursts through the garden gate.

'The water.' She dashes back out and returns with the bottle. I splash the water on the guy's face as the smoke begins to dissipate.

Bulging from his belly to his grey-bristled jowls, he looks like he rarely leaves the office.

'Booby trap,' he shouts, possibly deafened. 'They booby trapped the door!' His face creases in almost comical horror. 'My house! What have they done to my house!' He pushes us away and scrambles to his feet, racing inside.

A moment's silence, followed by a raw howl.

They – whoever they are – have certainly done their worst, or perhaps that should be best.

Through the front door, we step into a kitchen-diner still grainy with smoke. At first – at very first – it doesn't seem too bad. The round, plain white dining table is intact, albeit crowded with greasy bike parts. But then you take in the rest of the kitchen, and realise they've really done a number: the cabinets have been wrenched off the walls, along with half the plaster, baring brick and concrete, while red and black graffiti is sprayed across the rest. The kitchen surface – fake marble – is gouged down to its plasterboard, and the cabinets beneath kicked in. The stove is still apparently working, as a Moka is burning out on the gas, and the stainless-steel fridge appears to be functional, although scratched to fuck.

Across the kitchen island, the *soggiorno*, or living room, has been similarly vandalised, the synthetic suede sofa slashed, foam spilling from the cushions, and someone seems to have had a go at the arms with a saw.

The parquet floor has received the same treatment as the work top, and the TV is shattered. Slogans cover the walls, mainly political stuff:

HOMES FOR ALL

TOURISTS FUCK OFF

FUCK AIRBNB

RECLAIM BOLOGNA

The glass doors to the garden are kicked in and hanging open.

Lucia's bike has gone, along with the others that were beside it. A path has been trodden through the bushes at the rear, the wire fence cut and pulled back. I follow it, step on to the road. Nothing.

Dolores comes up behind me: 'What was so special about that bike?'

I head back into the house. The cop is sat on the edge of the sofa, shaking his head, sobbing. I go upstairs. They have even sawed sections of the banister out.

'Who the hell would *do* that?' I ask as Dolores follows me up.

On the landing, porcelain crunches beneath our feet. They appear to have taken a sledgehammer to the bathroom, enamel and glass fragments spilling out of the open door. The only thing left intact is the toilet, which, apparently, they still had in use. Presumably they washed their hands in the downstairs sink, if at all.

The curtains in the front bedroom have been pulled down and sliced to pieces, the wardrobes destroyed. The usual spray-paint adorns the walls, although the beds seem all right – they needed somewhere to sleep, I guess.

It's the same story at the rear.

'They're not squatters.' I shake my head: 'Not addicts either.' There would usually be syringes and other drugs paraphernalia. 'It's methodical. *Vindictive*.'

'The bike,' says Dolores.

'It was Lucia's,' I respond without turning around.

'Fuck,' I hear her whisper. 'So,' she says. 'You'll want to find them.'

'I will.'

'Yeah,' she says. 'I may be able to help you with that.'

V

That winter the shutters had frozen open and the snow had continued to fall during the night, piling up the balcony and against our bedroom window as if we were in a Norwegian cabin. Above this Artic horizon sat a moon-blue sky.

Lucia was wrapped around me, clinging on as if I might try to escape, so it was only by tilting my head sideways I could see that it was already 7:18. I gently lifted her arm and eased myself out from under her leg. She muttered something and turned over.

I stood by the window as I pulled on my sweatshirt, pants and socks – our venerable, second-floor apartment was not exactly freezing, but neither was it very well insulated. I gazed across the snow-covered rooftops towards the city centre with its domes and spires.

Rose's bedroom door was wide open. Despite knowing little more than *La Residenza Faidate* with its patchy frescoes,

Romeo and Juliet balconies, and courtyard wall with bricked together battlements, or perhaps because of this, the charm utterly escaped her. In fact her fondest memories appeared to revolve around her visits to our old ex-local authority flat in London 'where everything was new', and she had recently become convinced the Residence was packed with ghosts, insisting that we keep our door open, too.

I put it down to her reading material.

'*Basta*.' I meant the Harry Potter she was absorbed in as she laid in bed. She squinted at me – she had probably been reading for hours – and wordlessly followed me down to the kitchen, carrying the book with her.

I was not usually trusted in the vicinity of the stove, but winter mornings were the exception, when I was expected to produce 'sludge', as Lucia called porridge, for the pair of us.

I appreciated this time with Rose, albeit that I had recently had to compete for her attention with Joanne Rowling. It was us two Brits against the world. Well, three, if you counted JK.

'What have you got at school today?'

'Eh?'

I took the book away and replaced it with the bowl.

'School, today.'

'Maths.' She glumly spooned the porridge. Her face lit up as she remembered. 'Art.' She looked thoughtful. 'Matteo was saying that if it gets any colder they will have to close.'

'You would have thought they would be used to it by now.'

'Marisa was hit in the eye with a snowball with a stone in it. She had to go to hospital.'

'Is she okay?' Rose gave an Italian shrug. 'Who threw it?'

'One of the older boys.'

'Did he get into trouble?' Shrug.

Another telegram arrived: 'Stefania's going skiing this weekend. Her mum says I can come.'

'You don't have any skis.'

'They'll rent them.'

'We'll have to ask your mum.' Rose gave me a look older than her years.

'That's your way of saying no.'

'Maybe she's got something planned this weekend.' Now it was my turn to shrug. 'I don't know – no one tells me anything.'

'They do. You just have to learn the language.'

'What do you think I'm trying to do?'

'*Please*, Dad. Everyone else is going.'

'I'm sure they're not.'

'Dad.'

'Okay, I'll put in a good word for you. Mum can talk to Cristina at work.'

'Thanks Dad!' Mission accomplished, Rose reached for the book.

Lucia appeared in the kitchen, yawning, as we were preparing to leave. She smoothed Rose's hair, then checked her teeth as if she was a horse.

'Go on,' she directed Rose back to the bathroom. I bared mine. 'She always forgets,' she frowned. 'You should check.'

'And I always forget to check,' I said.

'And I always remind you to check.' She went on tiptoe to kiss me.

'Cristina and Rocco invited her skiing this weekend.'

'I think it's a good idea.'

'Aren't you worried?'

'I'll leave that to you – I realise you don't have snow in England, but here it's normal. If she learns now, she can go on skiing trips when she's older.'

'That's *precisely* what I'm worried about.'

A sly smile: 'Maybe we could do something together, go away somewhere. How about that?'

'Would your father have to come?'

She laughed. 'Even he might give us the weekend off.'

'Careful.' We had salted the stairs that ran down the two floors to the courtyard, but fresh snow had blown in to create an icy slush. We emerged at the bottom, yesterday's traffic thoroughly erased, and waded across the space like characters in a Bruegel. Certainly, in the snow-blown silence with that omnipresent smell of wood smoke, it could have been any time in the last millennia.

The sole tree, around which our cars were obscured by metre-deep drifts, drooped with the weight of the snow, adding to the wintry gloom, while in the two-storey workshop-cum-house where Lucia's cousin Alba had just moved in, a single, limpid amber light flickered like a candle. I drew back the heavy bolt from across the wicket door set in the main gate, and we stepped on to Via Mirasole.

Fortunately, the school was just around the corner in Via Paglietta. We walked along the centre of the road holding hands until we reached the vast arched entrance into the courtyard, where she ran to join her friends who were busy chasing each other with armfuls of snow as their parents called impotently for them to stop. The fear of them becoming wet from melted snow and being exposed to a *colpo d'aria* (literally, a 'hit of air') was a pervasive anxiety among Italian parents, much as the *cervicale*, which apparently existed around the top of one's spine, was usually the culprit of a stiff neck, although to my knowledge the 'cervical' had never actually been identified by medical science.

I waited until the teachers had ushered the kids inside and made my way out via the portered side door with the others, the huge oak gates having closed for the duration, then crunched back along Mirasole, passing the high walls of home, in the direction of work. There was no real hurry – given that my main job was to break up fights, there wasn't much call for me until the doors began to open at ten and the 'users' arrived at the welfare office to request lunch passes, receive help navigating bureaucracy, or just use the bathrooms – but I tended to pass the spare hour sat in the corner of a bar bent over my tatty Moleskine notebook with its ranks of cursive or shorthand English–Italian words as if it were a Hebrew or Islamic holy book.

My phone was flush on the right-hand side of the page to blank out the list of Italian words as I stared into space trying to remember them, when he crossed my sightline.

Alfonso Lambertini may have dropped into the bar before but until now I probably wouldn't have noticed him, engrossed as I usually was with vocabulary. His mischievous face was framed by a knitted black balaclava, his frosty beard poking down like an icicle as he stood at the counter in Wellington boots and a double-breasted navy greatcoat. If he hadn't been so plump, he might have been a straggler of the *Grande Armée* upon its treacherous trek from Moscow.

He approached with a teapot on a tray. I somewhat peevishly put my book aside – this was my sacred 'Italian hour', after all. I made a mental note to find another bar.

'Mister Lie-chester!' He removed the lid of the pot and dropped in the bag of Earl Grey. 'Am I disturbing you?'

'I was studying.'

'That is the point, yes? I do not see you working in the canteen as a fun job.' He peeled off his balaclava, the 'icicle' disintegrating in a sparkling cloud.

'It's all right,' I insisted. 'A means to an end.'

Alfonso ran a hand through his flattened hair, which sprang back to life. 'One of the many things I admire about Anglo-Saxon culture – your sense of an ending, or rather, should that be a destination? We Italians move forward crab-like, you know – from side-to-side – sometimes so much we forget where we are going. In fact, we wonder if we are going anywhere at all!' He gazed at me keenly. 'How about a swap?

'I'm sorry?'

'A conversation exchange. Fifteen minutes English, fifteen Italian.'

'To be honest, I'm not sure my Italian could compete with your English.'

'It's not a competition! Come on, what do you say?'

I glanced at the clock. I wasn't going to get much further with my studies this morning anyway. 'Okay,' I said. 'But you will have to bear with me.'

'Of course!'

Bouncing between his semi-fluent English and my ropey Italian, our conversation ranged from the evolution of the city's porticoes to the latest film by Nanni Moretti; from the likelihood of Brexit (never, I assured him) to the differences between common and Italian law; how Rose was settling in at school, to the work of Lucia's NGO. What we hadn't touched upon by the time I bade Alfonso farewell, was freemasonry. Perhaps he was keen to demonstrate he was more than just about that, which was partly true in the sense that the Pope might be a fly-fishing enthusiast. But, looking back, I'm not even sure his appearance in the bar was coincidental, or the topics of our conversation arbitrary. Alfonso Lambertini was a man who believed most of all in design, and little he did was by accident.

I suspect he had sussed me out and sensed, if not a fellow freemason, then a fellow traveller.

VI

'How long were they here?' Dolores asks the sobbing man.

'Two weeks, a good booking.' He wipes his face with a tissue. 'The centre's booming, but it's not so easy to get lettings out here.'

'Did they have references?'

'From two places they'd stayed at. Both in Bologna, nothing unusual.'

'So what made you suspect something was wrong?' I ask.

'The noise. The next door neighbour called me to complain about "the building work" in the early hours. I thought – there isn't any building work.' He shakes his head. 'I can't believe it. This is all my savings.'

'It's insured?'

'You know how difficult it is with these people, and in the meantime . . .'

'Can you send us the details?' asks Dolores. 'We'll look

into it for you.'

'And who are you?' It has apparently just occurred to him a pair of strangers are questioning him inside his wrecked house.

'We're private investigators,' I say. 'Although that's not why we're here – they've got something of mine.'

'What?'

'A bicycle.'

'Oh!' He throws up his hands. 'A fucking bike? Have you seen my house?'

'Be that as it may,' I say, 'give us the details and we'll fill you in on anything we discover.'

'What company? I can't afford PIs.'

'Faidate Investigations. And it's gratis.'

'I thought you had an accent – the bloody English detective! Have you taken over from the Comandante?'

'Hardly,' I say, unsurprised that our, or rather my father-in-law's, reputation has penetrated the precincts of the local police – they're the Carabinieri's biggest fanboys. 'The Comandante is currently cooling his feet in the Adriatic. I'm minding the shop.'

He takes a card. 'If you do find the bastards,' he says, 'a word in advance, eh? Folk think they can treat us Municipale however the hell they like, but only the once, if you get my drift.'

'We'll keep you in the loop,' I say absent-mindedly. I'm watching Dolores photographing the graffiti. I'm about to ask her why when there's the sound of a Vespa pulling up outside. I watch a young guy march down the garden path.

He peers in through the open doorway. His mouth falls open. He immediately whips out his phone and starts taking pictures too, oblivious to me and the *poliziotto* staring at him.

'And who are you?' I ask on behalf of the Municipale.

'Sorry!' He puts the phone down and holds out his hand. 'Maurizio Estiva from the *Carlino*. We got a tip.'

'A tip about what?'

'Well.' He gestures. 'This.'

'And what did they say, exactly?'

He looks at me like I'm a fool. 'That there was another one.'

Like most reporters, Maurizio Estiva thinks everyone follows the news as religiously as he does. 'This is the third let they've trashed. Haven't you read about it?'

'And who are they?' I glance at Dolores looking suitably deadpan.

'They call themselves "Reclaim Bologna". They're targeting tourists lets. They say they deprive students and ordinary folk of anywhere to live.'

'They smash them up like this?'

'Oh, yeah,' he nods emphatically. 'I've seen worse. They've pulled out the sockets in other places, and dismantled the plumbing. In the last they broke the stove. It was only when someone smelled gas they discovered what had happened. The whole building could have gone up.'

'The police are involved?'

'Ah,' he grins. 'Good question. Technically, maybe, but like the rest of "the establishment" they're trying to downplay it, hope it will go away. You won't read about it in the *Corriere* or see it on RAI. It's not exactly good publicity for "the City of Food", if you get my drift.'

'I suppose that's the point. Any idea why they should have targeted this place?'

'The other two were in the centre. I guess they're making a point that nowhere's safe.'

'Have they said anything else? Made any more demands?'

'You would know if you'd read my articles.'

'I'll have to buy the *Carlino* more regularly; in the meantime . . .'

'Not much. In fact, that's their approach – "the time for words is over", the guy said when he first called.'

'And it was a man. Bolognese?'

'Couldn't tell. Neutral. Anyway, that was it. "Nowhere's safe while there's nowhere to live." That's their slogan.'

'But how do they get away with it? They have to pay up front, don't they? Where do they get the money?'

'My bet is there's some fraud going on – these scumbags don't exactly look as if they're rolling in it. Stolen credit cards, maybe?'

'These will be friends of yours, I presume,' I say to Dolores as we leave the house.

'I recognised the designs,' she says. 'On the wall.'

'You mean the graffiti?' She nods. 'These guys are connected to your old squatting buddies, right?'

'Possibly . . . probably. The art seemed familiar.'

'There was art?'

'That snake design running around the holes in the

plaster? It's also on the bridge over Via Stalingrado. Goes by the street name of Quinto.'

'These "Reclaim Bologna" people, they've got to be linked with the group you used to belong to when you were living at the old hospital, right?'

She's quiet as she unchains her bike, straightens up. 'The point is to get Lucia's bike back, right? Not bust them.'

'All right,' I say. 'Like the gentleman said – he can't afford PIs.' She gives me a searching look.

'I'll ask about. So how are you going to get back?'

'I'll just . . .' I look around. The hire bike has disappeared.

Dolores snorts: 'At least you can't complain it was stolen.'

It is the hour of mad dogs and Englishmen, only no dogs would be mad enough to be out in this heat. I make it to the corner of Via Lenin and give up. I call a cab.

We cruise in air-conditioned comfort back to *La Residenza* in Via Mirasole. Dolores and I are taking turns to staff the office in Marconi, in case we get any 'walk ins', although from Ferragosto, one of history's first recorded public holidays – glory be to Emperor Augustus – we are officially shut for the rest of the month. Marconi, anyway – it looks as if I will still have to wrap up this job for the Contessa.

I pay the man and step back into the unforgiving heat, feeling wretched with sweat barely past midday. I click the fob and the old gates open automatically. I step between them. They freeze either side of me like an open mouth.

I see the courtyard as Lucia might. Gone are the cars on rough tarmac – they are tucked away in what were abandoned workshops. Now the courtyard is grassed over apart from a gravel strip between the garages and the gate.

A swing hangs from the branch of the single silver elm, with a bench set nearby. Alba's little house is still here, but it's been knocked through to the other workshops beside it in order to create a kind of ground-floor loft conversion, making space for the family my wife's cousin, who we always used to worry would remain single, came to grow – to age, like me, Rose, the Comandante, even this old tree. It is only you who never got to grow older, Lucia, who will forever be framed by the past.

I cross the courtyard and go up. The apartment might currently feel cool, not least because I have closed the shutters as well as the windows, but I know the heat will have impregnated the walls and wood so that by the time I step out of the shower, having turned on only the cold tap, which runs warm, it will feel as stuffy as if we are in mid-winter and the radiators are up to max.

I switch on the air-con as I pass the space I still use as an office between Rose's bedroom and my own. Through the window, rooftops roll in terracotta waves down to the bulk of the church of San Petronio, adrift in Piazza Maggiore.

The apartment has an odd layout, but it was constructed around four hundred years ago to accommodate lesser relatives (the Comandante occupies the frescoed *piano nobile* below) and adapted to suit the requirements of the centuries. The last time any serious work was done (apart from central heating and our own contribution – air-conditioning) was in the 1930s, judging by the wallpaper we discovered when modernising the kitchen. A wall or two might have come and gone since, but otherwise, give or take the odd crack left by a restive earth, it has remained more or less unchanged. I would like to get someone to look at the external frescoes along the balconies with their patchwork of biblical scenes, but I worry about the involvement of the *sovrintendenza*, which can multiply time and cost. For the same reason, I'm a little concerned about making any serious internal changes. I wonder what lurks behind those suspended (albeit high) ceilings, for example – the strong possibility of discovering venerable treasures is both an enticement and inhibition.

Emerging from the bathroom wrapped in a robe, I sit down at the desk and wake my computer, searching for *Associazione Studi Culturali Mazzini*. There's no website, just a series of listings picked up by the usual bots. Neither is there a description of activities, only a telephone number. I call it. I'm expecting an answerphone, so I'm a little thrown when someone picks up.

'Hello?' says a woman, sounding equally discombobulated.

'Hello,' I say. 'I'm interested in cultural studies, and I live in your area. I was wondering, how might I become involved?'

'Oh. Ah. I'm sorry, well, obviously, it's August . . .'

'Yes, I realise. I was just wondering if you have any events coming up in the future?'

'Ah, no. Not as far as I'm aware.'

'Okay . . . is there any way I could become involved?'

'I'm sorry, the membership is closed.'

I think about it. Without changing my tone, I ask: 'I apologise, I have probably misunderstood. Are you a masonic lodge?'

'I . . .' The line goes dead. I call back – and *now* I get an answer machine. Clearly a lodge, then. Usually, and legally, they would acknowledge the fact. I had probably been a little too sly – I'd counted on them just telling me. If I had asked them directly, they might have given me a straight answer, but I probably freaked the woman out. I wonder if it is a 'women-only' lodge. Despite the impression I may have given Ginevra, they are pretty rare, but it wasn't Alfonso's *Circolo sociale di Bologna Centro, Garibaldi*, and obviously not men-only.

Does it actually *matter* if Nancy Bonelli is a mason?

Apart from providing the Contessa with gossip, not as far as I can tell – it's about who she's screwing, not what else she's doing (unless the fellow under suspicion also happens to be a mason. Would the Contessa/her 'friend' know? Not necessarily).

But that's not what's really bothering me.

It's what Lucia's bike was doing outside.

It's the thief I couldn't catch.

It's the one that got away.

VII

The train sliced through the wintry landscape, the snow obscuring the topography and textures of the farmland beyond Bologna, absolving the suburbs of Florence of their ugliness. Just me and Lucia across the table, like once upon a time when we shot north to the Scottish Highlands or south to the English coast, or interrailed across the plains and valleys of Europe in unwashed clothes with a dog-eared *Lonely Planet* and coffee-stained map; when there was still a world to discover and the future was facing each other; before 'proper' adulthood burst forth between her thighs and life became bolted down. I felt a wave of nostalgia, reached out to take her hands.

A curious smile: 'What?'

'Thank you,' I said. 'For this.' She wove her fingers between mine.

'Poor Daniel – your Italy is all gloomy porticoes and

homeless.' She looked at me as if this was the antidote, and I felt bad she so clearly believed I required one.

Although we had actually visited Florence as backpackers, we had blanched when we had seen the queues for the sites. This time we had booked – the Uffizi that morning and the Accademia to see David in the afternoon, with the Medici palace at ten the following day. I would have preferred just one daily visit, with a long afternoon/morning in bed, but Lucia had clearly decided my educational requirements outweighed lazy time with the missus.

'This is it.' She squeezed my hand and let go.

Walking through *Firenze Santa Maria Novella*, I had the sense of being in a different Italy, a feeling compounded as we waited with the mob of tourists at the traffic lights. The sky was blue and Florence was glistening (not for nothing, Italians wear sunglasses in winter), its sandy complexion this side of the Apennines in contrast to the soil-reds of home.

An Italy of smart stores and bars, the Duomo looming ahead in all its Renaissance bling, as vulgar as Versace, before hordes of tourists. Instagram Italy, uncluttered by those pesky Italians I had once overheard a certain kind of English tourist complain about. Well, this Italy belonged to them, the locals existing solely to staff high-priced outlets or souvenir stores or herd crowds as if they were attendants at a museum. Central Florence felt a long way from the centre of Bologna, where foreigners were obliged to take Italians seriously.

It had probably been like this as far back as Helena Bonham Carter's ancestors had acted out their real-life version of *A Room with a View*. But it still took a little getting used to, even, I think, for Lucia, who was addressed automatically in

English everywhere we went. I, however, felt oddly at home, as if my wife, for once, was the outsider. After ordering lunch in Italian and being promptly answered in my native tongue, I cheerfully gave up. Lucia had once told me that Bologna was known as 'the city of freedom', yet here in Bologna I felt strangely free. While my wife complained about the crowds at the Uffizi, my tension melted away. I might still look forward to getting back to our hotel room and being with her without having to worry about our daughter popping her head around the door, but it felt so different to Bologna, like a proper holiday.

'Well?' We were sat looking up at David.

'It's certainly bigger than I thought,' I said.

'Everyone always thinks that the first time. Do you see, it's a single piece of marble? Imagine that.'

'It's pretty amazing.'

Lucia looked pleased. 'All this art, it's not boring?'

'Of course not! I'm just happy to be with you.'

She nodded thoughtfully. 'You look happy.'

'Don't I always?'

She hesitated. 'I'm sorry I don't pay you more attention. I know it isn't easy here. And I'm sorry about the Comandante. He can be,' she searched for the word, 'grumpy. He misses Mum.'

'I get that.'

Her hands formed a pyramid. 'And that I don't have much time when I get home.'

'*Basta*, Lucia. You don't need to say that. Let's enjoy ourselves this weekend, that's what it's all about.'

She considered this. 'You're right.' She reached behind the

back of my neck and pulled me towards her so the tips of our noses touched. 'I love you.'

'And I love you.'

She closed her eyes, as if to hold the words inside. They opened again, and she flashed a smile.

'Just checking.' She let me go and stood up. 'Well, I thought I'd take a look at the rest . . .'

'Go. I want to soak this up a little more.' I watched her weave between the crowd towards the other gallery, pulling out her phone to undoubtedly check the regular updates she was receiving from Cristina. *A revelation* – Lucia would prefer to be with Rose. Of course she would! But I couldn't ski, so instead of leaving me stranded back at the hotel or at home, she had entrusted her daughter to her friend so she could take her mopey English husband away for the weekend.

'Not bad for third time lucky. Agostino and Donatello had bloody given up.' I looked around. The words were unexpected, but I would know that Essex accent anywhere.

Inspector Brian Bull of the Metropolitan Police's Flying Squad was not a tall man but a very wide one, and his iron muscles strained against his brown leather jacket as he occupied the space of perhaps two people beside me. Certainly, the other tourists instinctively kept their distance. 'Then they left the block for a couple of dozen years until Michelangelo was given a crack.' He slapped me on the thigh with one of those big mitts. 'Bet you didn't expect to bump into me, Daniel.'

I cleared my throat. 'What are you—'

'Take it easy, old chap,' he chuckled. 'Off-duty. Mrs Bull.' He nodded at an attractive woman perhaps twenty years his junior. 'The third,' he winked. 'Wanted to do the Christmas market. Bloody rubbish, frankly – huts full of tat. It would be warmer at Bluewater. But I never need an excuse to visit *Italia*. Love the grub, and I'm partial to a bit of fine art. You caught *The Birth of Venus*?'

'You mean at the Uffizi?' He looked amused.

'*Bravo*, young man. If you haven't already seen it, I'd also recommend Masaccio's *Holy Trinity*, that's in the church of Santa Maria Novella, so you could probably catch it on your way out, right? You'll be returning to Bologna, I suppose.'

'You've kept dibs on me, then.'

'Nah,' he smiled affably. 'Not really. Your missus about? Lucia, is it? Maybe we could meet for an *aperitivo* tonight if you're still around.'

'We've got other plans,' I said coolly.

'Come on, old chap, it can't be all that bad – you're living the dream!'

I pictured the musty canteen. 'I wouldn't quite put it that way.'

He looked up at David. 'What is it with today's generation?' Now he turned his bullet blue eyes on me. 'I seem to recall that you were the one that got involved with that gang, Daniel, that participated in their nefarious activities—'

'As an observer.'

'So you said.' He shrugged, and a small continent may have trembled. 'Anyway, water under the bridge. Thanks to you – well, partially – they went down, and you're living *la dolce vita*. What's not to like?'

'You're saying the heat's off?'

He chuckled. 'Heat? You turned into Al Pacino? In your case it was never more than lukewarm, my friend, swimming-pool temperature. For all those illuminating articles of yours, I don't think you ever *truly* understood the criminal mind. The slammer is an occupational hazard for that lot and they're probably already planning the next one. You're long gone, mate, forgotten – they're not going to waste their time on speculation. It's not like the movies, or mafia.' A rumble began at his chest and resounded from his throat, which may have been appreciation. 'Now they're a different kettle of fish. You don't want to mess with them.'

'That's not exactly how you put it at the time.'

He held up his hands. 'Better safe than sorry, eh? I admit I may have mentioned you might want to watch your back.' His forehead formed great trenches as he frowned. 'In our game it's an occupational hazard.' He grinned.

'But how—'

'Bry.' Wife number three was standing in front of us. He shot up with astonishing speed. 'Who's this then?'

'Lori, darling, this is *Don*. We were just chatting about the best place for a steak Florentine. I was saying it's got to be the Vecchio Cancello, that place we went last night.'

'*Wonderful*,' she said. 'You should listen to him – he knows his food.'

'I'll check it out,' I said dryly.

'Oh, you're British. Are you a tourist, too?'

'Lori,' said Bull, 'he's here, of course he's a tourist!'

I spotted Lucia emerge from the other gallery. Bull's eyes darted the same way. He held out his hand. 'We'll be on our way, Don. Short for Donald, is it?'

'If you say so.'

'You take care now.' As the couple passed Lucia coming

the other way, he glanced over his shoulder. *Quack, quack,* he mouthed.

'Who were you were talking to?' asked Lucia.

'Just some tourists.'

True, I fell straight asleep that night, but was awake again at three, listening to Lucia draw deep breaths beside me. I had expected the meeting with the Inspector to catch up with me, and while I had done my best to delay it with wine and lovemaking, naturally it had nudged me awake in that airless room when my defences were down.

Logically, I should have felt reassured. I recalled the Inspector standing in Victoria Park with a cup of takeaway coffee as I passed on my morning run. 'You're too predictable,' he said, and worked his trigger finger with a snigger.

Word was a 'snitch list' was circulating and I was on it. A year earlier Bull had hauled me in on suspicion of drug trafficking and provided the option of wearing a wire or facing the same fate as the rest. Naturally, I'd whined freedom of the press, but he wasn't having it, and because I was a freelance, I didn't have a big media organisation to leap to my defence. Plus, I had a young family. So I did what he asked, and a few months later they were picked up. I'd feared being called as a witness, or the recordings being used in court, but it didn't happen. In fact, my 'evidence' hadn't been used at all. But, as a consequence, my work had dried up, or to be more precise – I had. I'd lost interest in the career I'd spent years cultivating. I had betrayed my professional code, my sources, myself. I felt ashamed, weak, and worried. What was I going to do?

'Are we talking witness protection?' I'd asked Bull. 'Is there a budget?'

'Come off it,' he laughed. 'They can't even keep us in knuckledusters.' His slap on the back felt like being hit with a shovel. 'You'll be all right, although if you're really worried, you might think about getting away. I hear Bologna's lovely this time of year.'

Lucia rolled over. 'What is it?'

'Nothing. Go back to sleep.'

'Is it that man?' she asked dozily.

'What man?'

'The one you said was a tourist.' She rubbed her eyes. 'I saw you with him before.'

'In the gallery, you mean.'

'No.' She sat up and reached for some water. 'In London once, when we were visiting. You got a call and said you had to go out. I watched from the window. I saw you both on the grass.'

'From the flat? But that was ten storeys up. You must have been mistaken.' Lucia switched on the bedside lamp, almost certainly to illuminate the fact that she was under no doubt whatsoever about what she had seen.

It was my turn to reach for some water in the hope it would buy me some time. It didn't, so I got up and went to the bathroom. Surveyed myself naked in the full-length mirror. I could equivocate, tell her a half-truth along the lines that he was an old police contact, which would obviously be true. I tended to be circumspect about honesty in relationships, which I felt one could have too much of. Women asked for the truth, men on the whole didn't want to hear it. Neither was being entirely honest. Intentions seemed more important – and my intentions had been good, to protect my family. I had done everything for them, so why should I have to carry this burden on my own? We were home now, safe. We were happy (well, at least Lucia and Rose were). And she was my wife: this was a secret I *should* share. It was now or never.

Or perhaps it was just because I was naked. When I came back into the room, Lucia had pulled on a T-shirt and sat up expectantly in bed. I felt obliged to put my discarded boxers on. I could feel myself backtracking but decided to press on, part of me taking a perverse pleasure in confronting her with the confession she was apparently so determined to hear.

'He's a policeman.' I sat gingerly apart from her. 'I know him from my time in London.'

'Why didn't you just say that? Why did you have to lie?'

'It's,' I wavered, 'difficult.'

'*Amore*,' she squeezed my hand. 'I can see it upset you. What were you so worried about?'

So I told her, without leaving a detail out.

Lucia raised a hand first to her chest, then her throat.

She swallowed. 'Is that everything?' I nodded. Her eyelids rolled down in the monochrome light as if she was a character in a silent movie.

I reached for her hand but she drew back. Then she gave me a look I had only glimpsed once before – when I had confessed to her I was really working in that coffee bar to write an exposé on the chain. Her reaction had been one of shock, disbelief, quickly followed by anger. This time it was as if I had just slapped her. Her cheeks seemed to burn with an emotion somehow worse than righteous anger – resentment.

'But you made me persuade you,' she hissed.

'I'm sorry?'

She cleared her throat. 'When I was offered the job in Bologna you made me persuade you to move here. I had to work hard to convince you, remember?' I shook my head. Her mouth curled. '*It'll be that chance to write your book.* I knew you weren't working, writing your articles any more. But you wouldn't open up, tell me why.' Her voice began to gather strength. 'And now we know. But you made me work for it. Oh, how you made me work! Made me feel like a shit, as if I was ruining your precious career, when in fact you had put us all at risk. You couldn't wait to get out!'

'Honestly, it wasn't like that—'

'Honesty? Who are you to talk about honesty? I was trying to help you, and you were quite happy to make me think you were making this great fucking sacrifice . . . *Son-of-a-bitch*,' she swore in Italian. 'My God, no wonder you're so fucking miserable! And all the time, there was me thinking it's all *my* fault.'

'Look,' I reached out, but she pulled back. 'I *honestly* didn't mean to. And I'm fine. I'm getting a grip of the language. I'm helping you out with your work. And sure, in time I could work for the family fir—'

'It's the *deceit*, Daniel. You had all this going on, and you didn't say a thing. It was *me* that lay awake night after night wondering if I was being fair, worrying about what you were going to do, whether I was being selfish, while you snored away beside me. I felt so, so . . . *guilty*. And even here, worrying all the time about your book, your Italian, *you*, Daniel, *you you you*. And you . . . *You just fucking let me*.'

'Lucia . . .' I tried to brush away her tears, but she batted my hand away. Her eyes widened; she shook her head, unbelieving.

'I'm seeing it all different. Everything different.'

'Lucia,' I said. 'Look – nothing's changed. We're still here. *Together.*'

'You're wrong,' she gulped. 'That's the problem. We were never together – you were just using me. You were just using *us* to escape, get away from these criminals.'

'*What?* Don't be ridiculous . . .'

She nodded to herself, nostrils flaring. 'Fuck you.' Her hands balled into fists. 'Get the fuck out.'

'What?'

'Out. Just get out.'

'Oh, *come on* . . .'

'Out!' Her shout must have woken half the hotel. As I began to protest, she let out a banshee scream, which might have roused the other half. She jumped up on to the bed and launched a hefty kick into my ribs.

'*Fine.*' I began to pull on my clothes, scattered upon the floor where we had left them after returning from the restaurant and making love.

As I bent to put on my shoes, I received a sharp shove from behind, followed by a string of Italian insults and a couple of well-aimed punches.

I had the presence of mind to grab my wallet, phone and, finally, overcoat as I was propelled out of the room.

The next thing I knew, the door was being slammed behind me.

Two doors down a bald man stood outside his room in pyjama bottoms with a bare, impressively hairy chest and shoulders. He raised his bushy black eyebrows questioningly. I lifted my hands as if to say: what can you do? He nodded understandingly and stepped back inside.

We had not been able to afford a particularly romantic hotel, which may have been for the best, all things considered. It was on the periphery of the centre, a modern, Holiday Inn-style establishment with a 24-hour reception and revolving doors.

The receptionist watched me push through them as if he had already been called about the commotion.

It didn't take long to make it through the crystal-cold streets to the River Arno. I was vaguely looking for a bar but it was too late. Even the nightclubs would be chucking out.

It was four o'clock in the morning in a freezing cold Florence and I was dying for a cigarette. I had given up smoking years before, around the time Rose had been due, but like a first love, tobacco always has a claim on you.

I leant over the wall with the Arno rushing by. I had done many stupid things in my life, I thought, this was simply the latest: I had allowed myself to be swayed by emotion, to believe in something for a moment – that I could trust Lucia, tell the truth – and had blown it. Would things have turned out better if I had told her from the outset, from when I had first been hauled in by Bull? Hardly. I could imagine her panic, fury. Should I have bitten the bullet and kept *schtum*, risked doing the slammer myself? It might not have come to that, but it could have. Would that have made her happy? I wonder how that would have gone down with her dad, the ex-Carabinieri.

I followed the path along the river towards the Ponte Vecchio lit up like a liner in the distance, while beside me the winter river stormed beneath a nondescript bridge.

Now here I was, stranded in an impossible country – an impossible language, an impenetrable culture . . .

Alfonso swam into view . . . crazy people . . . *Lucia's livid face* . . . a crazy wife.

La Dolce Vita? The Bitter Life, more like. I found myself translating it. *La Vita Amara.* I thought of those grim neo-realist films of the forties and fifties. This was *my* Italy – as hard and cold as the Florentine night.

Go, she'd screamed. Was that what she wanted?

I turned away from the river and began to head towards the centre. I would go to the train station. I would get the first train. I could be back in Bologna before it became light. I would grab my passport, catch a flight to the UK and arrive before lunchtime.

I hesitated.

But what about Rose?

That was when I got the call.

'Come back.' The line went dead. I swivelled on my heel and, accompanied by the sound of my soles slapping the cobblestones, almost ran to the hotel.

VIII

'You think I haven't tried?' Maurizio Estiva pushes back his chair and swings his feet up on to the desk. He puts his hands behind his head as if he's the editor of *La Stampa*, not a junior reporter on the local edition of a regional newspaper.

'What precisely have you tried?' I ask. We are in a windowless corner of the newsroom that takes up a floor in a tower block out past the suburb of Cirenaica. Frankly, I'm impressed that in this day and age the *Carlino* can afford to keep a whole floor of journalists going, but that's Italy – the rest of the world might be downsizing, but she hasn't got the memo.

'Have you any idea of the scale of what we're talking about?' Maurizio says. 'Five years ago, there were a couple of hundred apartments available for *affitti brevi*,' he means short-term tourist lets, 'in the historic centre of Bologna. Now there are more than two thousand five hundred. And of course, that's just inside the walls. Beyond the Viale—'

'Hold on,' I say. 'More than two and a half thousand apartments *in the city centre*? You're not including rooms in that.'

'Nah-ah. Counting rooms, that would be almost four thousand.'

'But there can't be that many places . . .' I felt dazed contemplating it. 'I mean – where do people live?'

A bitter chuckle: 'Not within the walls any more, that's for sure – ordinary families, students, basically anyone who doesn't already own an apartment or is a high-roller has to look further afield, and even then – well, you know there's been this huge tourist boom. They're competing with visitors, too. *Affitti brevi* actually account for over a third of all accommodation now in the centre – that's more than Florence.'

I think of our own home, how I often find cards from estate agents in the letterbox. How the sound of kids playing in Mirasole has been replaced by the trundle of suitcases and foreign chatter. The Comandante's old social centre is now an 'artisanal ice-cream laboratory'; I recall Giovanni's observation – 'many of the members are no longer with us' – and their old homes presumably converted to Airbnbs.

'Have you spoken to the site?' Maurizio looks at me as if I'm stupid.

'I asked them for a *comment*. They're looking into it, blah, have plenty of safeguards, blah, owners are insured, etcetera. We're talking a multibillion-euro business. It must be "a little local difficulty" to them, and let's face it, why would they want to provide the oxygen of publicity? You never know,' he winks. 'It might give other people ideas.'

'You sound as if you almost sympathise with them.'

He shrugs. 'It's not easy to find somewhere. You think I

want to live with my parents my whole life?' Anger inflects his voice. 'Even when I get promoted, what's my chance of affording a place to rent, let alone buy? I'll still have to live like a goddamn student.'

'And have you spoken to the police?'

He smirked. 'The *commissario* didn't seem very happy to be here over the holidays.'

'Who was it?'

'A right dragon, Miranda was her name.'

'Rita Miranda?'

'We're not on first name terms.'

'And what did she say, precisely?'

'She's like the rest of them.' He made a zipping gesture across his mouth. 'But the trouble's been going on for a while – the destruction of rentals is the only thing new. First there were the usual protests, graffiti. Then they took to placing objects on the monorail from the airport so it kept breaking down, although that was hushed up. And you must have heard about the train hijack!'

I frown. 'Well,' he admits. 'We're not exactly talking *Trenitalia*. It was the City Bologna Express, you know – that irritating train on wheels that runs up and down the streets with carriages and the tourists taking photos of ordinary people as if we're all Mickey and Minnie Mouse in Disneyland. The driver insisted he had nothing to do with it, but basically some chick waylaid him in a coffee bar, and the next thing he knew, when he got back to the departure point, where the train was already full of tourists, sixty of them in all, it was halfway down the road, toot-tooting and everything.

'What happens is, the kid in the driver's seat, he begins

taking them on the tour, complete with a commentary in English – here we have the church of San Domenico, where rests the sarcophagus of Saint Dominic complete with sculptures by the young Michelangelo, that sort of thing, but as he starts to take the more obscure streets and porticoes, the commentary changes to, "and this was once the old Carabinieri armoury, which was occupied by the heroic resistance to gentrification calling for the conversion of the building into affordable housing, but you know what happened? I am asking you, do you know what happened?" And the tourists gamely yelled "No!" "Of course, it was converted into another hotel." And so on, anyway, he drives them out through Bolognina, continuing his commentary about "and here we can see where the majority of Bolognese now live, there are really some of the very best restaurants here and coffee that is still affordable" until he reaches Pilastro on the outskirts of the city, and by now even some of the tourists must have been wondering what the hell was going on, and he finally parks at the shopping mall with something like, "Now your tour of the real Bologna is concluded. You can find some real bargains here, just like at home" and runs off. You're telling me you didn't hear about it? They had it on TikTok and everything. It was depicted as a student prank in the local media, but as you can see – it's escalating.'

'Do you think the company will give the police the details of the renters?'

'Who knows? I still can't see what they'd be able to do. From what I've understood, the company's a victim of its own success, there's so much going on, and Reclaim Bologna use different cards, IDs every time. The first was from a blonde

French woman with positive owner reviews. The next was an Italian businessman. A couple of positives from Turin. This one of yours – another Italian from Rimini, a couple. There's literally nothing to tell them from Adam, unless the company institutes a whole different system of checks, which obviously, they're not going to do.'

'But the people doing this must be local,' I say. 'That's got to be where to start. Reclaim Bologna are campaigners, protestors. They've got a cause, they want a profile. There can only be that many of these types in the city – that's got to be where the police would start.' I know Rita Miranda – she's on the ball. Would she have recognised the graffiti, spotted 'Quinto'? Maybe not, but she's shrewd enough to have someone take a look into it.

'Of course, I've asked around.' Maurizio says defensively. 'But it could be anyone. What I mean is – yes, there are plenty of political activists in the city, and they could be among them, but the *raison d'être* of this lot is "deeds not words". The medium is the message. Sure, they call me, but they don't seem to have a hunger for what you would call the normal kind of publicity.' He giggles.

'What?'

'Maybe it's an exaggeration, but they're more like terrorists than publicists, when you think about it.'

'It was pretty terrible what they did to that man.'

'Of course.' He forces himself to look serious. 'And in fact,' his face dims, 'it *was* pretty devastating for the other owners, too. I mean – they had time to do the full whammy on them.'

'They weren't discovered, you mean. Look – can you give me their details?'

'You think you can do better than me?' I'm amused by the kid's bravado. He almost reminds me of myself at his age.

'Two eyes are better than one. If I hear anything newsworthy, you're welcome to it. I was wondering – as we know, they were interrupted this time when the owner returned, so how did you manage to get there so quickly?'

'Oh, I get it, Sherlock. You think I'm in on it? It's just down the road, in case you haven't noticed. I got a call from a mobile – number unknown, VPN probably. They barely said a word – just, it's Reclaim Bologna. Go to the address now. They were actually panting. It was like they had jumped on their bikes and got out of there, which they clearly had. What?'

'You went to the scenes of the other incidents.' He nods. 'They were apartments, or houses like this?'

'Apartments.'

'Did they have gardens?' He shakes his head. 'So you saw nothing *particular* outside.'

He swings his feet down from the desk and leans forward. 'Should I have?'

'Not necessarily.'

'Come on, level with me – did I miss something?'

'Do I look like someone who wouldn't level with you?'

'Absolutely.'

I check Maurizio is not following me, more out of curiosity than actual concern. I don't care if he returns to the address with me, puttering behind on his Vespa. To be honest, in this heat, I'd be happy to give the kid a lift.

The metre-long ribbon of police tape draped wiltingly

from the front bush informs me that at least at some point they treated this as the scene of a crime. I open the garden gate and try the front door, but it's locked. Never mind – that's not what I'm here for.

I go round the back. I'm actually a little surprised to find the bikes still chained up. They're in various states of repair – some clearly cannibalised, others good to go. There are a couple of real beauties – brand new, top-of-the-range – the others more your student fare, battered and scratched but otherwise well enough maintained. These have doubtless passed through many hands, or legs, and could well date back to the seventies. A bike's a bike, after all. What's more surprising is that the kids didn't return for the newer ones, which are probably worth a couple of hundred.

I take in the sun-beaten garden.

A pair of black and green upright bins. Ragged, baked brown grass. Ants seeping from patches of cracked earth. Mean leaves of bushes wreathed with thorns. The rusty frame of what once may have been a lawnmower leans in a corner. The wall of sound from the cicadas.

I watch a lizard clamber up one of the pine trees that provide the garden with its needle canopy, follow its stuttering progress up the trunk until it reaches a nook between the branches. The gecko stops, flat as an empty glove. Will it choose the right or left branch? Or would it prefer the route between, into the safety and dark of the fork? Perhaps this is why it remains frozen – that choice is denied by the video camera.

It is not exactly hidden, but if you weren't looking for it, you probably wouldn't spot it, and that's what they would have counted on – the kids sneaking back, maybe at night, to grab the bikes. It's a pretty expensive system which definitely has night vision. They're lucky in a way they didn't decide to steal the camera itself, but there wouldn't have been a great deal they could have done with the hardware, and they would have no idea where the police were – close, presumably, if they wanted to catch them in the act, and not risk losing a pricey piece of kit.

Which means, they're probably checking me out, too. I'm about to give them a wave, but decide to cut out the whimsy. It's too hot to explain myself to a bunch of bruisers who have been stuck in the back of a van for heaven knows how long and have nothing better to do than pick on a PI, and a foreigner to boot.

I head out of the garden, my footsteps crackling upon the dry grass. I can't see anything out front, but once I'm back in my Alfa, I take a detour around the rear of the building, and in the street opposite spot a battered transit.

It doesn't look too new. I just hope to Christ they've got air-con.

I call Dolores. 'I may need your help.'

'I've just got back to the centre – signora Bonelli had a drink with another woman and then her husband turned up. Now they've gone home.'

'Separately, I take it.'

'Yup. I took a vid and pic of the woman.'

'Good. Then if the signora's with her husband, let's presume she's not going to slip out to see someone else's, at least at this time of the day. I'll come and get you. I'd like to try the New Market.'

'The New Market? What for?'

'The bike. I thought it might be worth a shot.'

'Which is why you need me.'

'Your presence may be helpful.'

IX

The blue sky of Florence followed us home, it seemed, not so much melting the snow, which continued to stand in grey drifts by the side of salted paths, piled up like termite mounds in Piazza Maggiore or crusted across parks and open spaces spattered with dog pee, but at least halting its advance.

It remained extravagantly cold, colder even – the loss of cloud cover permitting temperatures approaching minus twenty some nights, and at the canteen we took in extra coats and bedding for the rough sleepers, while the city came to resemble its August emptiness, only now the streets and porticoes were deserted due not to excoriating heat but cruel cold, and where heat might have drawn a scorched taint from the old walls and timbers, now black and grey wood smoke smudged the clear sky like ink in water; the ochre stucco became brittle and lumps fell off, baring ancient brickwork. The cracks on our external frescoes deepened.

When Lucia had summoned me back that night, I had hoped all would be forgiven, but it turned out she was keen to play the same side of the record, albeit this time at a lower volume.

She questioned me in depth about what, precisely, had taken place, why I had kept it from her, and how I could have allowed her to feel so guilty. On this last point I had to push back – she hadn't appeared very guilty at the time. On the contrary, she had seemed delighted I had acquiesced to her proposal so easily, although it was true, I may have slept through her late-night soul-searching.

She had got it the wrong way around, I continued. I'd been depressed about my work since the Inspector had ensnared me and had lost the will to keep going, but hadn't felt able to talk to anyone about it – *you could have talked to me*, she batted back – so when her job offer came along, it had seemed best for both of us. I had the book deal, and it made sense to live rent free. Once she had suggested it, I had no reason *to* tell her.

Lucia narrowed her eyes. 'You always were persuasive.' I made my best lost puppy eyes, made to kiss her.

She turned away and switched off the light.

'We have to get up in a couple of hours,' she said. 'We have that ten at the Medici Palace.'

Ever since, things had been like that following Sunday – nothing further was said but clearly nothing had been forgotten. The snow had stopped falling, but the ice endured.

Like the rest of the city, I would have to wait for the thaw.

Alfonso Lambertini had asked me to meet him at his 'apartment' before we went to the official dinner, but when I arrived at the doorway under the portico in Via San Felice that evening, there was only one bell, and name – Lambertini, A. I realised that unless I was otherwise mistaken, Alfonso had an entire palace to himself.

Certainly, we were not talking a house: the arched entrance was easily high and wide enough to accommodate a horse-drawn carriage. I would come to encounter all manner of living conditions in Bologna, but back then this was still a novelty. I rang again. The wicket door clicked open.

I stepped into a dimly lit, cobbled entrance illuminated by candles in cheap-looking lanterns that might have been purchased from Kasanova or IKEA.

'Hello?' I called. There was no response. I began to make my way up a sweeping stone staircase, the lanterns lodged in the alcoves together with the busts of old patriarchs, in one case, balanced precariously on top. The stairs scraped with grit. In the gloom above, I could hear the coo of pigeons, and when I laid a palm upon the handrail it was filthy with their mess.

I arrived at the top, faced on both sides by huge chambers, their faded olive-green doors now removed and tilted against the walls. All around that vast balcony, frescoes of grumpy deities were animated by the flickering light.

'In here,' Alfonso called.

He was stood at the far end of what must have been the ballroom, lined as it was by mottled mirrors and, unlike the rest of the *palazzo* with its stone *Veneziana* floor, laid with creaking chevron parquet. Above, a trio of massive Murano chandeliers hung unlit, while perhaps a dozen lanterns shone busily upon strategically placed stacks of books sprouting from the hundreds piled around the walls like unfinished foundations. There was a tatty leather sofa and old-style TV in the far corner, along with a battered occasional table and a threadbare rug. It was freezing.

Alfonso was stood with his back to a cast-iron, ornately decorated stove on four legs, its flue rising into the ceiling. He was wearing an overcoat and gloves above a formal dinner suit complete with floppy black velvet bowtie.

'Don't you have electricity?' I asked, words suspended on my breath.

'Yes, I have electricity,' he responded. 'How else would I watch television?'

'Don't you have central heating?'

'When it gets really cold,' he said confidentially. 'I use that.' He nodded to a convection heater. I also use them for meetings, of course.'

'Of course,' I said, not understanding at all.

'That's why I asked you here, I thought you might be curious. You didn't bring your wife?'

'She said she would meet us there.' Reluctantly, I might have added.

'Perhaps it's for the better. This is strictly forbidden.'

'I've no idea what you're talking about.'

He smiled confidentially and produced a torch. 'Follow me.'

The remaining rooms on the *piano nobile* were not lantern-lit. 'I switch the lights on when the members come,' he said as our footsteps echoed about us. 'But you see,' he swung the torch towards a socket with the wires hanging out. 'I wasn't going to go to all that trouble for a quick visit.'

'But why . . .'

'It's been in the family for many generations,' he continued. 'I may be the last Lambertini – I certainly will if they have their way – but I'll be damned if I give it up without a fight. *The eternal enmity of the profane.* They might think they are winning, without grasping what they have already *won*.' We passed through another doorless opening and he raised his torch hand pontifically, illuminating a library. '*They know not what they do*, as someone once said. But frankly,' he went to stand in front of a huge bookcase which smelled strongly of mould, 'I do sometimes wonder why we bother.'

He pushed.

Like the wicket door in the *palazzo* entrance, a set of bookshelves sunk back. Alfonso pulled it aside, revealing a black opening. He reached inside and switched on a light.

'Step,' he invited me, 'across the threshold.'

Gold signs of the zodiac ran around a vast domed chamber, cylindrically shaped like a giant baptistry or the cupola of a church.

Jewel-like silver dots sparkled above while below a dozen supporting Palmiform columns evoked ancient Egypt. Masonic symbols were inscribed in silver like hieroglyphs upon the emerald green walls.

Across the chequerboard marble floor, three rows of dark wood benches faced each other in a horseshoe. An ornately carved 'altar' table stood between them. Upon its white marble top: a closed book, which I saw was a Bible.

A golden throne was set upon a raised dais, high-backed

and baroque, flanked by a pair of lesser chairs. Studded in mosaic above the dais, an interlinked six-pointed gold star, with a silver compass and V-shaped ruler at its centre, a carefully drawn golden eye that might have come off the back of a dollar bill glaring out of the diamond shape they made.

'Impressive, no?' Alfonso's voice wavered with emotion.

'I never would have thought . . .' I turned slowly, trying to make sense of all the symbolism.

'It's entirely enclosed,' he said. 'At least, it was. You can probably see the dome from above now by helicopter, or satellite. My great-grandfather had concealed it with a false roof but, after the last earthquake, we were worried it was in danger of caving in, so we had it removed.'

He pointed. 'The compass symbolises the measure of our actions within moral boundaries. The square, straight dealing. The eye – the all-seeing eye of the Great Architect who watches and judges us, who some may call God.'

'I noticed the Bible.'

'More a tradition – it could actually be any holy book. The spiritual passages are meant to inspire. Certainly, when it is opened, it means a meeting is in session and outsiders are most definitely excluded, when it is closed . . .' He swept his arm around. 'I would like to show more people, even the *sovrintendenza* – the *palazzo* is of course listed – but they do not know anything about it and the lodge says no. We walk a fine line, it's true.'

'You mean because secret societies are illegal. And you've got to admit,' I nodded to the doorway behind us, 'this is pretty secret.'

'I told you about us when we first met, didn't I?'

'Only because you thought I already knew.' I frowned – there was an ornate oak door inset into the wall.

'May I?' I opened it. It was stuffed with black cloaks on hangers. Before Alfonso could stop me, I had taken one out. It had a pointy hood.

'Well,' I said, frankly lost for words. He returned it to the closet.

'We follow the tradition of the French rite,' he muttered. 'I appreciate this might seem a little . . . dramatic to a non-member, but the cloak is designed to symbolise the separation of the sacred and profane. When we occupy this space, we are within a different realm. Which reminds me,' he checked his watch, 'we should get going.' He began to usher me out. He reached back inside and switched off the light. 'I wanted to show you for context,' he explained, 'of course, were you to actually embark upon this path, I would never consider it. It is a question of awe, you see, the awe of the initiate. The revelation is a powerful symbol in itself. For it *is* "awesome" as you say, no?'

'Perhaps in the original meaning of the word.'

'Our path is difficult to comprehend to the outsider. But it is best understood as a lifelong journey illuminated by symbols representing and embodying the ancient wisdom shared by the masons who created the original temple – as one absorbs their profound spiritual and ethical truths, one becomes, to put it simply, a *fuller* person. One constructs the temple within, so to speak, and, most crucially in my opinion, the temple without.'

'Hence, for example, your charitable work.'

'That's it.'

'But you have to admit, hidden away like this . . .'

'We exist in the world of the profane. We require a refuge.'

'To be honest, it doesn't seem so very different from a religion. With those robes, a priesthood, even.'

'But we are focused on the *secular* world,' he insisted. 'We are temple builders, not worshippers.'

A string of cynical thoughts – of nudges and winks behind this secret bookcase – but I kept my counsel. Alfonso seemed so sincere I didn't want to disappoint him with cheap jibes.

It may not have been a priesthood, but he was undoubtedly a priest.

In contrast to the shadowy world of Alfonso's *palazzo*, the 'Agape' dinner was conducted beneath the dazzling chandeliers of the ballroom of Palazzo Gnudi on Via Riva di Reno. A riot of baroque, cheeky cherubs gazed down from puffy clouds upon Rococo stucco and dazed statuettes. Ten tables draped with white linen that seated six apiece ran along the length of the room, with a plinth at the end.

I wondered what the other masons must have made of Alfonso's place when they came for their fancy dress nights. Imagining them in those cloaks – let alone obscured by cowls – was almost as difficult as picturing them naked. They seemed so ostensibly, even oppressively, normal. But knowing what they were, or at least around half of them – this was meant to be an 'introductory' gala to allow prospective members to meet existing ones – I believed I could interpret the clues. Like Alfonso, I was beginning to see masonic influences everywhere. Even his eccentric style, the parody of a nineteenth-century English gentleman, provided a kind of key to teasing out the masons among us – he served as both an exception and a rule.

A certain over-attention to appearance seemed to distinguish the male of the species, who in his tailored dark-blue or charcoal suit, cut with the most expensive woollens, exuded the sobriety of the high-ranking government official or central banker. The evidence was the absence of the usual Italian slim-cut style. These suits were tailored in the boxy, English manner. Their style was power.

The women, too, were distinguishable in much the same way, although in truth it would be harder to tell the difference between them and other middle-class ladies. But instead of aping Englishness, they pursued a more French style in plain black, bottle-green and crimson gowns whose cut spoke of Chanel and Dior.

There was little of the usual Italian exuberance on display, yet they all exuded the air of satisfaction that came from belonging to a self-selected club.

Ages began at the late twenties, although the majority must have been over sixty, and while I knew very little about their British cousins, who I imagined consisted mostly of minor royalty, country publicans, and lord mayors, these seemed drawn from a very different social milieu – neither aristocratic nor petite bourgeoisie. This was very much the Latin middleclass at play – lawyers, notaries, dentists, doctors. While Britain's freemasons traditionally represented the old, conservative order, this was the class that had promulgated the revolutions that rocked the eighteenth and nineteenth centuries, and sought to obscure its activities beneath the cloak of masonry. Whigs not Tories, then, but still unmistakably powerbrokers in a nation that was, at least on the face of it, a secular republic.

Strictly speaking, Lucia should have been more uncomfortable there than me. She was as opposed to secret societies as she was to religion, and basically anything that was not secular and left-wing, but she seemed neither disconcerted nor intimidated. It may have been growing up as a Carabinieri brat, which must have constituted its own kind of cult, but the vaguely irritated look that met me as she waited bundled up in her long parka on the *palazzo* steps, transformed into a tickled expression as we handed in our coats and went for an *aperitivo* with the other diners. In her black lace-fringed dress, together with her usual minimal concessions to cosmetics, she was effortlessly gorgeous. For the nth time since Florence, I reminded myself of my good fortune, and cursed my over-disclosure.

Clearly, our table had been chosen because our hosts spoke good English.

'And what do you do?' The late-middle-aged woman who was a professor of law at Bologna University, asked Lucia.

'I work for an NGO promoting affordable housing for local people,' she replied as smoothly as if she was being interviewed on the radio.

'Now that's what we need more of – people *doing* things,' she said to the suave man beside me, who had introduced himself as Michele. 'It sometimes feels as if we just talk.'

'But we fund a lot of "doing" work as you say, Leticia. Charity brings to life those who are spiritually dead.'

'Ah,' she said, 'but if a thief helps a poor man out of the spoils of his thieving, we must not call that charity.'

'Speak for yourself,' Michele said good-humouredly. 'My accounts are fully audited.'

'And in fact,' she looked at us, slightly flustered, 'the lodge's accounts are also fully audited.'

'Under the auspices of *Circolo sociale di Bologna Centro, Garibaldi*,' I said.

'I shouldn't have put it that way,' she added quickly. 'One can get a little carried away with the verbal sparring sometimes, among friends.'

'It can be easy to forget you are among the "profane".'

'It's not meant to be rude,' she explained. 'It's just the word we have always used for the . . . uninitiated.'

'Your mention of the thieves was from Dante,' said Lucia. Michele and Letitia nodded approvingly. 'I'm not sure I caught the first . . . ?'

Michele smiled. 'Aquinas, *Summa Theologica*. We are honoured to have a Faidate among us. It is only a shame the Comandante isn't with you; we have much to thank him for.'

'He's a strict Catholic,' said Lucia.

'Opus Dei?'

'The Comandante doesn't believe in secret societies.' An uncomfortable pause.

'Although I do frequently bump into him at Cisalpina.' Michele smiled. He meant the members club in Via Castiglione.

'I don't think he's necessarily got anything against *exclusivity*,' I said. Lucia laughed. 'The restaurant's excellent,' I continued. 'And he claims it's got the best card room in

Bologna. So,' I addressed the young woman opposite me in an attempt to shift the spotlight away from us, 'what makes you interested in joining?'

She was dressed for dinner but looked as if she was set for an interview. 'It's my fiancé,' she explained with a lipstick-smeared smile, indicating a rather dull-looking young man on another table. 'But it's also for self-improvement,' she added emphatically. 'I want to become a better person.'

'And how do you think it will make you a "better person"?' Michele asked playfully.

'It's access to,' she looked around, 'the learning. The lectures you hold, papers you present on all kinds of issues: art, architecture, history, literature . . . *esoterica*.' The word came out a little mangled in her mouth – I wasn't sure whether it was her English pronunciation, or the novelty of the word in both languages.

Michele nodded warmly and looked at me. 'You're sure you don't want to join?'

'I'm still grappling with Italian. Italy is mystery enough for me.'

'We are a force for good,' he said somewhat insistently.

'I don't doubt it.'

He laughed. 'Of course you do! Honesty is one of our cornerstones, so let's be honest.'

'Like P2?' asked Lucia. There was another hush around the table.

'You know why it was called "Two"?' said Michele. 'Because there was a Propaganda One a hundred years before, when "propaganda" simply stood for good PR. It was about promoting the good we could do. Of course, Gelli twisted that into something bad – he went against all our tenets to blackmail people into belonging.'

'The "bad apple" theory,' I said.

'Something like that.'

'You don't have bad apples now?'

He laughed. 'Oh, I'm sure. But to be fair, that was an entirely different lodge – the Grand Orient – and those were different times. What organisation doesn't have "bad apples"? The Church? Politics?' He looked meaningfully at Lucia. 'Carabinieri?' Then at me. 'National Union of Journalists?'

'I left that ages ago.'

'But you get my point.'

'These were powerful people,' pressed Lucia. 'Politicians, policemen, businessmen, judges. *Berlusconi.* Even the old king was one of them. They pulled the strings.' She gave him an angry look. '*People like you pull the strings.*' I couldn't help feeling proud to see Lucia take on a pair of classics-quoting masons. Hell, I realised, she would have taken on the whole room.

'Which is precisely why we are required to abide to a strict moral code,' Michele replied, apparently unruffled. 'It's funny – no one seems to object to those same kinds of people – politicians like Prodi or Andreotti, policeman like your dear father – believing in a sky god and "the certainty" of believers coming back to life. Don't you think it's a little . . . *fishy* that all the suspicion should fall on us?'

'But . . .' Lucia hesitated.

'But you do believe in a "higher power",' I said. I almost added – I just saw His Cyclops eye glaring at me in your temple.

Michele brushed this aside. 'So do members of Alcoholics Anonymous. It's a handy check on the ego.'

'And Christians don't keep themselves a secret,' said Lucia.

'They used to when they were the persecuted rather than the persecutors. Our discretion springs from that same necessity. Freemasons have been relentlessly persecuted – by the Church, monarchists, communists, fascists, every single totalitarian organisation sees us as a threat. Now, of course, with the advent of the internet we are the inevitable font of any conspiracy, let alone the fodder of *pulp* authors.' He almost spat the words.

'I do grant you,' he continued. 'Our – any – lodge could provide certain unsavoury types with an opportunity to exploit the situation, but we do our best to weed out undesirables.'

'Membership takes a considerable commitment,' cut in the professor tartly. 'It's not a supper club.'

Michele continued: 'And further the well-being of humanity. We keep to the shadows, and neither expect, nor seek, praise.'

I took in the spectacular venue. 'That's very humble of you.'

'By improving ourselves,' he beamed. His teeth were very straight and white – I remembered he was a dentist. '"We improve the world."' He looked at the young woman. 'Persuaded?'

'Absolutely,' she smiled tightly.

'And how about you?' he asked Lucia.

She raised her glass. 'This wine is certainly very good.'

'What did you think?' We were outside, a couple of kilos heavier and almost certainly over the limit. For once I was glad of the ice – it forced us to walk home arm-in-arm in fear of slipping over.

'I felt as if I was doing an *orale* at university,' Lucia said. 'I'm exhausted.'

'But they weren't all that bad.'

'No,' she admitted. 'They certainly weren't demons like in Dan Brown.'

'I don't think they were exactly that in his novels, to be fair.'

'But, Daniel – this is how Italy works. It's all like this, groups of people doing things behind doors. They're just a more extreme version.'

'I get that.'

She looked up at me, the top of her nose red with the cold. I couldn't resist kissing it.

'Do you, though?'

'But you can't deny they also do good,' I said. 'It's thanks to them we keep the canteen going.'

'Of course they do,' she said, sounding like an impatient professor herself. 'But it's complicated.'

'I'm sorry, I don't get you.'

'All of them – the Church, fascists, communists, even the mafia, do "good". But what difference does it make?'

'The intention behind it, I suppose.'

'And what do you think their intention is? "To be the best one can be, and thereby assist others" like your mate said?'

I considered this. 'I believe he believes that.'

'You know why Bologna ended up being run by the Church in the old days?'

'No idea.'

'Because before that, it was a republic of guilds. The furriers, ironmongers – I don't know – merchants, all the rest. They were the ones who built the towers so when they fell out with each other and started to fight they could run into them and throw rocks down on each other. In the end, it got so bad they called on the Vatican to take over like a sort of UN.'

'And?'

'That's what these people really are, just one of those guilds – Christ, they've even kept the name. Sure, they do good, but like all the others it's a means to an end. Backing charity justifies their expensive dinners, because everyone wants to think they're the good guys, but if that was what it was all about, then join the Rotary.'

I thought of Alfonso making his way between the tables, gladhanding fellow members and chatting jovially with newcomers – true-believer, evangelist, *Worshipful Master.* Arriving at our table delighted to share this evening with me and, in that moment, I wished I could share it fully with him. But it would never happen: I might not have much in common with the Comandante, but I knew I could never be part of any gang, especially not now.

'Fair enough,' I looked into her gleaming eyes. 'But if we follow your logic, everyone's bad and no one's good. Everyone's simply in it for themselves.' I looked into her gleaming eyes.

'No, Daniel.' Lucia shook her head firmly. 'That's not it at all.'

X

It would not surprise me to learn Bologna is Italy's, if not Europe's, capital of bicycle theft. Almost everyone I know has had a bike stolen, regardless of location or elaborate (and expensive) security. Bologna is not only considered the 'city of freedom' by young runaways, but also many of the nation's drug abusers and petty criminals, who can rely on rich pickings and a vibrant re-sale market. In the absence of any interest whatsoever by the authorities, vigilantes and Facebook groups fight a seemingly futile battle against what is almost as Bolognese as *tagliatelle al ragú*.

There was a time when to get hold of a stolen bike, or buy one back, your best bet would have been to head down to Piazza Verdi. There, if you were quick enough, you might find it being wheeled conspicuously around and could either pay a bounty, or wrestle it from the seller (although given that they could probably call on the support of other lowlifes peddling everything from essays to heroin in the square, that was easier said than done). This had been our first stop when Lucia's original bicycle (secured to a parking sign with two chains) had gone missing. We hadn't had any luck then, and in the years since, the authorities had made an effort to clean up the area around the Teatro Comunale – which is, after all, the world's second oldest opera house – with mixed results (the bicycle thieves had been moved on, but the drug dealers had apparently proved harder to shift).

These days, if you want to get your hands on a 'second-hand' bike, you have to head to what is parochially known as 'the New Market' in an old light-industrial site just on the wrong side of the tracks beneath the bridge at the beginning of Via Stalingrado. Many of the old factories and warehouses have been converted into artist's studios, galleries and music venues, with stalls for biological produce at the weekend and similarly hipsterish happenings, while the streets in between have become known as the place to pick up a new (old) pair of wheels.

'The students will be away,' says Dolores as I park the car in a nearby side street. 'And even bicycle thieves need a holiday.'

'I'm not sure "need" is the right word. And aren't most of them students, anyway?'

'They're probably in Albania.'

'Ironic, really.' I open the door, pausing as the cool, air-conditioned breeze meets the heat of the late afternoon. 'All their criminals come here, and ours go there.'

'Boh.' Dolores puts on a huge pair of mirrored Aviators. 'They've probably gone home, too. It's just us chumps working.'

We get out. 'You'll be away soon enough. Off to the cold and rain; Wills and Kate.'

Dolores lets out a long breath, fanning a hand in front of her face. 'Promise me that's true. I'll send King Charles your love.'

'Please do, I'm sure he'll remember me.'

We walk deserted streets. Certainly, there's no sight of pallid youths stood tentatively beside suspiciously expensive-looking bicycles.

The rumble of a train drones upon the drunken air, the sigh of the evening breeze – *il vento della sera*. Dust gets in my eyes. I put on my own sunglasses.

'Your bet is that the people who trashed that place are also bike thieves,' says Dolores. 'I'm not sure it will earn them enough to pay for renting all those apartments.'

'You saw the parts on the table. The bikes are still chained up around the back – and Rita Miranda thinks so, too, that's why she's got a camera up there. That must narrow it down a little – politics, theft, "property is theft". Wasn't bicycle thievery a sideline of your squatting pals back in the day? A means to fund the "revolution", at least for the more hard-bitten ones?'

'But these ones haven't bitten. They didn't go back.'

'They can apparently afford to lose the bikes, including a couple worth a bit.'

The muffled boom of Italian rap and the whiff of marijuana draws us around a nondescript corner. A table and trio of stools set outside a converted workshop. A couple of black-clad guys leaning back with their feet up, beer bottles collected on a table in front of them.

'Let me do the talking,' says Dolores.

'That's why you're here.'

They peer incuriously up at us. Outfitted in classic *punkabestia* summer-wear – shabby T-shirts and cargo shorts – one is a grizzled, unshaven type in his fifties with tied-back grey hair. The other might be his son, although I doubt it.

'Dolores,' the older guy says. 'What are you doing here this time of year? I would have thought you'd have been with the rest of the jet set in Miami.' He pronounces each syllable contemptuously – Mi-Am-Eee.

'Lorenzo,' says Dolores. 'Ta, we'll have two beers.'

His head twitches backwards. 'Take a couple from the fridge, and leave the cash on the counter – five euros a pop.'

'Discount for old times' sake?'

'Make it cash. We haven't got the card machine working yet.' He eyes me while Dolores goes to get them. 'And you must be the boss. The corrupter of young minds.'

'We have something in common, then.' He smiles thinly through pot smoke, offers me the joint. I decline.

'Haven't we met before?'

'News to me.' He shrugs, passes the joint to his companion. Dolores returns with the beers.

'I didn't know you'd moved out here,' she says, taking a hit on the bottle.

'Just doing up the place. Where there's life, there's hope. Dolores here,' he addresses the youngster, 'was one of our best, helped convert the grounds of the old hospital.'

'That's the courthouse now?'

''sright. Once they had kicked us out, they planned to make it into a hotel but ran out of money, so the taxpayer stepped in because that was precisely what the city needed – more courts. Back then, Dolores was a dairy farmer.' I give her a wary glance. That didn't end well, but she appears to keep her cool, although I can't see what's happening behind those shades.

She smiles. 'And you and the other "organisers" were happy to live off our milk and eggs. Along with everything else your young skivvies could scrape together.' She nods appreciatively. 'But it looks like you're doing all right, Lorenzo. I'd heard you'd opened a bar.'

'A venue. Want to promote young talent. The young are all about entertainment now, what with their phones and TikTok. You need to draw them in if you want to have a chance to educate them.'

'Free entrance, then?'

'Well, we need to pay the rent. And anyway, putting a price on things adds value to the events – "social marketing" it's called. The relentless algorithm of the worldwide web has *mutated* the young into such exquisite consumers, such *quintessential* capitalists they don't see the value in anything if it hasn't got a price tag. Even politics, so we have to *sell* it to them. *Social marketing.* Not to be confused with "social media marketing".' He waves at the lad. 'That's his realm.'

'I'm impressed,' says Dolores.

'And I'm disappointed,' frowns Lorenzo. 'Did I ever tell you how disappointed I was – we all were – in you?'

She shakes her head, takes another hit. 'I didn't have much chance to hear, mind you. After the raid you and the other organisers were nowhere to be found – you didn't get arrested, weren't at any of your usual haunts in the city. It was just us kids that ended up in court.'

'We had to make ourselves scarce,' Lorenzo explains to his companion. 'We were already well-known to the filth. They were just looking to trump up charges, send us down for a lengthy stretch.'

'I heard most of you managed to escape to Mario's chalet in the mountains of Veneto,' Dolores continues, 'where you had a very cosy Christmas, by all accounts.'

'He had inherited it,' Lorenzo explains to the youth. 'We needed somewhere to get away.'

'Anyway, those of us without chalets or rich parents needed to work when we graduated, and it was this or a call centre.'

'Really?' I ask. Dolores shrugs.

Lorenzo smiles meanly. 'An agent for the bourgeoisie it was, then.'

'Anyway, we're looking for something,' she says.

'Naturally.'

'Specifically, a bicycle.' Lorenzo coughs on his smoke.

'That, I wasn't expecting.'

'It's an English bike.' Dolores looks at the kid. 'Racer, a Raleigh. Green. Sentimental value. A client lost it. They're willing to pay to get it back.'

'It's not yours, is it?' Lorenzo asks me. 'Being English.' I shake my head. He turns back to Dolores. 'How much?'

'I'll discuss that with whoever has it.'

'But since they've hired you, and I'm sure you don't come cheap, comrade, it must be worth a lot.'

Dolores finishes the bottle. 'Maybe it is.'

Lorenzo sucks in the end of the joint, which blazes blood orange, and flicks the roach just past me.

'I don't see what harm it can do to ask about,' he says. 'We can always do with a contribution to the cause, even if it's to make some rich bastard happy.' He turns again to the youth. 'You'll notice that – the wealthy have a habit of funding their downfall.'

Dolores sends him her Telegram info ('WhatsApp? Are you kidding?') and we leave them to it.

Once we're out of earshot, I remark: 'It seems you're not so popular among your old buddies these days.'

'Only the assholes.' Her Aviators glint with a sideways glance. 'And they were always assholes. But despite what you might think, that wasn't them all. There were some good people, and we're still friends. You know, a couple even remember Lucia.'

I stop in the shadows, remove my glasses. 'You never told me.'

Dolores takes off her own. 'It didn't come up.' Her chestnut eyes flicker away. 'I don't like to mention her, Dan.'

'Who are these people?'

'Just a couple of the older ones, on the fringes. Friends of friends, they were at university together, did some squatting, that sort of thing. *Nice* people.'

I have vague memories of us dining with some of her old university friends, picnics in the park. Hands and hugs at her funeral. Faces faded away.

'I'm sorry,' she says. I'm startled back into the present.

'What about?'

'Not mentioning it.'

'I understand.' Do I still appear so raw? Apparently so. 'But was it really a toss-up between us and a call centre?'

A smile darts across her face. 'All I'm saying is, I didn't have a lot of other options.'

'Really?'

'I had a degree in Ancient Civilisations. I was only really qualified to teach others, or time travel, and that hasn't been invented yet.'

'You were qualified to *excavate* the truth, though.'

Dolores winces. 'Terrible. Although I may have *dug up* a clue.'

'Oh?'

'Turn around.' Across the street, side-on to the row of one-storey buildings, is the exposed side wall of the building hosting Lorenzo's bar. A ladder set on the neighbouring roof rests against it, by a half-finished mural three-storeys high. The outline of the entire mural has already been worked out in white paint, its borders comprising the iconic buildings of Bologna, from her two ancient towers, Asinelli and Garisenda, to the 'wedding cake' view of the hilltop church of San Luca with its escalator of porticoes and the modern crop of Japanese-designed, tubular 'Kenzo' skyscrapers with what looks like Godzilla looming behind them. These sit upon an oval horizon of white lines that become more richly detailed vines or creepers in greens and reds that, as more detail is added, transform into the yellow eyes of serpents.

A pair of stubby, beige fingers pull back this viper curtain and a single eye gazes out, its golden pupil on velour blue.

WE ARE WATCHING is outlined below in white capitals perhaps a metre high.

There is a graffito signature in the corner: *5th*

Quinto.

XI

I parked our Fiat Punto outside Villagio Nuovo Bentivoglio, or New Village Bentivoglio, although it was still known by most Bolognese, including its residents, as ex-Fabrica Bentivoglio – ex-Bentivoglio Factory.

I'd been trying to persuade Lucia to learn to drive, without much success. Before she left for the UK, she had ridden a Vespa but now she had become more eco-conscious she rode her (well, my) bike everywhere, so claimed she didn't see the need. In the past I'd have been tempted to moan that 'with me as your chauffeur why should you?' but this time I was happy to help out – anything to get back into her good books.

She certainly would have normally ridden to the ex-Fabrica, but she had promised to give one of the residents, an elderly lady who couldn't walk far, a lift.

The comune had decided to hold a public meeting to discuss the claims surrounding the site, and rather than organising it somewhere nearby, naturally we had been summoned to its headquarters in the splendour of Palazzo d'Accursio in Piazza Maggiore.

The ex-Fabrica was not exactly as I had imagined from Lucia's stories. I had pictured a Dickensian warren of converted workshops with raw, sulphurous bricks and sooty windows. Pallid, whey-eyed children would watch unblinkingly as we walked crumbling halls, eerie echoes punctuated by hacking coughs.

Instead, the 'Villagio' seemed like a modern, tasteful development comprising of half-a-dozen four-storey yolk-yellow apartment blocks around three ample open areas, complete with children's playgrounds, albeit they were now under six inches of grey snow. The old factories had apparently been entirely demolished and the developers had built afresh on the 'brownfield' site.

Seeing the place with its thick walls and top-notch windows, smoked-glass-fronted reception with a gleaming intercom, it was difficult to give the residents' concerns a great deal of credence. It had been a private development built on public land, so both had an interest in everything being hunky-dory.

Despite my poker face, there was nowhere to go in the mirrored lift to the fourth floor, and Lucia didn't need to read my expression to know what I was thinking.

'What did you expect?'

'It makes you realise how much money they've poured into it,' I said diplomatically. 'You've certainly got your work cut out.'

'Haven't we always?' The doors opened. 'You should know that.'

I followed her along the floor-lit, cream-walled corridor that might have belonged to a hotel had it been carpeted instead of tiled. Everything seemed high-spec, down to the wood-effect security doors on every apartment.

The old lady's apartment was ajar when we arrived. Lucia knocked gently.

'Ludovica?' she called.

'Come, come, I'm just getting myself together.'

Ludovica already had on her coat and shoes – in fact, black trainers. The living room, with its parquet floor, low ceilings and modern windows was predictably spotless, the old-fashioned furniture as out of place as an uninvited guest. An ebony display cabinet took up most of the main wall, while a flowery sofa and armchair bulked out the rest of the space. There was a flatscreen TV on a stand beside the windows, but it was not plugged in or hooked up to cable. I suspected the signora spent more time listening to the radio on the sole shelf of the cabinet that was uncluttered by family photos and memorabilia. A coffee cup and saucer were set upon an antique side table by the chair beside the weekend's copy of *L'Unita*.

Some way north of eighty, bone-thin signora Buccanni seemed a jittery mix of tenacity and vulnerability. She had the air of an old professor, although it turned out that, like her late husband, she had been an engineer, a rather uncommon profession for a woman of her generation: 'I go in the factories,' she said in English, 'and they said but where your boss? And I say – that's me!'

'Ludovica was also the leader of the local party section,' said Lucia.

'Oh yes!' She pointed to a black and white group photo in the cabinet. 'There is trip to Moscow, but only men permitted. They say women stay home with children. I say bullshits, but no difference. I think Ruski know how to fool men easier!'

Through the windows, I could see a banner hanging across the way. Limp with ice, I couldn't make out what it said.

'Squatters,' Ludovica said approvingly. 'Move in when family move out. No one else wants place – worry about getting sick.'

We made our way slowly downstairs, taking extra care on the gritted path, me supporting Ludovica on one side and her walking stick the other. Lucia helped her into the front passenger seat. I got in the driver's side.

'Why she not drive?'

'She not want to,' I replied. 'She too lazy.' Lucia cuffed me. I heard her explain to Ludovica in Italian something along the lines of cars being bad for the environment.

'Important that women independent,' said Ludovica. 'Can't depend on men.'

'*Grazie*,' I said, as we turned onto the Viale.

'*Prego.*' She bowed her head. 'You nice boy,' she said. '*Un bravo ragazzo*, Luci.'

'*A volte*,' replied Lucia.

Sometimes.

We parked at the rear of Palazzo d'Accursio. Unlike its ornate facade on Piazza Maggiore, the rear of the building that ran the length of the car park revealed its true nature – as a late medieval fortress for the rulers of Bologna, constructed to project their strength and provide a redoubt should invaders breach the city's two defensive rings. There was nothing ornate about those walls, guard towers and battlements. They were built to withstand a siege from without or, should the people or one of the powerful families get restless, within.

I supported Ludovica across the gritted road and through the dark passageway at the side of the *palazzo* into the rear courtyard that, in contrast to the handsome, high-porticoed front entrance, was strictly business – dozens of offices looked on to a barren square serving as a car park for comune staff. I had learned on the drive over that Ludovica was one of the prime movers behind the campaign, her husband having died suddenly just a year after they had moved into Nuovo Bentivoglio of leukaemia. He had been ninety 'but as strong as an ox!' It had been this that had sparked her suspicions, and as deaths and illnesses began to mount, she had contacted Lucia's charity. How much this had to do with Ludovica's grief, and providing her with an outlet, was moot – there certainly seemed to be a lot of anecdotal evidence and support for the campaign. But *Bologna dei Popoli* had yet to commission a health statistician, and the soil samples were still at the lab. I got the vibe that the mayor, who was chairing the meeting alongside a representative of the builders, was trying to get ahead of the issue, especially now professional campaigners were involved. He was seizing the initiative before Lucia's lot had got their ducks in a row. Did this infer guilt? Not necessarily – just good politics.

'Ludovica, you're such a star!' Cristina met us in the courtyard. This was Lucia's boss, and mother to Rose's school friend Stefania. Despite both women being precisely half

Bolognese on their father's sides, Cristina and Lucia could not have looked more different – if Lucia took her height and dark looks from Puglia, Cristina's tall stature and long blond hair spoke of her mother's Tuscan origins. Smartly dressed and always carefully made-up, she looked a lot like what she was – a lawyer.

Bologna dei Popoli was a strange beast, set up by the city's ruling Communist Party in the 1980s as a sort of pressure group to ensure the comune, which it had run since the end of the war, maintained its commitment to preserving the city as a place for its residents and didn't suffer a fate similar to the likes of Florence or Venice, where tourism and high prices had already begun to drive out ordinary people. This was regarded as an eccentric gesture even at the time, although chiefly because the national party believed history was on its side and the downfall of capitalism was just around the corner, so creating a watchdog was largely unnecessary.

In those early years, *Bologna dei Popoli* was a sort of political nursery for would-be Communist Party activists, paying its way by running training courses for housing managers and receiving (untendered) commissions to inform residents of their rights, conduct consultations, and organise local festivals and events. This changed in 1989 when the Italian Communist Party experienced a kind of nervous breakdown following the end of the Soviet Union and, appropriately at a meeting in the working-class Bologna district of Bolognina, dissolved itself.

Following the *svolta della Bolognina* – Bolognina turning point – the party rebranded itself the Democratic Party of the Left, going on to drop 'the Left' as, over the years, it moved ever further to the right. But in the chaos of that initial move, the activists who found themselves in charge at *Bologna dei Popoli* had the foresight to argue for ownership of a number of party properties that would give the organisation financial independence and a future.

One of those activists now happened to be mayor.

I was a little surprised Carlo Manzi had called the meeting at the headquarters of the comune. It was in one of the frescoed anterooms where clergy and aristocracy had once convened and was lined with portraits of the self-same, ermined schemers glaring disdainfully from gilded frames as if it had been downhill ever since and, considering the two dozen or so of us taking orange plastic bucket seats in our dark winter clothes to discuss housing, I could sympathise. Bologna's communists may have been long gone, but I couldn't help feeling as if we were in one of those scenes from Dr Zhivago when the peasantry had occupied the palaces.

Was this Manzi's strategy, or did he simply not want to get cornered in a chilly party HQ in the sticks? He stood at the front, smiling welcomingly as the crowd took their seats, helping with the coats of older people (and it was mainly old people – it was in the middle of the day) and sharing the odd intimacy with an old comrade.

'Ludovica.'

'Carlo. Thank you for coming all the way down the hall to meet us.'

He pressed his hands in front of his chest as if in prayer. 'I thought I was doing you a favour holding it here. In any case, Oslo Homes have developments all over Bologna, so we thought it would only be fair to convene the meeting centrally, and a good way for you to meet each other.'

Ludovica turned to Cristina. 'But I thought this was to discuss the ex-Fabrica.'

Cristina scowled at Manzi. 'So did I.'

'We will, ladies. Only I thought it would also give other residents the opportunity to confront Oslo, too.'

'You'd better not shaft us,' said Ludovica.

Manzi laughed. 'I wouldn't dare. All will become clear, comrade.'

Ludovica went to sit at the front, with Cristina taking a place beside her. I was in the second row behind them with Lucia. 'Comrade my arse,' Ludovica muttered.

'Did you understand?' Lucia looked concernedly around the room.

'I did,' I said, a little surprised. 'It was probably the vulgarity. That's the kind of Italian I'm used to.'

Manzi had turned away from us. He appeared entirely at ease, his cheap, smart-casual clothes – sky blue OVS jacket and open-necked soft white cotton shirt, jeans and trainers – belying his former role as a university professor and a reputed *palazzo* tucked away in the ex-Ghetto, acquired through marriage to a millionairess.

A mike stood upon a desk like a black tulip. Manzi tapped it. It was apparently working. He nodded to an attractive young woman in tight skirt and cream, low-cut mohair sweater with a Chinese word tattooed up her neck, stationed by the side of the room holding a handheld microphone.

'I think we're ready,' said Manzi. Lucia began to translate with a whisper. I enjoyed feeling the warmth of her breath, her lips occasionally brushing my ear. I felt like a teenager in class beside the girl I had a crush on.

'To begin with,' said Manzi, 'I would like to thank everyone for making the effort to come here.' That fixed smile settled on Ludovica. 'I realise that for some of you it may have been difficult, but I thought it would be a good opportunity to bring everyone together to discuss some issues that have been brought to our attention concerning Oslo Homes, and signor Molino here, CEO of Oslo Homes, has kindly agreed to join us. I apologise that I only have an hour available on this occasion, but I have instructed my staff,' he indicated the woman, 'to arrange further meetings, should you require them. Signor Molino, would you like to say anything?'

Signor Molino, who with his square head and face reminded me of a Lego model squeezed into a blue suit and tie, leaned towards the mike: 'Thank you for having me here.' He cleared his throat and looked out at the audience as if we were a firing squad. His already flushed face turned puce. He nodded to the mayor.

Carlo Manzi's smile vanished as sharply as a fox clamping its jaws shut. 'Now, these very serious concerns about the cases of illness at Nuovo Bentivoglio.' He shifted some papers. 'I would like to say, especially as a former member of *Bologna dei Popoli*, that this matter very much concerned me. I remember even back in my time, there was a lot of discussion about what to do with the site of the old factory, and safety was a big topic, so when the proposals came in, I took a direct interest, especially in the health implications, so it is a great sadness to me that this has come up. As such,' he shuffled some more papers, 'I have once again looked very closely. Now, we know that the soil samples we commissioned came back negative. I have also had a health statistician conduct a study.' I nudged Lucia. 'Which I am happy to share with you.' The tattooed woman landed a heavy booklet on our laps. 'And you are welcome to interrogate at your leisure. I must say, I do find the outcome a little concerning.' He glanced at the Lego man, who looked down.

'In short,' continued Manzi. 'Although it is early to say anything definitive, there *are* indications that the levels of some diseases may be higher on this site than in the general population.' There was a collective gasp. 'But let me add that further work is required to see if this is due to natural variation, which I of course immediately commissioned.

'Obviously, the Comune of Bologna is one hundred per cent committed to the welfare of its citizens and I promise you I will leave no stone unturned to get to the truth.' He looked directly at Cristina. 'I expect you will have questions?'

'Yes.' Her voice wavered with surprise. 'What diseases are we talking about?'

'It is all in the report,' he said officiously. 'Various cancers, mainly. But the important thing to remember is that this is preliminary – further work is required.'

'That's not very reassuring if you are living there; if you have children.'

'I fully understand that, Cristina, which is why we will be offering a temporary resettlement scheme for any resident that applies for it, funded by Oslo Homes, I might add.'

'An apology,' said Ludovica. 'This was a council project – will we be hearing an apology from the mayor for his lethal partnership with the private sector?'

Manzi nodded. 'I am very, very sorry for your loss, signora, as you know, although we certainly cannot say that had anything to do with our initial findings. Your husband, Giorgio, was a personal friend. But I can assure you I did, and am doing, everything in my power to ensure the well-being of the residents, along with all the people of Bologna. That was why as soon as I heard of your concerns, we looked into it, and will continue to—'

'*Bologna dei Popoli* would like a one-to-one meeting with the mayor to discuss this issue in detail,' called Lucia.

'Of course, my assistant will organise it.'

'What about the rest of us?' An old man's voice from the centre. 'Are our buildings safe?'

'That is a good question, signor Testoni, and why I have invited you all here. As part of the analysis, I have commissioned a study on all Oslo developments, alongside other projects, which we will use as a benchmark. Be assured, we will leave no stone unturned.'

'And will we get access to this resettlement scheme?'

'Not in the first instance, no.' He was interrupted by grumblings of discontent. 'But I have asked for a similar "quick and dirty" analysis of your buildings, and if something emerges, then certainly.' Signor Testoni appeared satisfied.

'And has signor Molino got anything to say?' asked Cristina. The mayor pushed the microphone across to him like a loaded gun.

Molino cleared his throat and leaned forward. 'Only that we did everything, absolutely everything in our power to ensure the building was safe. And remember,' he glanced at the mayor, 'these are preliminary findings, eh? It doesn't mean—' The shouting began. 'It doesn't mean that there's anything wrong. We did all the studies that the law required, and more . . .'

The meeting dissolved rather than ended, with the mayor and builder being surrounded by concerned residents, while the four of us stood apart. There was no sense of triumph. Cristina and Lucia were pale with shock, while Ludovica seemed to have visibly aged – the fight had drained from her. I wondered if the battle against the comune had been keeping her alive.

After Cristina exchanged her details with the assistant, we made our way out of the room and along the long corridor where for centuries scribes and petitioners had sat on stone seats by the windows. As we waited for the lift, Cristina said: 'Why does it feel as if we lost?'

'Because we're so unused to winning?' asked Lucia.

'If that's what happened,' said Ludovica. 'If that man said black was black, I wouldn't believe him.'

The lift arrived. It was tiny considering the scale of the rest of the *palazzo*, but then I don't suppose they had designed it with one in mind.

We squeezed in and descended in silence.

Of the four of us pressed into the lift, two would be dead within the decade. Ludovica – well, I suppose at that age, she was always on borrowed time. And, of course, Lucia.

But there was also signor Molino of Oslo Homes, who would be found hanging from a beam in the attic of his family's summer house in the mountains just a week or so after Lucia's accident, a yellow Post-it note helpfully left on the front door warning neighbours or family not to enter, to call the police.

And Carlo Manzi, albeit somewhat later.

In fact, just before the Comandante and Alba had left for their vacation in Cesenatico, Giovanni waved a copy of the *Carlino* at me.

Manzi was no longer mayor by now. He had long since resigned following publicity surrounding his involvement in a scandal that our own Faidate Investigations may have played a small part in exposing, but this being politics, he had been booted upwards to the PD's seats in the Senate.

On the few occasions that he had ventured back from Rome, however, he had been known to visit the party's offices in the Kenzo Tange Towers, and it was from one of these he had apparently fallen while struggling to open a window. There were not said to be any suspicious circumstances, although when I read the news, I couldn't help recalling his remark to me once in that very building:

'Defenestration, they say, is the Italian way.'

XII

I haven't been entirely alone at the Residence – Claudio, Alba's boyfriend, father to her daughter, 'Little' Lucia, has also been knocking about. His business is never short of work, although a description of what his work actually is would be tricky. The clue is probably in its name – Gaspari Solutions.

I first encountered him when he came to install our satellite TV back in the days before digital when I was trying to pick up (i.e., steal) British channels. We got talking and it turned out he could also fit and (he boasted) disarm alarm systems. We began to use him for various hardware 'challenges' and enhancements, until one day he began dating Lucia's cousin and became permanently installed, so to speak.

Not that he's been exactly rushed off his feet this summer. Like many fathers to young children, I suspect he is partly pleased to have an excuse to stay at home while Alba and the Comandante (but clearly, mostly Alba) look after three-year-old 'Little' Lucia at the house in Cesenatico. I know the coroner and his granddaughter (along with her husband and two small children) with whom we share ownership of the sprawling beachfront villa are also down there, so I'm sure they have plenty of company. Claudio is only too happy to spend the weekday evenings in Bologna at the pub with his old pals from the motorbike club and head down to the coast at the weekends.

I managed to lure him away from Il Moretto one evening and we drove his van down to the New Market, using his collapsible ladder to climb on to the roof where Quinto had yet to finish his mural and install a camera at the base of a satellite dish.

Sure enough, as I step out of the shower at nine the next morning, my phone pings – movement on the roof. There is Quinto, naked except for a pair of Speedos and a kind of respirator, halfway up the ladder, spraying away at the mural, a sack slung over his side containing cans of paint. The colour and definition of the camera is excellent, although it is about twenty metres away and Quinto is working in the shade. A small, skinny fellow, his bare, outstretched arms appear the same length as his legs and he works flattened against the wall in stops and starts like that gecko.

I hadn't considered the sun – clearly, he will down tools when the wall becomes exposed to direct sunlight. Will he return once it has moved around?

Another notification. A video from Rose. I open it – a panorama of green valleys, the breath of wind, sonorous clank of cow bells.

'Say hello to Dad,' Rose says in English as the brown cow

munches disinterestedly on the pasture. She swivels the phone around to her boyfriend Antonio who is wearing ridiculous wraparound sunglasses instead of his habitual goggly specs below his curly black hair. He grins in his customarily gormless fashion and waves. Finally, my eighteen-year-old switches the camera to selfie mode as they carry on up the mountain path. It's only been two weeks but they might as well have been years – I can't help thinking of her as a child, and it is always a shock to see this young woman, her pale skin freckly from the sun (I must remind her to wear sunscreen – shouldn't Antonio tell her? He does want to be a damn doctor, after all) trekking this path hundreds of miles from home – from me – cheerfully chatting away about how many kilometres they've walked, her blisters and muscle ache, and did I see her Instagram of the food at the refuge? And what a great house Antonio's family have up here, you really must come. Then she flicks the view back to the path ahead and with a 'that's it for now, don't get too hot!' she's gone. *Done*, I'm sure she thinks, *that chore out of the way*. I've only received one 'live' call since she's been away. But what do teenagers know about the wrench of parental love?

I flick back to the feed. The Gecko's still at it. I message Claudio, who I presume is actually in his apartment on the ground floor of the Residence.

'Seen this?' I don't receive a reply, which hardly surprises me – he's no early riser. Although I like Claudio *in principle* – he's an avuncular, can-do sort, with a personality as big as he is – I can't say we are friends. Sure, we might share a cold beer in the courtyard one evening, but he has never invited me out with his mates, and the thought has probably never occurred to him. He is motorbikes and gizmos and soccer scores, while I'm the English widower, the former journalist (and therefore, apparently, an 'intellectual') who lives upstairs and successfully argued against him and his girlfriend taking over the *entire* ground floor of the Residence for their housing extension; together with the Comandante, effectively his boss, or at least main client.

It is only now, with Rose away for her first summer holiday 'alone', I'm beginning to realise the extent of my isolation. Do I exaggerate? On any non-holiday at the *La Residenza Faidate*, you're likely to find the place packed. Even Lucia's younger brother Jacopo has apparently met his match with Dolores' feisty Neapolitan cousin Celeste, who has also moved in, incidentally. But despite the numbers, there always seem to be less people around our dinner table, and with Rose increasingly staying over at Antonio's, I find myself banging about the apartment as the Comandante must do one floor below, albeit I have a mutt for company. Of course, I do have friends – Luca, for instance, who I met all those years ago at the canteen – but he now has young kids, which create their own climate. My musician pal Vesuvio, I guess, although with the advent of streaming he makes most of his money from touring, so is constantly on the move in order to maintain his ex-wives and children. In fact, I spend most of my time socialising with clients, especially 'the ladies that lunch' like Ginevra, which I'm not sure is particularly healthy, or that I would like to hook up with one of the single friends who she paints as *Sex and The City*, Bologna Chapter.

I might have spent the years following Lucia's death

focusing on work, and just bloody fitting in, but my main job has actually been raising Rose, and it only now dawns on me that I've been made redundant. Had everything worked out as planned, I suppose I would be sharing this time with my wife. We might even have another fledgling beneath our wings. Instead, I wake alone on a foreign shore.

Is it time to return to Britain? This prompts a smile – I might be 'Bologna's English Detective', and my application for Italian citizenship still languishes in the bureaucratic purgatory that is after all a necessary stage in a Catholic country; my claims to Italian identity may prompt hilarity among native-born Italians and Britons alike, but something about me has definitely changed, there's been a tweak to my DNA.

I might still see the world through English eyes, but I interpret it like an Italian. And once you've lost a certain islander innocence, there's no going back.

I take another look at the photos Dolores shared from the wrecked Airbnb in San Donato. Her purpose had been mainly to record Quinto's signature, which she had then compared with other photos she had taken around town. His preference for greens and reds, the cursive, serpent-like R in RECLAIM, the style certainly seemed to be his, but it wasn't that I was now drawn to, it was the squiggles around those words, which I, and doubtless most people, would usually dismiss. Those inverted pyramids, for example: are they the usual Extinction Rebellion symbol? Or could that be a different form of hourglass, symbolic of another kind of subversion? And the parallel lines running up the wall – is that actually a ladder? A ladder leading up to a house? House *boat*, actually? Three rungs. *Jacob's ladder*? The house – an *ark*? And look there, hooked under the C – an anchor. I could almost hear Alfonso in my ear: *The anchor for hope, the ark, faith, the ladder, a life well-spent.*

Squiggles, obscure architectural features. Meaningless to the uninitiated, but the initiated, thanks to my unofficial baptism, saw them everywhere. Be it the square and compass at the base of the statue of Italian patriot Ugo Bassi along his eponymous city centre street, or even the Comandante's club, Cisalpina, named after Napoleon's short-lived Italian republic. Although not all of the club's members had been masons, its founders, champions of a bourgeois revolution, certainly were and had redecorated the un-consecrated monastery in a nineteenth-century celebration of the Society – that eight-columned card room, the five-pointed star and honeycomb stucco all symbols of their secular faith.

And what did we have here? An anchored house (or house boat) you could reach by a ladder.

All it needed was a massive bloody eye.

WE ARE WATCHING.

'Are you following this?' I open Claudio's message and flick back to the rooftop, but the feed has been replaced by a bird's eye view of the bridge, moving in the direction of the centre. Quinto is apparently on the go, and Claudio has activated the drone we hid on a neighbouring rooftop.

I wouldn't be able to tell it was Quinto if there wasn't a purple triangle hanging menacingly above his head as he weaves between the queuing cars at the red lights, jumping them to go on the pavement, then crossing the Viale on the zebra along with the pedestrians. Because the drone is helpfully synchronised with Google Maps, the street names appear as he passes along them. He seems to be zipping across the city in my direction.

Keeping an eye on his progress, I quickly pull on some clothes. By the time I'm ready to go, Quinto has crossed Piazza Maggiore. A message from Claudio:

'Twenty minutes flight time remains.' That's the trouble with drones – for all their technology, their battery life is limited.

Quinto has hit an alley running parallel to the pedestrianised stretch of Via D'Azeglio, which is packed with tourists. He passes it, then cycles up D'Azeglio, going against the cars and busses.

I cross the courtyard. The back of Claudio's head is visible as he sits on his Lay-Z-Boy recliner in only his pants with his computer on his lap, working a joystick on the tray in the armrest. He raises his free hand as I pass.

I couldn't have asked Quinto to be more accommodating – I thought I might have to pursue him in our little white Alfa Mito, which I share with Rose to get around town, but he has come to a halt near the top of D'Azeglio, just around the corner.

This is one of the shortcomings of drones, however, and why, apart from their limited battery life, they won't be able to replace flesh-and-blood PIs just yet: while it can zoom in as Quinto rests his bike against the drainpipe and steps beneath the portico, it can't float down and follow him underneath without being noticed.

And I will need to get a move on if I want to find out precisely where he's headed – that part of the street is mainly upmarket stores, but there are enough residential doors in-between, and like everywhere else in the city, those seemingly anonymous entrances can lead to the long dark hallways of former convents and monasteries, branching off at all angles. They are little worlds within themselves, with any number of possibilities.

But as I round the corner at the top of the road by the bar, there's an explosion.

It's not like the booby trap before – this delivers a proper punch. Having almost run around the corner, I find myself crashing into the platform set on to the street for the summer custom, cowering instinctively. There is no one actually sat outside – it's too hot – otherwise, as I straighten up, I'm pretty sure I would have found them on the floor.

The explosion had been loud enough to make my ears ring, but apparently not shatter the glass of the bar or any nearby shops. Car alarms sound, and there's a kerfuffle inside the bar, which had its double doors closed to keep out the heat. They open as I get to my feet, a welcome blast of cold hitting me along with the despairing cry from an infant woken by the blast. Along with other onlookers, I feel more curious than afraid. Ahead, the portico is billowing red smoke, as if football supporters have let off a flare. I step on to the street where I catch sight of Quinto speeding towards the centre on his bike. Well, I know where he's going.

I keep to the middle of the road as there's too much smoke beneath the portico; in fact, it's beginning to drift across the street, causing cars to slow. Horns now join the car alarms.

I was wrong – one store front has shattered, glass fanning across the portico and on to the road.

A car beeps, and I stumble back to stand on the opposite side of the road. From here I can get a better idea of what has happened – an entire store front gone, red smoke billowing from its broken mouth. In white paint sprayed between the portico's arch (probably by Quinto):

RECLAIM BOLOGNA.

The store's sign is visible through the billowing cloud in silver lettering upon a tasteful mole-brown background – BAB.

I have never noticed the place before, but that means nothing – if it was a fancy women's wear store, like many in this neck of the woods, why would I? But then, why would Quinto's mob want to wreck a fancy women's wear store? Gentrification? A little late for that in these parts, gecko boy.

Weaving my way back through the now-stalled traffic with my hand across my mouth and nose, I get closer.

Written beneath BAB is my answer: *Bologna Affitti Brevi*.

Bologna Brief Lets.

I'm back at the bar, treating myself to a cannolo and cappuccino in the absence of my daughter/in-house dietician, and monitoring Quinto's return to the mural via the static cam (the drone must have long since landed at the Residence) when I have company.

'The best cannoli are in Via Saragozza.' Commissario Rita Miranda of the Polizia di Stato pulls up a seat. I hide the cam footage. Fortunately, my phone is propped against the napkin holder, away from her.

'That's a bit far to go for breakfast,' I say.

'Anything interesting?' She means the phone.

'English news.'

'How's your citizenship application coming along, by the way?'

'It's not you holding it up at the Questura, is it? So you can get a little more leverage over a humble private detective?'

'When I meet a humble one, I'll tell you.' She's as elegant as ever, although more casually dressed than a Nancy Bonelli or the Contessa di Castiglione, in baggy khaki cotton trousers and an ivory T-Shirt, albeit with Aquazzura sandals, a Prada bag (which presumably contains her cuffs, handgun and goodness knows what other accoutrements of the trade) and huge, square D&G sunglasses. In short, she's a senior detective dressed for work in this impossible climate, which does not honestly seem to bother her, but then she's from the far south, with a bloodline likely stretching back to the Trojan Wars, and gives off the impression she's remembered every moment since.

'I thought we were friends, Daniel.' Beneath those glasses she smiles like Atalanta outwitting one of her suitors.

'What has friendship got to do with it, Commissario?'

'Ooh, listen to you – I wish I had my stamp right here, I would *definitely* say you qualified as an Italian.' She pulls out a sweetener from her cavernous bag and adds a drop to her coffee. 'You saw it, then, did you? The attack?'

'I *heard* it, you mean. That's why I'm here. You know we live around the corner. There was this big bang, so I came around to find out what was happening.'

'Terrorists.'

I pause the cannolo halfway to my mouth. 'I think that's a bit strong, Commissario. Vandals, apparently, judging from the graffiti. The usual suspects?'

She produces a cigarette. Another late-middle-aged smoker, skin leathered by the sun. Yet I suspect she will still be puffing blithely away when she's wearing a one-piece on the beach, playing cards with all the other old ladies.

'That was a bomb, Daniel. That's terrorism. More your mate the *Ispettore*'s territory, frankly, but the powers-that-be left me to cover while the men bugger off for the month. In Italy, a childless spinster is at the very bottom of the pecking order, it goes without saying.'

Sadly, I suspect she's correct, so I move swiftly on: 'But terrorism, I mean – it was a smoke bomb.'

She tips her glasses forward to reveal gently mocking eyes. Twists the napkin holder around and deals one out, reaching across to wipe my nose. 'Cream,' she says. 'Reclaim Bologna, they call themselves. Who would you say they want to "reclaim" Bologna from?'

'I guess they're to do with the protests about people having nowhere to live.'

'Reckon your associate Dolores knows any of them?'

'I could ask her,' I say. 'But I get the impression she's not as involved with that lot as she used to be.'

'Hm.' The *commissario* pushes her glasses back up and takes a thoughtful puff. 'What about you?'

'What about me? I told you – I just heard the—'

She raises her hand. 'What were you doing in the garden of the house in San Donato?'

Of course, she saw the CCTV footage.

'I was looking for my bike, if you can believe it.' She doesn't look convinced. 'I'd heard it had been spotted in the back garden.'

'Your bike was stolen?'

'That's it. A Green Raleigh racer, an English brand.'

'So this had nothing to do with the incident at the house.'

'You mean the one with the tape outside?' She nods, contemplating the cigarette rolling between her the tips of her fingers. I realise if she's got this far, she's also spoken to the homeowner and knows about us.

'Look, it's true, it really is for the bike. Full disclosure – I saw a kid riding it, chased him to that place at the same time as they were discovered. The kid got away on it, and I returned a bit later to see if there were any clues to where he might have gone.' I hold up my hands. 'That's it, I promise.'

'Because we're pals, right? And you know if you help me, I might be able to get your wife's bike back.'

I have to ask: 'How do you know it was Lucia's?'

'You really want to get your hands on this bike, so I had a look in the files.'

'Do you know how it happened, then? How the police managed to lose it in the first place?'

'I considered this,' she says. 'I suspect it was placed aside at the time of the incident, then got missed in the handover between us and the Polizia Municipale. It happens. By the time anyone realised, they may have returned to the scene to collect it but it would have been long gone – no lock.' She lowers those glasses again. 'Cock-up over conspiracy, Daniel.'

XIII

The woman behind the Plexiglass glared at me with a look of sheer hatred. I attempted to explain again in my shaky Italian that there really wasn't a problem, that this had already been agreed; that despite not having an Italian employer I was self-employed (which had apparently been how they had managed to hire me at the canteen in the first place: don't ask – it was complicated) and therefore entitled to health care as an EU citizen, but she was having none of it. While I desperately plucked words out of the air, she was shaking her head.

Her hand slapped on the bulging white folder in front of her.

'It's not in the book,' she yelled. I believe she yelled because she didn't think I could understand, but I understood that much. Neither of the immigrants on either side of me flinched. This was par for the course. They had taken the precaution of coming with people who could speak the language well enough to navigate a bureaucracy that even Italians found intimidating, and arrived armed with their own stuffed folders. I was also supposed to have one – an Italian, I mean – Lucia had been meant to accompany me as she had before when, faced with the same 'not in the book' speech, she had demanded to see the boss who turned out to be an old school friend and said leave it to me. A week later I had received my renewed *tèssera sanitaria*, or health card, in the post.

But now it was up for renewal again, and I was on my own.

As I had sat in the dingy room with twenty others waiting for my number, my alchemist had not materialised. I had messaged Lucia to remind her my time was approaching, but she replied that something had come up. 'Anyway,' she added, 'it's all sorted now. You just have to give them your card and say "*per il rinnovo*". If there are any problems explain Dino Farinelli agreed it. Your Italian is better now.'

Trouble was, when I had mentioned Dino, the official shook her head even more emphatically.

'*You deal with me.*' She shoved the expired card back across the desk.

'But . . .'

'Basta!' She slammed the folder closed. This time even my fellow supplicants jumped. She stalked off to stand by the rear doorway, arms crossed, muttering bitterly. I smiled wanly and got to my feet, my heart beating fast. My grasp of the language fell to pieces when seized by emotion, and there were just two ways to maintain a *bella figura* – launch a tirade of invective, of which I was entirely incapable, or keep my cool and remain polite, which I could just about handle. I backed out, a smile plastered across my stupid face, until I reached the hallway.

The rage, silently brewing as I had tried desperately to make myself understood, hardened into a sense of injustice, impotence, abandonment.

Had Lucia any idea how hard it was? How could she just have left me to it?

I began to make my way to the exit, past the somewhat brighter room reserved for Italian citizens, where fewer people waited for more officials to become free although, to be fair, I doubted their experience of AUSL, *Aziende Unità Sanitarie Locali*, was a great deal less onerous than my own – the gatekeepers of Italian bureaucracy were equal opportunity disciplinarians. In that sense, Italians were never truly able to escape the rigid pedagogy of their education system where sometimes prickly, often jaded, occasionally inspirational functionaries would school them in how to behave. It all depended on what counter you ended up at.

It was then that I spotted the fuzzy head of hair cupped by the upturned collar of that blue greatcoat. Sure enough, Alfonso Lambertini was sat mid-way along a row with a bulging lever file on his lap. He was staring ahead with the customary zombie-like gaze towards the digital numerical display, his fist presumably closed around a ticket. I waved but he didn't see me.

'Alfonso,' I said. A couple of people in the row looked my way, but he remained in profile like a well-fed king on the side of a coin. '*Alfonso*,' I repeated. I indicated to his neighbour to give him a nudge.

He roused as if from a trance; blinking, finally looking my way. He initially failed to recognise me, but then it clicked, and he appeared to force a smile. This was followed by a resigned shrug. He pointed to the display and shook his head. I had wondered whether he might be my saviour and I could send him into combat against the functionary but, seeing that huge file on his lap, I understood he had his own battles to fight.

I had waved him goodbye and was halfway down the road, when I heard puffing behind me.

'I thought,' Alfonso struggled for breath. 'I . . .'

'Take it easy.'

'I . . .'

'Let me take that.' His folder was in a straining shopping bag. 'My God,' I said. 'Even by Italian standards, you've got a lot of paperwork.'

He shook his head mournfully. 'I thought . . . that you might be . . . of service to me.'

We went to a nearby bar. The colour returned to Alfonso's cheeks, the glint to his eye. Although he was a chubby fellow, he had an animating vigour as if there was some kind of dynamo inside his barrel chest. He was one of those sixty-somethings you wouldn't be surprised to hear had made a century, or dropped dead the following day.

'When we are young we spend our time as if we are millionaires without realising it is not wealth we possess but credit, and then arrives the time to pay the bill.' He gazed at me. 'Have you exhausted your credit, Daniel?'

'If there's a time to miss-spend, as you put it, it might as well be when you are young. I guess I was lucky – I met Lucia.'

'Ah yes, the love of a good woman. For me it was the brotherhood, although with the admission of ladies, I suppose I should call it something else. I had, of course, been initiated as a youth – with my father as the Worshipful Master it was more or less obligatory – but I did not take it seriously. In fact, I rejected it! Fell into bad company at university.' He glanced at the shopping bag. 'The truth is, I took illegal pharmaceuticals, which resulted in me falling gravely ill.' He sighed. 'There was something inside me, apparently, which "broke".'

'Do you mean you became addicted?'

He chuckled. 'That would be the usual path, I grant you. The dissolute son of the aristocrat who becomes a drug addict. Heaven knows, it's easy enough in this city, and the toleration of drug abuse is one of our worst scandals, but no, that was not my particular road to Hades, although it might well have been, had I persevered. No, in my case, it was a single dose of Lysergic Acid Diethylamide, or LSD, the mind-altering drug. I remember taking it and,' he glanced again at the bag, 'in short, nothing was ever the same again. It triggered what was diagnosed as a "psychotic episode". I won't go into details, but it led me to being physically restrained and admitted to hospital. Unfortunately, it was down the hill, as I think you say, from there. Whether the proclivity was underlying and always likely to emerge, or whether it would have remained dormant, we will never know, but in any case, this led to the development of other delusions and periods of psychosis. In short, I spent much of the remainder of my twenties in a state of some distress and undergoing various treatments, which is why,' he smiled wistfully, 'my file is "bulging", as I think you say.'

'And which was what you were doing at AUSL.'

'Yes, and no. As I was saying, I have long since returned to normality. The treatments were eventually successful. Either that or I grew out of it, assisted profoundly by the structure, the rites, the support of freemasonry. I have not required pharmaceuticals or any other form of therapy for over two decades. My purpose in visiting AUSL was to secure an official recognition of this.'

'Great.' I frowned. 'But how can I help you?'

'You, and perhaps your dear wife. I suppose the pertinent question to ask is – why? Why is it necessary for me to require this official documentation?'

'Okay.'

'Because certain actions are being taken against me, certain legal actions, which are placing in doubt my, um, state of health.'

'You mean your mental health?'

'That's right – they are questioning that.'

'Who are they?'

'Who else would "they" be? They are my family.'

Moves were afoot to put Alfonso's sanity to the test. From what he told me, various witnesses had attested to his unorthodox behaviour. For example a neighbour he had never even seen before had testified to a notary that he had turned up at her door one evening, brushed past her and behaved as if her apartment was his own. She had been about to call the police when, having sat upon her sofa, put his boots on to her coffee table, and turned on the TV, he had muttered to himself, switched it off, and marched out again. Another witness had claimed that while waiting at the bus stop he had seen Alfonso stood nude at his window, masturbating. He had been about to call the police himself, but then his bus had arrived.

'And you have no memory of this?'

'Of course not! Why would I do such a thing?'

'And how did they find this person? Or the neighbour?'

'I have no idea.'

'Has anything else occurred,' I chose my words carefully, 'you have found . . . unusual recently?'

'What do you mean "unusual"?' He held my gaze a little too intently, I thought.

'You know, things that have struck you as out of the ordinary.' He looked away. 'You have misplaced things, perhaps?'

A genuine smile. 'That is not out of the ordinary, Daniel. I would lose my own head if it wasn't screwed on.'

'Any odd experiences, then?'

'What are you, my doctor?'

I opened my hands. 'You asked for help.'

He sighed. 'Obviously, this has all been very upsetting. And I admit, there have been things. I suspect, caused by the stress.'

'What things?'

'Little things.'

'Like?'

He shuddered. 'Flashbacks, perhaps. Of my previous

experience. Or more like echoes. After I have fallen asleep, I wake up. Waking dreams, so to speak. I wake –' Now he gave me a desperate look, a look I had never seen before but which seemed to come from some hidden place – *'But my dreams pursue me.'*

'You see things, you mean. Hallucinate.'

'It has only happened once. Well, twice. No, three times.'

'What is it, Alfonso?'

'It began one night. I woke up. I was very cold. I could feel the shadows. Well, you've seen my place. It is cold and shadowy. But I had this terrible . . . feeling. I went to the stove. I kept stoking the stove, but still couldn't get warm. I . . .' He closed his eyes. 'I embraced it.' He gave me another wary look and rolled up his arm. It was bandaged. 'I only came to when I smelled the burning. I wondered what was cooking. Obviously, it was me.'

'Oh Jesus Christ, Alfonso.'

'There was another time, I realised, before then. I had woken up in front of the television, but for some reason, I believed I was in the teledrama itself. *Un Posto al sole*. I believed I was one of the women, which was odd.'

'I suppose it might be.'

'What I mean was, it was odd because I had never seen *A Place in the Sun*, yet I appeared to know all the characters, including my own, and their back story, along with my lines before I, or she, as I was watching her simultaneously on the television, while also being in the television, said them.'

'I can see why that might strike you as strange.'

'Then I was in the hospital. This was the dream. I was in the hospital, restrained. Doctors were coming with scalpels.

They wanted to see what was inside me. They began to cut me open, even though I was fully awake – although obviously, I must have been dreaming – and discussing my inner parts as they took them out, while completely ignoring my pain and protests. Finally, I managed to wriggle free of my restraints, and run from the room. I arrived in my own bathroom and switched on the light, expecting to wake up, but instead looked down and saw myself in my hospital gown with all my insides exposed, my heart pounding away at a rate I thought was unsustainable. Can you believe I was afraid I might have a heart attack? It was only when I attempted to slow it down, by grasping hold of it, of all things, and I felt the damp cloth of my pyjamas, that the vision melted away.'

'It might be stress,' I said. 'You didn't have this before your family took this action against you?' He shook his head.

'The accusations came out of the blue.' His eyes flickered upwards as if he remembered something.

'What?'

'Although I believe I understand what has caused them: in short, I have no wife or children, siblings or parents, so I am not obliged to leave any part of my estate to my extended family.

'I think there may have been the assumption "eccentric uncle Alfonso" would pass it to his family. But as it turns out, eccentric "uncle" Alfonso is not disposed to leave anything whatsoever to the spoilt brats of distant relatives. Instead, I intend to bequeath the entirety to my true brotherhood, with the understanding that the temple will be preserved accordingly, and any other assets are used to support the canteen.'

'That sounds reasonable. And can't have been entirely unexpected.'

'Yet I now find myself in a position where certain claims are being made to undermine confidence in my sanity and even, if my guess from the questions being asked by doctors is anything to go by, that I am not even capable of showing myself at the window without performing an act of obscenity.'

I was puzzled. 'But how do you think I could help you? Or Lucia's organisation?'

'*Bologna dei Popoli* because I am one of the people, am I not? I admit, not one of their usual clients, but equally entitled to be treated fairly. A lawyer would be a good start.'

'I can ask.'

'Then I require the support of respected witnesses who can attest to my state of mind. You are a journalist. You are *English*. We Italians are tremendous Anglophiles. It could help.'

'I don't see a problem with that,' I said. 'But how about your "templars"? Aren't they drawn from the great and good?'

His mouth twisted sourly. 'That would play into the hands of my family. You know there is tremendous prejudice against our kind. If I asked one my brothers or sisters, I do not doubt they would stand by me, but they would risk exposure. They could lose everything. And it might not even do our cause much good – who, now, can trust the word of a mason?'

'You're hoist by your own petard.'

'Ah, Hamlet! Albeit I feel more like Ferdinand – "Hell is empty and all the devils are here." There is another thing, too. A personal thing. I was wondering if you might . . . monitor me.'

'What do you mean, exactly?'

'Watch me, stay with me, reassure me, Daniel. That I am not,' his voice broke, 'actually going mad.'

XIV

I walk into Alba and Claudio's place bearing the landed drone and a bag of cannoli for its pilot, Claudio, who hasn't moved from his Lay-Z-Boy. He accepts the cannoli I place on his stomach with a satisfied grunt and directs me to one of five chargers plugged into an extension.

In Alba's absence, Claudio's office on the mezzanine above the *soggiorno* has drifted down to the living room, which is carpeted with work stuff. Laptops, their leads stretched across the parquet, are busy running mysterious programmes. I have to pick my way gingerly between boxes of routers, phones, CCTV cameras, hard drives, and drones, surplus plastic parts scattered between them like bones.

I attach the drone to its pad. It winks ruby.

'He's back.' Claudio nods at their huge flatscreen TV on to which he is casting video from the static camera.

Quinto coolly picks up the canvas sack of paint and climbs

back up the ladder. 'He didn't get nabbed then.'

'But I met the police. Commissario Miranda.'

'You told her?'

I tut. 'We have different priorities.'

'She won't be too happy if she finds out you know *whodunnit*.'

'I think it would take more than that to make the *commissario* happy.'

'So you want to carry on with this? If you don't mind me saying, Dan, it seems like a lot of hassle just to recover a bike.'

Claudio is remarkably guileless for someone with no shortage of schemes. To him, a bike is just that – spindles, spokes, metallic and rubber tubes. A means of mobility, a means to an end. The solution to a problem, not the problem in itself.

'I'm a sentimental guy.'

He shrugs. The only thing he loses sleep over is an undercooked sausage and little Lucia's night terrors.

'I'll be upstairs,' I say. 'Let's put the drone back this evening. Then maybe we could grab a beer?'

He frowns. 'I can do the drone, but after, I'm meeting up with a couple of mates from the Pigs out at Boscuri. They're having a barbie. If you'd like to come . . .'

'Don't worry.' I have less in common with the members of his boar hunting club than his biker pals.

Outside, the cicadas are turned up to full volume. I stride across the exposed slice of courtyard back into the shade. This time of the day, the sun's rays beat as hard as tropical rain, but our apartment remains cool because, in my haste, I forgot to switch off the air-con. I head straight for the bathroom for my second shower of the day.

The flat seems especially lifeless without Rufus, our Lagotto. I regret letting them take him, although he's much better off by the sea. I vaguely wonder if I should get a cat. But then, I realise, I would simply be living with two creatures that ignore me.

Claudio may have a point, however. It won't be easy to justify all this effort over the bike once I've tied up Ginevra's job, which will have to be soon, if only because I will take all the strain once Dolores has left for London.

Which reminds me: I open my email and go to the surveillance file she's sent.

It's labelled MEETING WITH WOMAN.

There are actually three files: photos from when she was trailing Nancy Bonelli, then after she had entered the bar and Dolores had followed her inside, presumably taking a cold drink at the *banco* while Signora Bonelli settled by the window with the other woman. Dolores has recorded them chatting over a glass of white wine, and then, because she's bold, filmed them, using the mini directional mike which Jacopo and Claudio created to appear like a pen. Unfortunately, on this occasion it didn't work very well because of the bar music and a group of Dutch tourists who came between Dolores and the women, making a lot of relieved noises about the air-conditioning.

Dolores moves around the Dutch, but it is not a big space, and because she is already on Nancy Bonelli's tail, she can't linger long in case she is recognised. In any case, their conversation does not seem particularly pertinent – just holiday plans.

'. . . in Peru, and then Bolivia. Chile, too, I believe . . .'

'I've always wanted to visit Chile, I hear it's lovely.'

'For me, Peru . . .'

A blast of Dutch. Then we're back out on the street.

I call her. 'What are you doing?'

'Wilting, outside the target's home. When will we be done with this, Dan?'

'Soon,' I say. 'Just sit back and think of England.'

'You think that's funny, I'm the one stuck here beneath the portico.'

'Did I mention you'll be getting a daily €50 hardship bonus?'

'You didn't. But thanks. Anyway, she's not been out this morning, wisely. You'll take over after lunch, right?'

'I was also going to treat you to lunch,' I say.

'Ah, I'm sorry. I'm meeting my friend to plan our trip.'

'Okay, but there was one thing I wanted to tell you: well done.'

'What for.'

'That woman you spotted the signora with in the bar. I know her.'

In a sense, it all began here, outside this anonymous, graffiti-riddled door beneath a low, oak-beamed portico in the ex-Ghetto; that tangle of streets in the very heart of the city where they once locked up the Jewish population at night. I had done my fair share of work for the Comandante up until then, but it was only now that I fully took the reins, and began to discover how little I really understood.

The door is ajar.

I push it open. I don't bother with the intercom. I never

do if I can help it – I prefer not to provide the caller with an option, or warning.

I walk down that improbably long, cave-cold corridor. In the insipid light, it is a dingy, greenish cream like tainted dairy, as if there's nothing good to find down here.

Forget it – don't waste your time.

Turn back.

A stone staircase curves upwards, but it is the frosted glass door in front of me I try.

It is also unlocked.

The door opens on to a park. Only it is not a park, but a private garden constructed before parks were common, when natural pleasures, as opposed to the more common pains associated with the countryside, were viewed as almost eccentric, and certainly elite. Crafted centuries before Marie Antoinette created her little toy farm in Versailles, this 'garden' manages to convey the impression you are not visiting a city centre *palazzo* but have stumbled across one of the Medici's country retreats, the distant house as pretty as a watercolour.

When I first saw this place, it shocked me. Later, I came to understand there were many hidden gardens and cloisters, courtyards and inner sanctums built to conduct business away from prying eyes. All the more so for this *palazzo*'s owner in the heart of the Ghetto, who had absolutely no desire to draw unwanted attention.

The gravel path winds between shaggy perennials and riotous shrubs – bougainvillea, oleander, hydrangea – dazzle the visitor in hues of magenta, indigo, lemon, ushering them towards a Giambologna fountain populated by baroque, spouting nymphs and chortling child creatures. Beyond, the garden opens into an uneven expanse of trees, statues, and benches fronting the three-storey *palazzo*. The cicadas are simply deafening.

The front door opens.

Although she must now be approaching her seventh decade, Marta Finzi bears few signs except for her grey hair, quite a rarity for an Italian woman of any age, which she has cut shockingly short. Shocking to me, at least – I remember it long.

But she's as stunning as ever – the image of her biting Paolo Solitudine's cheek in the throes of passion almost fifty years earlier. Has she ever read the diaries Dolores found hidden in his old radio? Dee would have told me if she had requested them, so no. Marta Finzi is not the curious type. There remains a visceral quality to her. She is an agent of change, for whom the time is always now, so of course she wouldn't be interested in what Paolo might have written about what they got up to in the eighties, or indeed what we thought about it now. She only cares about the taste in her own mouth.

Marta leans in the wide doorway, barefoot in beige shorts and a plain white T-shirt, her tanned ankles and arms crossed. She does not look hostile. On the contrary, she looks as if she's been expecting me.

'You didn't ring,' she chides. 'How did you even know I was here?'

'The front door was open. I was passing a bar the other day and saw you chatting to a friend. I was going to say something, but decided to leave you to it. You seemed deep in conversation. How *did* you know I was here?'

'A camera,' she holds up her mobile phone, 'I knew from the moment you came into the garden.'

'Not your second sense then.' I extend my hand. She closes slender fingers around it. We are not on kissing terms, but neither are we exactly adversaries. 'I read what happened to Carlo,' I continue. 'So thought I would convey my condolences.'

'Really?'

'Is that all right?'

'Well, I suppose so.' A wry smile. 'Coffee, then? Something cold?'

'Coffee would be fine.'

I follow her inside. Nothing has changed. From the outside, you might expect the *palazzo*'s Renaissance theme to continue, but neither Marta, nor her late husband, former mayor Carlo Manzi, much venerated the past, hence the whitewashed walls, abstract art, dark-stained chevron parquet; the brushed-metal 'industrial' feel of the kitchen.

She loads up a Nespresso machine. 'I admit,' she says, 'it was a bit of a shock after everything. Don't get me wrong – the thought had crossed my mind someone might try to knock him off. Gun him down, that kind of thing. But that was back in the old days, when people gave a shit. Now I suppose I was resigned to him just growing old, although his bitch appeared to be keeping him young, and the little boy, of course.'

'Oh, his girlfriend had a boy, did she? You didn't divorce, then.'

'We both had too much to lose. It would have been highly inconvenient, and I guess I was hardly one to judge his . . . indiscretions.'

'That's understandable.'

'I suppose you're really here because you're curious. I never did thank you for getting to the bottom of Paolo's death. And I suppose, after your dealings with Carlo, you weren't likely to show your face around here again.'

'You can't say he didn't get what was coming to him.'

'You probably did him a favour – he loved Rome. I loved him staying in Rome. In fact, that's where the bitch is now; he moved them down there. Fortunately, we had separated our assets on marriage – my parents, God bless them, insisted – so she doesn't have any stake in the Finzi family holdings. But Carlo had his own patrimony, which we are in the process of liquidating. Her kid is entitled to his pound of flesh according to the law. There was no point disputing it, he hadn't updated his will, but there was a considerable paper trail . . .' Her face remains an amused mask. 'It's funny, isn't it? If he had fallen out of that window before, my life could have been entirely different. Perhaps even Paolo wouldn't have died, he would be here with me now helping with the gardening.'

My life would have been different too, I suppose. I wouldn't have Dolores Pugliese working for me, for one.

'And how do you feel?' I ask. 'You still think about him? Paolo, I mean.' A tight smile. 'And even a little about Carlo?'

'Now I'm an official widow. Like you, huh? But that was my proper widowhood, when Paolo died. After my little "performance", let's call it, by the graveside, I did my best to keep it properly bottled up. The favour Carlo has done me is to allow me to express it formally. It's a style I'm still adjusting to, to be honest. Any tips?'

'Me? You know what I've spent half the week doing?

Running after my wife's old bike, which we thought had disappeared, but then I saw some kid riding.' I expect her to laugh, but she looks at me very seriously.

'And did you recover it?'

'Not yet.'

'But you will.'

'You can count on it. And you – that friend I saw you talking to. Holiday plans?'

A puzzled look sweeps her face. 'Where was this?'

'Strada Maggiore.'

She reaches for her cigarettes on top of the machine.

'You don't, do you?'

'And you still do.'

'If it hasn't killed me yet, it's probably not going to.'

'I'm not sure I follow your logic.'

'Not logic, philosophy. Your Italian has improved.'

'After all this time, I would hope so. You're still lecturing about Marx?'

'It's a little late to teach this horse new tricks.'

'The other lady is a lecturer, too?'

'Nancy's an "events organiser", at least that's how she puts it. Actually, she's married to a rather successful plastic surgeon and views her purpose in life to arrange cultural activities. In fact, that's what we were talking about – a trip to South America. I can't wait to get away, especially as the kids are circling. "What are you going to do in this big place alone, Mamma?" "Have you thought about how much you would get for it if you turned it into a hotel?" They so take after their father, I almost wonder why I bothered. If *I* happen to tumble from a tall building, can you investigate?'

'You don't suppose someone actually *did* launch Carlo from the eleventh floor?'

She looks down her long nose at me. 'The real question is – do I care? Does anyone care enough to look into it? Apparently not. The safety of Italian windows is a scandal waiting to be exposed, Daniel.'

As usual with Marta Finzi, I have received half-truths, which in Italy are often more revealing than whole facts. Carlo Manzi is Schrödinger's ex-mayor: simultaneously assisted and not assisted out of the window. Context is everything – because his fate appeared fixed, everyone apparently agrees that the means by which he arrived at it is irrelevant.

More to the point, Marta has confirmed the audio from the bar. After all, Bologna is not a mega-city, it contains only a few hundred thousand souls, and a lot less bourgeoisie. Her meeting with Nancy Bonelli is probably a coincidence. On the other hand, *precisely because* there are only so many atoms bouncing around in what is left of the city walls, I can't dismiss synchronicity either – the crisscross of trails, collision of interests. Bologna exists within its own dimension, apparently free from time's gravity . . .

Marta Finzi and Nancy Bonelli. The bicycle outside the masonic lodge.

Carlo Manzi meeting his fate upon unyielding concrete.

Apartments wrecked, housing developments poisoned.

Signor Molino strung up in his holiday home.

Alfonso's hidden temple, Quinto's graffiti.

Lucia tossed on to the tarmac.

I move them around in my mind like a model in 3D.

One thing I suspect – Marta Finzi isn't planning a holiday.

Another – I'm getting close. To precisely what, I can't quite say.

A third – the missing element is Alfonso Lambertini.

XV

'I'm not sure who's the mad one, you or him.' Lucia had her back to me, finishing the washing-up. I had offered to help, but she had insisted: 'Oh no, you go and pack.'

I could hear Rose in the *soggiorno* along the corridor, entranced by the *X Factor* auditions. Thank heaven for small mercies.

'It'll only be for the night. Well,' I admitted, 'maybe two.'

'Stay as long as you like.'

I put the bag down. 'Come on, what's all this about?'

She turned to me, sleeves rolled up, sponge in hand. She placed it in the sink. I reached for the towel, handed it to her.

'Grazie.' She wiped her hands, then folded it thoughtfully.

'Lucia . . .'

'I'm just wondering if you could be spending your time a little more usefully.' She looked at me challengingly, barely holding back, it appeared, her fury.

'What more would you like me to do? I'm learning the language. Soon I'll find a job.'

'Oh yeah? And what will you find a job doing? Sweeping the streets? That's about all your Italian is good for.'

'*Now hold on.* I'm doing my best, I'm studying every day. Believe me, I know how important it is . . .'

'Or do you think you can just live off my wages, rent free, like you have been, while you go off and play bloody masons with your crazy friends?'

'What? You mean the crazy friend I met after being kicked out of AUSL because my wife couldn't be bothered to show up?'

'Because she had better things to do than waste an afternoon acting as a translator for someone who should know the language by now, you mean? Because she had to earn the money to put the food on his daughter's plate?'

'Hold on,' I said. 'You mean you *deliberately* didn't turn up? You made me go through that alone, on purpose?'

'It's about time you took responsibility for yourself instead of expecting other people to take it for you.'

'Jesus,' I gawped at her. 'You must really hate me.'

We stared at each other, the bridge I thought we had begun to reconstruct after Florence now floating in pieces downstream.

'Dad? Mum? What's up?' Rose stood in the doorway. 'Why are you shouting?'

I swept up my bag and came over and kissed her on the forehead. 'Mamma doesn't want me to go to the funny man's house. It hasn't got much heating and she's afraid I'll catch a cold.'

'But you'll wear your big coat,' said Rose with concern.

'All night long, if need be. And don't worry, I'll be back in time for sludge.'

'It's all right, Mum,' said Rose in English. 'Brits don't get colds like we do.'

Lucia responded pointedly in Italian: 'But they're really more used to the rain than the snow.'

'That's true,' Rose said thoughtfully. 'Make sure you don't get too warm, either, Dad. Sweating then getting cold can make you sick, too.'

I saluted her, before nodding warily at Lucia, who was already turning back to the washing-up.

'You are so very, very kind.' Alfonso greeted me at the wicket door in his great coat and a muffler, wearing what appeared by the look of them to be felt boots. There had been fresh snowfall and the porticoes were once again deserted and grainy with wood smoke.

As I entered his candle-lit *palazzo*, I couldn't help feeling as if I'd stepped on to the set of that old Polanski movie *The Fearless Vampire Killers*. I wasn't given to being afraid of the dark, but I couldn't deny that a small part of me wished I'd packed a mallet and wooden stakes. Perhaps a little Holy Water, just to be on the safe side.

'Your wife wasn't too aggrieved?'

'I will need to leave first thing as Rose will expect her breakfast.'

'Of course!'

We arrived at the top of the staircase, those grumpy gods looking particularly put out. Above, the pigeons were cooing insistently and I considered raising my hood, but decided it would be harder to get any stain off my coat than to simply wash my hair. I noticed the doors to the room on the right side of the landing had been, well, not affixed exactly, but were leaning across a doorway containing an amber glow. With some effort, Alfonso shifted one aside.

'Please,' he chuckled, 'honoured guest!'

Shrugging off my backpack, I stepped into the room, blanching at the heat. Flames were licking a pile of logs beneath an ancient stone hearth. Angled before it was a pair of age-scuffed Chesterfield armchairs.

A long oak table ran the length of the oval, eight-columned room. The mosaic floor featured a sun, its caramel and topaz beams ending at each column.

Two places were set across from each other at the centre. A pair of silver menorahs sat on either side, providing ample light, while the usual excessively large Murano chandelier loomed far above in the company of cracked frescoes, only this one, I noted, was also suffering the indignity of a scruffy pigeon's nest among its grimy pink and blue fronds. I glanced at the table. I couldn't see any signs of droppings.

'Here, let me take your coat, your bag?', said Alfonso. I hesitated, although I was not exactly sure why – I had also forgotten my crucifix. 'You will be relieved to know I have set the stove and thoroughly aired your room, so it should be neither cold nor damp. I appreciate that on the surface this may all seem somewhat rudimentary, but these places *were* actually built with comfort in mind, it's just that I am used to making do and mending, which is what I think you say, no?'

'More or less. Although since I'm here, I should take advantage of your Italian.' I sighed. 'I really need to improve.'

'That incident at the AUSL? I think they place the very worst functionaries to deal with the immigrants. A sort of punishment battalion.'

'I'm not sure who's being punished.'

'Well, everyone, obviously.'

Alfonso poured a ruby Sangiovese Reserve into a pair of crystal glasses. 'I will look into your situation at AUSL. We are not without influence.'

'*Grazie.*' I didn't need to ask who 'we' were.

'*Tigelle* are also known as *crescentine*,' he explained, holding a pair of flat dough patties between his fingers. Having removed his great coat to reveal a somewhat threadbare chef's uniform, Alfonso had also returned to the table with a hat balanced upon his head along with a stack of *tigelle* on a silver platter. I realised our meal was going to be as much masonic allocution as a gastronomic *tour d'horizon*. 'They're especially typical of Modena. Here, try them with *stracciatella* cheese and *prosciutto*.

Tigella probably comes from the Latin verb *tegere*,' he continued. 'Meaning to cover. They are baked between terracotta discs two centimetres thick so they can withstand high temperatures. They have a handcrafted engraved "frieze", that leaves a symbol on the *tigelle*: see, the most common is the star-flower, *Trientalis boreali*, better known as the flower of life, a symbol of fertility. Don't eat them all, Daniel! This is just the appetizer!'

Next up was tortellini in broth, which I didn't have the

heart to tell him I wasn't a fan of. I had no doubt it was excellent, but I had always found something unappetizing about pasta floating in soup. Heresy in Emilia, I knew, but it just seemed wrong.

'This is of course the classic winter dish. The pasta is made by ladies using a rolling pin, which makes it both thin and flexible.' His eyes gleamed with enthusiasm as my spoon poised politely above the bowl. 'The "meat broth" is just that – usually created from a mixture or chicken and beef, together with the bones, to provide the fullest flavour, along with salt, carrots, onions, celery, and stock. You like?'

'Delicious!' Put that way, it wasn't bad. In the meantime, we had a minor thesis on the roots of its accompanying, unsalted bread. 'Dante writes in the *Divine Comedy "Tu proverai sì come sa di sale lo pane altrui,"* – You shall experience how the bread of others tastes of salt – which is a euphemism for exile, because Florentine bread was also unsalted. It is said this was to avoid the Pisan tax on salt arriving into their ports, but it wasn't just them – the Perugians rose against the Papal State's salt tax in 1540 – the so-called "Salt War", which the Pope won – but they, too, still forsake salt in their bread.

'However, personally, I believe the tradition is simply due to our tasty food. Unsalted bread goes better with the likes of *prosciutto*, cured meats and flavoursome cheeses, and this would not be inconsistent with the observation that the tradition dates even further back. You see,' he held up a bun of *pane comune*, 'there is a theory that long before all the trouble over taxes, the Etruscans ate their bread just so, and the locations where the tradition endures map out their former homeland. So even if their writing did not leave much of a trace, perhaps their cuisine did.'

As we finished up, he gave me an odd look. 'Still have some space?'

'Some,' I said cautiously. 'Although don't pull any surprises like another couple of *primi* as if we're at an Italian wedding, or I might have to report you to the police.'

He giggled: 'You're right – it should be outlawed by the European Court of Human Rights. I'm sure if the French would, they could – you know they hate our food more than anyone, because they stole most of it. Even their forks were introduced by the Queen of Parma, let alone their chefs. But what is France, after all, but the land of the *Franks*? No,' he waved his knife dismissively, 'the French are just Germans *trying* to be Italian . . .

'Now,' he lowered his voice, 'the secret of surviving the Italian wedding is to pace yourself. *Don't* leave a clean plate. Traditionally, people over-catered at weddings to demonstrate their wealth, or rather, lack of poverty. It was often the only occasion at which the guests would eat meat. Speaking of which.' He got to his feet and trotted off to the kitchen.

Lulled by the food, fine wine and flickering fire, I couldn't help feeling a little amazed to find myself beneath those blackened frescoes in that antique *palazzo*. It certainly seemed a long way from London, the daily grind of what had once constituted 'real life' that I had given up for . . . *this*, which would have certainly seemed unreal to my former self. I had become so used to regarding Bologna as a kind of obligation and encumbrance, I had somehow forgotten how enchanting it could be.

*

Alfonso returned with a large steaming pot. If I had been hoping for something a little lighter, I was about to be disappointed. He began to serve up that most traditional of Bolognese dishes – boiled beef.

'I expected you had already enjoyed our traditional *cotoletta* so I thought I would continue the winter theme. Other regions mix their meats. You might find pork or veal, but in Bologna it is strictly beef, in this case the shoulder, tenderloin, socket of the eye . . .' He sighed contentedly. 'Of course, the recipe has been annotated by our Chamber of Commerce, of which this is in strict accordance.' He doled a huge chunk into my bowl, and then spooned some carrot, celery, and potato.

I looked dubiously down. 'Is there a story behind this?'

'Ah, not really. Except it must be served with this.' He pushed the porcelain jug toward me. 'Green sauce.'

'Like mint sauce?'

'With the lamb, yes? No, not at all – parsley, capers, onions, and so on. More like pesto. You like?'

I gamely sliced into the meat and tried it. 'I do.'

'You are not just being English-polite?' I was a little – it tasted like seasoned shoe leather – but I was too English-polite to tell him.

'So,' I said, chewing, 'is this how you dine every evening?'

He chuckled, almost infernally – framed by the firelight his springy hair seemed busy with flames. 'To be honest, I rarely eat in the evenings. Well, perhaps some cheese and biscuits, a little brandy and a good book.'

'If you aren't attending an Agape, or one of your mysterious ceremonies.'

'They are really not so mysterious,' he winked, 'to the initiated.'

'But do your fellow masons know you're . . . in difficulty? With the property, I mean. I know you don't want to involve them for reputational reasons, but you yourself just admitted your "fraternity" has some influence.'

'They may be able to assist you, Daniel – precisely because you are not associated with the lodge – but you can be sure intense attention will be applied, and it is vital that there is absolutely no inference of their involvement. That would be a disaster, even worse, perhaps, than me losing the building. It would only take a single spark to ignite all the old suspicions we have worked so hard to address . . .'

'So your family know you're a mason.'

'As I said, I've never kept it a secret, although admittedly some do, even from their kin. But we are an old masonic family. Not only my father was Worshipful Master, but also my grandfather, his father, and so on. However, the rot began as far back as granddad's generation – of his two brothers, one was a fascist, the other a communist, both driven by hunger for power and power alone, I might add, and neither therefore particularly keen to be associated with freemasonry, which their creeds both viewed as a competitor to their hegemonizing ambitions. Their children were raised to feel similarly, although my father's cousin – the son of the fascist one – was an active member until his death, but he had daughters, who were not permitted to join back then, so in short it was left to me.'

'And you never,' I chose my words carefully, 'wanted children?'

He looked amused. 'Why, Daniel, I have been married twice. Surprised a fatty like me in a run-down old house should be such a *bon vivant*? How about Toulouse Lautrec?'

'You mean an alcoholic who frequented prostitutes and died of syphilis?' I glanced at my glass and realised we had somehow gotten through a bottle a-piece of Sangiovese.

'Touché. My great-grandfather actually met him in London, you know. Admittedly, probably in a brothel. As for me, I was first married as a young man. She left me when it transpired I couldn't give her children. The second I married in an act of gallantry – a Russian, passport wedding, although I can't pretend part of me didn't hope she might fall in love. But she soon realised I didn't have much spare cash, and wasn't about to sell this place. Still, we've remained friends – she continues to do the cleaning.'

'You mean, you married your cleaner.'

'Isn't that what every man dreams of?'

'I suspect many women think so.'

'And you?'

'Lucia?' Tears sprung to my eyes. I really had been knocking it back, and noticed a refill being poured into my glass. 'It was love,' I said apologetically.

'Like my first, then. I dare say it might have stayed that way if we had had offspring, but it became . . . stale.' His eyes grew misty in the flickering candlelight. 'It wouldn't have been fair to stand in her way.'

'And there's no one now?'

'Apart from Olga, you mean?'

'You mean your Russian? I thought you said you had broken up.'

'We have, but we're both single. It's nice to have someone to keep your feet warm at night.' He frowned playfully. 'Your prudishness surprises me.'

With some effort, Alfonso got back on his feet. Rocking slightly, he reached for my bowl.

'Can I help?'

'*No, no*. You are the honoured guest.'

'You haven't got Olga slaving away in the kitchen, have you?'

'Gave her the night off,' he said solemnly.

Although this was more fun than I had expected, I knew by the amount of booze I was consuming, never mind the bowling ball in my stomach, that this was a disaster in waiting and I would encounter the full consequences the following morning. On the other hand, I was enjoying Alfonso's non-censorious company, and pleased I wasn't about to roll home drunk, although I wasn't sure that either my body or relationship would survive more than one evening of his hospitality.

Given everything that had preceded it, our final dish came as no surprise: *zuppa Inglese*, 'English Soup'.

Alfonso was about to declaim, when I stopped him.

'Allow me. Basically, it was invented by Bolognese chefs to mimic the English trifle British visitors requested. And it doesn't do a bad job, to be honest.'

'Bravo,' said Alfonso. 'Although there is another theory, that it was created by the Neapolitans to celebrate Nelson's victory on the Nile.'

'Touché to you.'

'Speaking of Nelson,' he said. 'I don't have any Napoleon

brandy – heaven forfend! – but I do have Bologna's own *Vecchia Romagna* . . .'

I tried half-heartedly to stop him, but didn't require much persuasion.

I awoke confused and semi-dressed, reaching into the empty space where Lucia should have been, and only gradually coming to appreciate where I was. I was less hungover than I had expected, but that may have been because I was still drunk. I scrabbled for my phone set on the bedside table. It was 03:42. I switched on the lamp. It gave off a timid light from its wonky, flowery shade. I picked up the large glass of water I had filled when I had finally accompanied Alfonso to the kitchen which, in contrast to the decrepit dining hall, had been jarringly up-to-date with a white marble work surface strewn with the vestiges of chopped vegetables, and no Olga anywhere to be seen.

The bedroom had returned me to the eighteenth century. Wallpaper, which was a rarity in Italy, lined the walls with faded gold damask flowers, the ceiling frescoes aped the designs of the excavations at Pompei. A delicate, Empire-style powder-blue wardrobe and a dressing table with an age-tarnished mirror faced the bed, from which I blinked back, consumptive-pale. The corner stove had ceased crackling, but continued to radiate an impressive amount of heat. The sole window looked across a courtyard at others dark as the night.

Now I remembered what had kept me sat on the side of the bed, gazing up until I could no longer keep my eyes open and it was the best I could do to peel off my trousers and shirt before crawling beneath the covers – that small painting in a dark wood frame.

I turned on my phone's light to inspect it more closely. At first glance, it might not seem so special – just a young woman and man – or was it another woman? Their hair was short, but the profile quite feminine – facing each other in bed. A waxen, unhealthy-looking pair with messy 'bed hair'. The suggestion was they were naked beneath the cerise duvet, but their bodies were not visible, simply three-quarter profiles against a grubby pillow.

Darkness had closed around them as if they were illuminated only by candlelight. This was an intensely private moment one rarely saw in any form of art: a communion impossible to put into words, yet so commonplace it would likely be forgotten by the time they had risen or fallen asleep; a shared gaze that might be fleeting or lingering, mean nothing or everything, but most of all was so modestly, carelessly, poignantly human.

'It's an earlier version of the one in Musée D'Orsay,' Alfonso had said. 'Although I don't think there's much to choose between them, and I don't think the Conte really cared.'

'Lautrec, you mean.'

'Yes, my great-grandfather bought this at a knock-down price, but he was a huge collector of art, albeit it was hit and miss. His purchases were shared between the family. They grabbed the inoffensive – and expensive – stuff, or so they thought. Morandi – all those jugs! – De Maria. All right, a couple of early Picassos. Whereas my father selected for taste – Sickert, Hammershøi, Bonnard, Beardsley. To be honest, it's what's kept me going, parting with them. But this one, never.'

I reached again for the water, finished it off but still felt parched.

I reluctantly pulled on my trousers and socks, picked up the empty glass and, guided by the light on my phone, opened the door to the hallway.

As in the bedroom, the floor was a swirling stone mosaic and the hall itself broad and mausoleum-cold, with a high vaulted ceiling that could have been a portico were there not doorways on either side. My breath hung before me like a veil.

I reached for the switch but discovered it hanging off the wall. Alfonso might not be mad, but he was certainly as mean as hell. I swept my light up and down the corridor before setting off, stockinged feet stung by the cold stone.

Dust sparkled in the light. I very much doubted Olga had had the energy or inclination to cover this part of the house. As I made my way down the service staircase that led on to another set of abandoned chambers, I heard the slumbersome flutter of a disturbed pigeon.

I passed room after room where the forms of furniture, covered by bed linen, loomed in my phone light; squares of sold-off paintings patched grimy walls, and rodents ran, I didn't doubt.

I arrived at the rear of the dining room. The dying fire cast a plaintive light. Alfonso was asleep on one of the Chesterfields, snoring heroically.

I bordered the uncleared table and made for the kitchen at the end of a narrow service corridor.

The door was open, light on. It was only as I was about to enter that I realised there was someone inside.

XVI

'Just because Quinto's here, it doesn't mean the guy who has your bike is.' Dolores waves out the match and flicks it into the gutter. She draws on the roll-up.

'I don't know how you can smoke in this heat,' I say. We are standing in the shade of the trees opposite the mansion block in Bolognina our drone had tracked Quinto to. 'It's hard enough to breathe.'

'Practice.'

Bolognina is, literally, on the wrong side of the tracks. There are few porticoes here: built 'outside the walls' to accommodate workers during the industrial revolution; the blocks continue to serve this purpose for ordinary folk priced out of the centre, alongside immigrants, students and, no doubt, an increasing number of *affiti brevi*. This one, however, appears to have been seized by WE OWN BOLOGNA, another bunch of squatters, their red banner strung between windows and decorated with hammer and sickles alongside the Anarchist symbol. If the revolution ever did materialise, the two philosophies would be mutually incompatible, but they have presumably put their differences aside until then.

'So what's the plan?' asks Dolores.

My sunglasses glint in hers. 'Go in, find the bike – hopefully in the hallway – and get the hell out.'

'Which is why you've brought the bolt cutters.' She looks down at my CONAD shopping bag.

'That's right.'

'And if it's not in the hall?'

'We knock on the doors until we find Quinto, and I ask him where it is.'

'You think he'll know?'

'He was definitely at the other place, so if he doesn't know the bike, he should know its owner. In fact, perhaps we'll find him there, too – don't they all nest together?' Dolores' mouth hardens. These are still her tribe, technically. 'Like fluffy fledglings,' I smile. 'Like cuddly cutie pies.'

'And you think Quinto's just going to tell you?' She eyes the bag. 'Look, Dan. You're not going to threaten—'

I shake my head. 'I'm sure we'll be able to work something out.'

We begin to cross the road. 'Be nice,' she murmurs.

To my surprise, the front door is locked, but Dolores has recently completed a lock-picking course and breaks it with ease. A bog-standard Yale, they may as well have left it open.

The typically dingy hallway is crowded with bikes, many stolen, I suspect, and probably upon dozens of occasions. At first, I'm delighted, but quickly realise Lucia's Raleigh is not among them.

The back door opens on to a small, unfenced garden spotted with dog shit, empty cans of Tennent's Super, cigarette and roach butts, and rusty bike parts. It is busy with flies. Their neighbours must love them. I quickly close it and turn to Dolores.

'Looks like we'll have to do some knocking.'

'But we'll ask nicely, right?' Another glance at my bag. 'If this place is full, we'll be outnumbered.'

'Good point.' She winces, wipes her forehead. 'What?' This time I hear the splash on her shorn scalp.

'Leak somewhere?' She looks up and a drop splashes her face. She steps aside as rivulets fall between the stairwell, sounding like Morse code on the stone.

A steady stream is slinking down the stairs. 'Someone must have left a tap on.'

Although I'd planned to go door to door, we're naturally drawn to the source of the flood, which turns out to be an apartment on the third floor.

We arrive on the landing with a splash. The door is open, water shifting across the grubby chequerboard linoleum. I know instantly this is Quinto's place – the hallway walls and ceiling are alive with a mural of rope-thick vines that weave in shades of green and blood vessel red to form the capillary of a jungle, as much animal as vegetable.

'Quinto!' I call. 'Are you here?' Dolores also gives it a go. 'We're coming in.'

The reek of paint and stale cigarettes.

'Quinto! Anyone?'

The theme changes in the living room, where night-blue walls are decorated by silver moons and yellow, radiating suns around a battered leather sofa and eighties smoked-glass-topped coffee table littered with druggie detritus. Lotus columns rise to the ceiling where an emerald eye gazes down, its pupil, bizarrely, a globular, gold-painted crepe lampshade.

But no Quinto.

We can hear, however, the splash of running water.

'Quinto?' Dolores calls. We pass a bedroom where cobalt, yellow and red flora spring between those ubiquitous vines. The tangle of grey sheets on the double bed. A discarded plastic tobacco pouch floats on the flooded floor beside a soaked T-shirt.

The bathroom light is on. Its brash fluorescence makes us blink despite the auburn and khaki leaves apparently intended to evoke a hidden jungle pool.

I realise Dolores' face is streaked raspberry from the reflection of the water.

She grabs my wrist hard, her face transforming into a series of Os. There's a body in the tub, taps still running, intestines bubbling, ballooning with fresh water.

His naked feet and legs point rigidly upwards like a dead donkey, torso and head bob just above the waterline, tap water splashing on a startled, waxen face.

The mason – Michele – cut in two.

XVII

'Olga?' I didn't want to frighten her, but who else could it be? Although Alfonso had insisted the lengthy meal had been entirely his doing, he had remerged so promptly from the kitchen with dishes prepared to perfection, and the kitchen had been in such good order when I had accompanied him, it would not at all have surprised me to discover he had had a helping hand after all, and that Olga, his ex-wife and apparent 'friend with benefits,' had a room of her own in the vast building.

The black-cloaked form was frozen before the open fridge in a surreal tableau – the medieval monk, complete with a cowl covering their head, reaching into the fridge as if they had had a case of the munchies.

I had time to utter *'What the—'* before, head down, they barrelled into me, knocking me to the floor and making off back down the corridor. I twisted to watch the rear of their flapping cloak reveal modern jeans and trainers.

I grabbed my phone off the tiles and scrambled after them.

'Alfonso!' I shouted as I ran past him. The figure was already around the table and heading out of the doorway. They might not have been Olga, but they clearly knew their way about. I heard a snuffle from Alfonso, but not much else.

I made it to the landing and was plunged into the frozen dark. I raised my phone, half expecting the figure to step in front of me and thrust a dagger into my guts, but there was nothing except those gloomy frescoes, pigeons scuffling.

I descended the steps, my milky phone light brushing the faces of the marble busts, alcoves looming behind them as if they had cowls themselves. I kept a firm grip on the crusty handrail, straining to hear, to see below as the stairs curved down to the courtyard.

Were they already outside? It was hard to believe that I wouldn't have heard them descending the stairs, the groan as they opened the front wicket door and its resounding slam behind them. Then they must still be here somewhere, pressed into a murky corner, the cloak not just a prop but perfect cover.

I had almost reached the bottom of the stairs, my light bouncing weakly around the entrance and inner courtyard, when I heard it behind me, above: the distinct scrape of wood against a stone floor.

'Alfonso?' Nothing.

I ran back up the stairs, reaching the top in time to hear another sharp scrape. Only it wasn't coming from the dining room but across the landing.

My light bounced wildly around the ballroom, dazzling in those old mirrors, but I couldn't see a thing. The next room appeared similarly empty.

It was only when I reached the library, dust dancing around the disturbed bookcase, that I understood.

Where else would an intruder outfitted like a mason go?

My fingers ran along those cold, greasy spines. I wished I had paid more attention when Alfonso had opened up the bookcase.

I pulled out the damp volumes, clearing one shelf after another. Peered beneath, above. They certainly weren't making it easy.

Calm yourself. Take a step back.

I tried to be more systematic. Finally, there – upon the shelf above the one I had just cleared: hand-size smears upon the green spine of a book embossed *The Temple of Solomon.*

I grasped hold of it. Although the cover was like the others, there was no give – its content was wood.

I reached around and wrenched. The bookshelf rumbled, scraped aside.

Whoever was inside the temple must have heard. I was afraid they would make another run for it, barge past me. But as I opened up, this time – nothing.

My phone couldn't penetrate that indomitable darkness, which together with the temple's chill, seemed almost like a force in itself.

I lingered by the threshold. 'Come on,' I shouted in Italian. '*Basta*. Enough. *Out*.' Even my words seemed eaten by the black.

I reached tentatively inside, feeling for the switch. But, of course, it was hanging from the wall.

I stepped forward, waving my light warily before me.

The weak beam brushed benches, columns. Those thrones, that all-seeing eye. It shone upwards to the grey, lightless miasma where a blue dome lurked with masonic symbols and painted stars. Dipped back down. They had to be here somewhere. Behind a column? They didn't appear large enough. Crouched between the benches? That appeared more likely.

I knew that if I moved to one side of the horseshoe, they could make a run from the other, but I had no choice.

I was about to move to the right when I heard the rasp of stone on stone. I swung the light back towards the altar.

The clang of footsteps on iron.

I felt the exit before I reached it – fresh air rising behind the main throne.

A paving stone had been removed to reveal an iron spiral staircase like a fire escape. I could hear their footfall hammering downwards.

I stepped forwards – and slipped. It was only by grabbing the pole that I saved myself from a catastrophic fall. The stairs were slick with frost.

My phone had fallen face-down below, providing me with just enough light to make my way tentatively down. As I picked the phone up, the sound of the escaping footsteps on iron ceased – they had not stopped, presumably, but had arrived at the bottom.

It felt as if I could have descended forever until there I was – stood on gritted ground. I shone the phone around, found myself facing the mouth of a tunnel glistening with masonic symbols. The zodiac – rams, lions, scorpions – together with suns, moons, anchors, squares and compasses set in mosaics of gold and silver, pearl, olive, sable.

But I didn't have time to admire it. I made off along the gritted path. I soon reached a kind of crossroads: there were a further three tunnels, each marked by a different symbol picked out in tiny gold stones above each entrance – the all-seeing eye, an hourglass, and a point within a circle set between a pair of diagonal lines.

I shone the light warily along each, but it only penetrated a few metres. Listened, my breath spouting before me. Did the symbols provide a clue?

Only to the truly initiated.

Then I lowered the light and saw it – the trainer mark on the gravel.

I began to make my way along the one with the circle.

'Come on,' I called. 'Come out.' My light played across the mosaics, glinting with ice crystals like a diamond crust.

'Show yourself. There's no escape.'

How far could this tunnel run? I didn't know then that the city was riddled with passageways, as busy below ground as above. Re-purposed, multi-purposed. This one might have had many uses over the centuries. Roman, Etruscan. Now it was masonic.

In my shaky light the symbols began to take on a life of their own. Constellations shifted. Aries aligned with Taurus, Gemini with Cancer. The deeper I went, the more the tunnel seemed to close around me, less a tunnel, in fact, than a hole.

Was I moving upwards or downwards, forwards to an exit? Or was it sucking me in?

A creeping, imponderable panic – would I emerge in a

different time? Place? I shook my head. Fucking mason mind-tricks.

Movement up ahead.

Darkness shifting.

They were making a break for it, their cloak flapping like a monstrous, scuttling raven.

'No! Stop!'

I was running . . . running . . .

A burst of light, the bite of fresh air.

Was I ducking or diving through that opening? Or was the tunnel itself expelling me?

I lost my footing, I was stumbling, I was hitting the ground with a hard smack, a crack.

I rolled on to my back, gasping.

A blank night sky reflecting gaseous amber. The sound of a trolley bus pulling out nearby. A hooded figure bent over me.

Faceless, until something began to emerge from the darkness. An all-seeing eye, jade green, with a pupil that glittered gold.

Lucia's face was drained phantom-white in the dawn light. She looked as if she had emerged from a night at the disco when in reality I had called her from Pronto Socorso, or Casualty, at five in the morning. By that time, Alfonso had left – in fact, I insisted he leave before Lucia arrived – I sensed him being there would only make things worse.

The room smelled of disinfectant and an insidious vanilla that drilled into my sinuses making me weep as the nurse applied the cast around my wrist. Noticing my tears, he asked if the pain killers were wearing off.

Lucia was talking to the doctor. I hadn't understood a word, although I wasn't making much of an effort. I was exhausted and woozy and a little terrified about how she would react. She turned to me while the doctor watched her translate.

'He says it's not as bad as it might have been. The x-rays indicate a fracture near the wrist joint. It's more like a crack than a break, but you will have to keep it immobile for . . .' she turned to him and there was an exchange of words, 'At least a month,' he says.

'I'm sorry,' I said to her. She tutted, shook her head. 'I'm sorry,' I said to the doctor.

He chuckled. 'You English, drink much, yes?'

I pleadingly addressed Lucia: 'I did drink but by the time this happened, I was sober, I . . .' I glanced at the doctor. 'I woke in the night and went for some water, I slipped.'

They both looked at me as if this was a likely story.

XVIII

'You have got to be fucking kidding me.' The hate-filled look from Commissario Rita Miranda is not unfamiliar, but at least I can see where she's coming from. She stops the recording machine and pulls out her cigarettes, lighting up despite the No Smoking sign behind her. I doubt she'll get in trouble – the grey linoleum is covered with scorch marks.

She scowls at me through the smoke. 'For fuck's sake,' she hisses. 'You're sure of this?'

'I'm afraid so.'

'*Unbelievable.* And how many other people know?'

'Apart from the killer?'

'Don't be an ass.'

'Probably only me,' I say. 'Dolores might have clocked the masonic influence on the murals, but she hasn't mentioned it. I did discuss some similarities—' I stop myself. I had had a chat with the Comandante about Nancy Bonelli, but I can't see how that can be related and I don't want the Polizia di Stato elbowing into our client work, not least because it would be professional suicide – clients often came to us precisely to avoid involving the police.

'What?'

'With the Comandante – about the graffiti in the Airbnb, I mean, it's possible masonic symbolism.'

'Your father-in-law's not the leaking type,' she says. 'I don't doubt you'll tell him about this, but keep it between the two of you. He'll understand.'

'Will do.'

'Do you? Understand, I mean.'

'Sure.'

Commissario Miranda gives me an appraising look. 'You've come a long way, *caro* Daniel, but I'm not convinced you truly get it. A mason carved up like this, that's a huge deal. As soon as it's out it'll light a firecracker up the arse of the media, the whole country, especially now everyone's at the seaside and nothing else is happening.' She checks her watch. 'I'll have every fucker with an epaulette on the blower. From the beach, mind you, although I don't doubt a few might race down to get their fat faces in front of the cameras.

'So what is it?' she continues. 'You think this Quinto is killing masons? I saw all that shit in his *soggiorno*. He's clearly an obsessive.'

The *commissario* may be right about how much I have yet to understand, but if there's one thing I've grasped, it's that information is the most precious currency, and not to spend it all at once.

'I can't see how Quinto would know that Michele is . . .

was a mason. Also, the drone followed Quinto from the mural to home. We came along perhaps a quarter of an hour later. What we saw in the bath– that's not fifteen minutes' work.'

'He could have done it before.'

'And left the door open and the bath on?'

'Who did it then?'

'I've no idea.' Miranda narrows her eyes.

'What is it you're not telling me, Daniel?'

'Honestly, I was just trying to get my bike back.'

A smoky laugh. 'You know what? I actually believe you. I mean, I believe that. That's precisely the kind of thing a bull-headed Englishman would do. But what led you there? You lied about turning up at the incident at the lettings place. You've been following this guy since you were spotted in the garden. And where does all this knowledge about the mother-fucking masons suddenly come from?'

'Dolores recognised Quinto's "signature" in the busted-up house,' I say. 'That was how we came to follow him.'

'And you didn't think to tell me that?'

'It was just a bit of vandalism, Commissario. It's not actually my job to help you solve crimes.' Her nostrils flare; she makes a mean smile.

'Now – thinking you're the smartest cock on the walk, that *is* very Italian. But if you had coughed up this little morsel earlier maybe your pal in the bathtub wouldn't be in the morgue, and,' she says in very passable English, 'all the king's horses and all the king's men cannot put Michele together again.' She returns to Italian: 'So how come you recognised him?' She drops the cigarette stub and grinds it beneath her heel, points a crimson talon at me: 'Mark you, *caro*, the answer you give to this question will affect the rest of the time you have in this country. Perhaps this planet.'

I give it due respect. 'A long time ago,' I say, 'I came into contact with the masons through my work at the canteen for the poor in San Donato. It was funded by them and I was invited to one of their meals – this Michele was sat at the same table as us.'

'Us?'

'My wife and I.'

'And they didn't want you to . . .' She frowns. 'You *didn't* join, did you?' I shake my head. 'There was always talk,' she says, 'the Comandante . . .'

'Not him, either. Against company policy.'

'You'd better tell me about them, then. How I can find them. Who was your contact?'

'A man named Alfonso Lambertini.'

'You have his contact details?'

'It was a long time ago. I've no idea what happened to him.' Rita Miranda gives me a long look, but moves on.

I receive a message as I leave the Questura. Dolores is nearby, in the bar of the Salaborsa, the old corn exchange now home to the public library. I'm relieved to hear from her – the sight of Michele was strong stuff, and I would have understood if she had wanted to go and lie in a dark room. But I find her in a corner of the air-conditioned bar on the ground floor of the covered *piazza*. She is not alone, there's an older woman with her – well, older than Dolores, probably early forties – in a khaki vest and shorts, her skin baked brown and her sun-bleached straw hair tied back with an African-style cloth.

She is wearing old military boots. She might have been a *kibbutzim* returned from a day building irrigation trenches, although the comparison would probably horrify her. I buy a coffee and a large glass of water, and join them.

'This is Sofia.' The woman radiates hostility, although I have a feeling this is how she views anyone outside her tribe. 'She was staying at the squat because she'd brought some goods to sell at the biological market. I met her on the way out of the Questura. They had picked her up along with the others. She thinks she might know where to find your bike. I explained that we didn't want anything else.'

'Nothing.' I return Sofia's scowl with equanimity.

'I said we'd pay,' adds Dolores.

'A contribution,' Sofia corrects her. 'To the collective.'

'That's what I meant,' she says. I pull out my wallet and produce a fifty. Sofia looks at Dolores.

'From me,' she says. I hand the note to Dolores and she passes it to Sofia.

She looks satisfied; at least the corners of her downturned mouth rise to mid-way point. 'I've told her we need a dairy expert,' she says. 'That she doesn't need to be doing this dirty work in this dirty city. She could help us improve our cheeses. But for some reason, she doesn't want to.'

'Like I've said,' says Dolores, 'I like the work, I like working with people.'

'The lowest of the low, though, Dee.' She glances at me. 'With the lowest, for the lowest, no matter how rich they might be. I never figured you for such a petite-bourgeois.'

Dolores bites her bottom lip, a sure sign she's holding back. 'I'm sorry to disappoint you.'

'Oh, you don't disappoint me,' says Sofia. She gets up. 'It's yourself you should worry about.' She heads for the bathroom.

'Another telling off,' I say. 'What fun you must have with your former comrades. Although she has a point – it wasn't just a choice between us and the call centre, you could have joined their cooperative in the countryside. Not that we'd want to lose you,' I hurriedly add.

'Sofia, all the rest,' says Dolores as she watches her go, 'have money behind them – this "cooperative" is actually a farm left to her girlfriend. They share what they eat, but what they sell barely pays the water bill. You're expected to "rent" your room out of your own pocket, and pay your share of the bills, and if you haven't got an income how can you do that? And they can kick you out if you rub them up the wrong way.' She asks the passing *cameriera* for another coffee. 'No – she calls me bourgeois,' she says. 'But what does she think she is?' She lowers her voice as Sofia reappears. 'They're all so fucking self-righteous.'

'This person you mentioned,' she prompts Sofia. 'With the bike.'

'Ottavo, he calls himself.' I frown. 'They've all got numbers. I suppose they have real names, but they don't share them. Security. And it's non-binary,' she adds approvingly.

'Although you said he's a he,' I can't help remarking.

'Well,' she says uncomfortably. '*They've* never mentioned pronouns. Anyway, it sounds like them – they've ridden out to the farm a few times on that bike, I remember it because of the curvy handlebars. I can't see them giving it up. Anyway, Otto, that's what they like to be called, mentioned that if things went pear-shaped, they would meet at the Oratorio dello Spirito Santo.'

I look at Dolores. 'It's that creepy little church up from the Questura,' she says.

'At midnight,' says Sofia. 'Just to make it even more spooky.' She glances at the clock. It was two in the afternoon. 'You've got plenty of time.'

'Thank you,' I say. 'That's something to go on.'

Sofia shrugs. 'I suppose he must be out by now. I mean, if he ever went down.'

I look at her. 'I'm sorry?'

That humourless smile again. 'To prison, I mean. I know you, you see. Or at least, I knew your wife, if only by sight. We were squatting ex-Fabrica Bentivoglio before they were forced to pull it down. In fact,' she turns to Dolores, 'that was how we came to occupy the old hospital.' She thinks about it. 'And probably how Otto ended up with your bike, although *they* certainly weren't among us back then, they would have probably still been at school.'

'You knew Lucia was working for *Bologna dei Popoli*?' I ask.

'We knew she was involved in some NGO the residents had got helping them. She called around a few times for a chat. I was actually stood by the window when it happened.' Her cockiness melts and it's as if there's a real person behind the mask, finally viewing me with something approaching compassion. 'I heard it, I mean, I didn't actually see it, but it was right after, and I called to the guys in the apartment who had a phone to call the emergency services but . . .' She looks vague. 'Anyway, I had to go and find my phone and call. Then, as I was doing it, I looked back out, saw Lucia lying there. I can't say whether she was alive, but she was very still.'

Her eyes glaze with the memory. 'Look, I'm sure she didn't suffer. The man was still behind the wheel, fiddling with the gear stick, it looked like . . .'

'No no no,' I say. 'It was a woman. You must have thought it was a man.' She gives me a condescending look.

'It was a man, believe me. I can see him now through the windscreen – shaved head and a beard. I mean,' she glances at Dolores. 'There wasn't any . . . ambiguity back then.

'I remember smelling burning, at first I thought it was the accident but of course it wasn't because it was cold and the windows were closed, it was from the kitchen where someone had turned the toaster too high. Anyway, by the time I got back, there was the ambulance, police, onlookers. Nothing much else to see.'

'Dan?' Dolores' voice from far off, but I'm in the canteen all those years ago, chatting to a couple of the regulars, my bandaged wrist sufficient explanation for my recent absence, when Luca approaches and begins, miraculously, speaking to me in English, even though he's never uttered a word in my own language before. He says: 'Daniel, you have to come to the office, there's a call.'

And gently ushers me from one world to another.

XIX

I was truly good for nothing. With just one working hand (I mostly carried the wrist in a sling), I couldn't even write the English section of Faidate Investigations website, let alone force myself to crank out some words on a book. At least I was able to make Rose, with a little assistance, her sludge, then walk her to school, albeit that she told me she didn't need me to, it was treacherous out, and I couldn't risk falling down again, 'Although,' she reflected, 'I suppose you're not drunk in the morning.'

Given that I wasn't much use at the canteen, after a few days moping around the house, with Lucia decidedly short on conversation, I announced that I would go to the Comandante's office in Via Marconi to see if I could help out.

'Does he know?' Lucia asked sceptically.

'I'm sure he can find me something.'

'You would be better spending your time studying Italian.'

'I do – but I can't manage it all day.'

She spat out the toothpaste. 'And whose fault's that?'

'Oh, come on,' I stroked her arm. 'How long are you going to be like this?'

She wiped her mouth on the towel, frowned in the mirror and reached for a hair brush. She ran it through her hair. I honestly couldn't see what she was trying to achieve.

'What do you mean?' she asked distractedly.

'You're annoyed with me, clearly.'

Now she scowled, although I couldn't tell whether it was at me or herself. She opened a jar and began to dab the contents on to her face.

'Is that foundation?' I asked. 'I didn't know you used that.'

'I'm not twenty-five any more. What's the problem?'

'Come on. Maybe you're not so young, but neither am I. This is childish. I understand you're angry, but I apologised. It really wasn't that I was drunk, it was the crazy goings-on, and,' I could see this would get nowhere, 'and I am *totally committed* to us, to everything working out here. It was you who mentioned me working for Giovanni.'

'He hates it when you call him that.'

'Well, you know what? Maybe he should lighten up a bit, too. You – the whole lot of you – you're so fucking heavy. So much for fun-loving Italians!' I followed her into the bedroom.

'If you want dancing, go down south.' She began to get dressed.

'Aren't you supposed to be half-southern?'

'Yes, that would be the damn furious half.'

'Can we have a bit of the northern part, too, then?'

She turned to me as she pulled the black roll neck over her head. She narrowed her eyes. 'That would be the sulky side.'

But she couldn't help smiling.

'Come on,' I held out my good arm for a hug, but she stayed put.

'It's just,' she wrapped her arms around herself. 'I'm not sure.' She shook her head, her eyes welled. 'I don't know what we're going to do.'

'Oh, come on.' I put my arm around her anyway. 'We'll be fine. You're doing well.'

She looked up at me. 'But what about you? It's not just about me – if you're not happy, how can we be happy as a family?'

'I'm fine.'

'No,' she pressed her face against my chest. 'You're not fine. You keep saying *fine, fine, fine,* but you're not fine at all – you haven't been fine for a long time. You drink too much—'

'It's just that—'

'At night, I know you do. I smell it on you when you come to bed. Sometimes I can even smell it in the mornings, it's like living with an alcoholic.'

'Oh come—'

She beat a fist upon my chest. '*Basta*. Admit it!'

'Okay,' I said. 'I'm not fine.'

'Good. That's good. You are not fine. And if you are not fine, we are not fine.' She sniffed. 'Do you think we can fix that?'

'I'm trying.' She gave me a searching look.

'I think maybe you are. But you need to do some things.'

'Like what?'

'No more drinking.'

'Ever? That's a tough ask, I'm an Englishman.'

'To make yourself feel better. Accept that you're a miserable bastard.'

'Am I really a miserable bastard?' I asked. 'Does Rose think that?'

'I don't think so,' Lucia said thoughtfully. 'But she has noticed your drinking.'

'So I gathered. But really, in England, it wouldn't be so—'

'*But you're in Italy now.* I think maybe that's part of the problem – you haven't accepted it. You're an immigrant. I know you go on the internet and watch your football, but England's thousands of miles away. *This* is what exists. *This* is your life, here and now.

'And this silly man, all this masonic claptrap. That's no more real than Rose's ghosts. It's a lot of hocus-pocus created so a bunch of bourgeois can do their business deals while thinking they're serving a higher purpose.' She shook her head. 'No more of that.'

'I think Alfonso's pretty sincere, though, I—'

Lucia pressed a finger upon my lips. 'Italians worship complexity, *amore*. There's something behind everything – *dietrologia*, we call it – behind-ology. It's a common pastime, almost a field worthy of study. To us, the Devil always lurks in the detail. Who killed Aldo Moro? Was it really the Red Brigade? But didn't Andreotti interfere with the investigation so his political rival would be killed? Or the military themselves, half of whom were *masons*? Or the Bologna station bombing. They sent a couple of fascists to prison for that, but weren't they linked to the secret services, who were fuelling "a strategy of tension?" On and on it goes. A mundane solution is never permitted where the baroque will do. Poor Meredith was killed in a "satanic rite" – you see, *literally* the Devil! No wonder the case collapsed. We believe in this rubbish so much, you're almost obliged to belong to a secret society to protect yourself from the secret societies!

'But the old families, well, most of them – all that remains are their names on the *palazzi*. I know you think the Comandante's a pompous one, *but we're still here*, the Faidate, living in the very building our ancestors built, precisely because we've always avoided all that. We don't belong to anything, we don't owe nothing to no one.' She used the Italian double-negative. 'Which is why people trust us.' Another snotty sniff, she wiped her face on my T-shirt, leaving it streaked with make-up, and broke away.

'I'll speak to Dad, ask him if you can come to the office. Maybe you can study there, and help out if he needs it. Okay?'

'Okay.' She nodded, business-like. I took her face in my hands. 'Friends?'

'Okay.' I kissed her forehead, her nose, finally her lips. She closed her eyes.

'I really love you, you know,' I said.

'Me, too.'

'You mean you really love you, too?'

She giggled. 'I mean I really love you, too.'

Mamma mia, though, it was quiet. Although I was pleased to have apparently patched things up with Lucia, I wondered if I had made a rod to beat myself by volunteering to come into the office.

Faidate Investigations occupied the fourth floor of a mix-use block along Via Marconi. This area was among the most modern part of Bologna 'within the walls', having suffered a combination of fascist-era redevelopment and bombing when the Allies had targeted the nearby train station. The canal which used to run down the centre of the road had disappeared, but Marconi was as broad as a boulevard, and altogether somewhat soulless.

I would have liked to have had a cubicle on the south side of the floor where the security part of the business was located and plenty of ex-cops came and went. These weren't uniformed store or bank guards, but plain-clothed body-guards to the uber-wealthy, visiting celebrities, or tasked with transporting large sums of cash, precious metals or jewels across the country. Even though my Italian was pretty terrible, it *sounded* like they were a lot of fun, and I would have enjoyed getting to know them and, who knew, even making some friends.

However, as the Comandante's son-in-law, I was expected to occupy the north wing of the floor alongside his office. Here was the long, marble tiled reception staffed by Alba, Lucia's cousin and office administrator, who was friendly and (perhaps overly) respectful, but responded to each of my attempts at Italian with an *'Eh?'*

I sighed like a schoolboy over the grammar primer, my wrist throbbing relentlessly. It was bright outside, sunlight reflecting off the snow piled along the sides of the street and bouncing off office windows.

The clock marked another minute. Would this be it, then? My life from now on, stuck here counting the hours? I stared at the subjunctive form and the subjunctive form stared back at me.

I got up, reached for my overcoat, and walked along the corridor, past the Comandante's empty office, which was more like a gentleman's study, full of leather-bound volumes and age-darkened portraits, including one of Dante Hercules Faidate, *Cavaliere* and clan founder, glowering above his mahogany desk as if his grave, grey-bearded countenance was about to be served up on his enormous white ruff, although the wily dog had managed to die in bed at the then-venerable age of sixty-seven.

The reception was empty except for Alba, who was wearing headphones as she worked through some figures on the computer.

The dusty metal blinds cast noirish shadows. I passed the huge fifties diptych the Comandante had received in lieu of payment by a bankrupt client (a Pollockesque splatter of maroon and brown Jacopo would come to call 'the shit storms') and stepped on to the landing.

The door to the other wing was open and I could see the guys (and it was all guys) looking busy and interesting, but that was not for me – I was now pegged as the English son-in-law, the subject of respectful smiles and muted conversation.

I took the stairs down, buttoning myself with some difficulty against the cold, and opened the door. There was a bitter breeze, but at least the pavement beneath the portico was snow and ice free. It was a hardy, black-mottled rubber that must have been fashionable in the sixties and, although it wasn't especially attractive, it at least provided grip.

I walked south with the idea of getting a coffee, although

in reality none of the bars seemed especially appealing – despite the freezing winters we still had back then, Bolognese bars lacked the snugness one might find in northern Europe. Typically furnished in white leather with a tendency towards chrome and mirrors, while the seasons might change, Italian taste seemed permanently set for summer. Be the rain thundering or the snow a metre deep, Italians – even Bolognese – appeared to derive a sense of comfort from the impression that they were never more than a cheeky stroll from a sun bed.

I carried on to the intersection then swung west down Via Ugo Bassi towards the two towers, crossing over to Piazza Maggiore and plodding up the steps to Salaborsa, the public library. Beneath the Art-Nouveau-tiled roof, the air was stale like a charity store packed with second-hand goods, or in this case second-hand books *and* second-hand people, although that was not entirely fair – there were probably twice as many students hunched over desks on the upper floors along the sides of the building – but it was the aged, unemployed, and escapees like me who occupied the open areas, flicking through old magazines or newspapers, sat tracing the small print of a reference book with a stubby finger, or just having a nap. I grabbed an empty seat and found myself facing Alfonso Lambertini.

His greatcoat folded over the back of the seat, he was in a canary shirt, leaf-green waistcoat and corded fawn trousers stuffed into riding boots speckled with dried slush. His head was bent over a science magazine, a *pince-nez* pressed solidly over his nose. He was mumbling to himself as if he was commenting on the article as he went along. I began to discreetly push myself back up when he looked directly at me.

'Ah! I wanted to ask you . . .'

'Sorry, I didn't notice you there.'

'What were you doing down there?' He laid the magazine on the table between us. The olive-green banner read in English: *Frontiers in Psychological Medicine.* 'I couldn't get much sense out of you at the time.'

'In the tunnel, you mean?'

'Of course.'

I explained what had happened. Or at least, what I thought had happened. It was so bizarre, even I was beginning to wonder if my chase through the *palazzo* had been an especially vivid dream.

'If it was a dream, how did you manage to get into the temple?'

'Some kind of hallucination? I had been in there with you, so I would have known there must have been some way in.'

Alfonso nodded thoughtfully, then narrowed his eyes. 'But that doesn't explain how you found the secret tunnels.'

We contemplated this while the tramp on the swivel chair beside us began to snore. 'There was no possible way,' I agreed. 'But if this . . . person *was* real, that still doesn't explain what came over me. The actual hallucination – the sense that the tunnel was closing in around me, the vision of the eye, and so on.'

'You had gone down there half-dressed. You were in your socks and a shirt. It must have been below ten down there. Some kind of cold-induced hysteria?'

'It's a possibility,' I admitted. 'But that doesn't explain this person in black. And how did you find me, anyway?'

'The lights. I went to the window to see what was going on and came down.'

'So you didn't know about the tunnels?'

He looked offended. 'Of course I knew about the tunnels – they've run beneath the *palazzo* for centuries, long preceding the construction of the temple. They were used to transport goods directly into the kitchens from the canals and dispose of waste. And provide a handy exit should the city be overrun. It was only later that my great-grandfather converted them into a mode by which the brotherhood could enter the *palazzo* unseen from prying eyes, of which there were many. You were found outside Alpha and Omega, basically the entrance and exit.'

'That was what the symbol meant? The point within a circle within those lines?'

'It doesn't actually mean entrance and exit.' He sighed tetchily. 'It means much more, but for your purposes—'

'Does Olga know about them?'

He looked genuinely surprised. 'Olga? She is most definitely not a mason, Daniel.'

'You've shown her the temple, though.'

'To clean,' he said. 'What?'

'I suppose that's something one never thinks about. Who cleans the evil genius's lair? Who puts the rubbish out.'

'You still believe we are "evil", Daniel?'

'And the tunnels? Did she know about them?'

'I didn't show her,' he said. 'And I doubt she would have discovered them. To be honest, she did little more than dust and vacuum. And put the rubbish out, as you say.' He permitted himself a wry smile. 'Although she may have occasionally taken the cloaks to the cleaners.'

'But don't you also talk about having these "waking

dreams"? And that is certainly how it seemed to me. Not the chase stuff – how else could I have found the tunnel if that hadn't been real? – but the other, *surreal*, stuff. What were they doing in the kitchen? They were reaching into the fridge. Were they taking something out?' It began to dawn. '*Or putting something in?* What did you have in the fridge?'

'Oh, that evening, many things.' His face reddened. 'It's true, I may have had a little help, with the preparation – Olga and I had worked during the day to prepare the dishes. The broth, the beef, you couldn't do it just like that! So everything would be ready when you arrived.'

'And you placed it in the fridge?'

'Some of it, yes. Especially the *zuppa Inglese*, for example.'

'But you were saying that you don't eat like that every evening.'

'No, not at all.'

'What, then, is always in the fridge?'

He puffed his cheeks. '*Beh.* Some cheese. Fruit. Perhaps milk. Wine. Other ingredients . . .'

I thought about our meal. 'The water was cold. You keep that in the fridge?'

'Yes, I like cold water.'

'So you always have it there.'

'I do.'

'Do me a favour, will you? See if you can ask one of your contacts to have it analysed.'

XX

The smoked-glass doors of the Salaborsa are scorching hot. I emerge into unblinking light. I reach for my sunglasses. My lips smart.

I veer beneath the shadow of Palazzo D'Accursio, weaving through knots of tourists as I take D'Azeglio towards home. I don't believe Dolores' friend, Sofia, and I do – I don't *want* to believe her is the thing. She had no reason to lie, spin a tale. Lucia's death meant nothing to her.

It was a man who killed my wife, not a woman, which begs the question: why? I stride up D'Azeglio in a rush to get to my computer, my phone having yielded only rudimentary results. I need to go deeper if I want to find the woman's address.

But of course – she will be on holiday!

There was no gaol time for signora Guerra, even though she was convicted of 'vehicular homicide'. She had been speeding, but claimed Lucia had run a red, which was difficult to prove either way. She then panicked, backing over her, which probably finished her off.

Three years, suspended. We didn't contest it, it was one of those things. Lucia was gone, what else mattered? Even the speeding we knew everyone was guilty of from time to time, and of course Lucia had not been wearing a helmet, because in Italy who does?

Except – the driver was not apparently signora Anna Guerra.

It was a man, who may have got away with murder.

The fob leaps from my hand like wet soap, springing in front my fingertips as I try to scrape it off the road. I finally grab hold and squeeze. The gates shudder open.

As I walk up the gravel drive my forehead begins to prickle feverishly, and my guts rumble. I take the steps up to the apartment two at a time and burst in. It is fridge-cold – I have forgotten to turn off the air con-again – and dash to the bathroom.

I pull myself up, pull myself together. Gaze back pale, maudlin in the mirror as if I've received a righteous slap, and deserved it.

I sit at the laptop, Google her name.

Anna Guerra – there are very few names that are unique. There are fat Annas, slim ones, old ones, young, light-skinned, dark, American, Argentinian, French, Spanish, Portuguese, Brazilian.

I refine the search to Italy, Bologna.

There is still a fair raft of Annas, but the one in question appears on the second page of *Images*. Nothing more than a blurred snap of an unremarkable late-middle-aged woman tagged in a Facebook photo of a Christmas lunch, in this case for a stationery supply company out at Sasso Marconi. She is raising a glass of cheap fizz with the pained jollity of a woman trailing a hen-do in midwinter.

It is nevertheless odd seeing her smile – she looked suitably defeated when I saw her 'live' on the sole occasion I turned up to court – for her sentencing. Her grey roots showed from red-tinted hair pulled back from a saggy face. Her black XL T-shirt, spelling ONE LOVE in sequins, contoured rolls of fat. Lucia would have appreciated the irony – genuine conspiracy manifests in the dismal court case coming to a close on a wet Wednesday afternoon.

There is nothing more about Anna Guerra. When I try her Facebook page it no longer exists. I check the stationery company. There's no website, just an address and telephone number. I'm about to call but think better of it. I should take a shower. Cool off, in more ways than one.

The water pounds upon my upturned face until it has dredged so deep in the earth it finally runs properly cold.

I let it run on and on.

I finally step out, wipe off, wrap the towel around me.

The colour has begun to return to my cheeks.

I was shocked. Dehydrated. Over-heated. Or put the other way – over-heated, dehydrated, shocked. Hit for six by truth rushing through my punctured carapace; the conviction that *everything* has been a lie.

Everything I've believed until now.

Which in turn throws into question everything else. Am I really so deluded to believe that Lucia has been listening all these years? Witnessed all we've done, Rose and I? Despite that sense of having her constantly by my side; feeling the heat of her gaze?

Merely the heat of *dolore d'amore* – Love grief.

I was a fool to believe that, just as I was a fool to take the explanation of her death for granted.

I should know by now to take nothing for granted, and yet when it came to Lucia, I believed what I was told.

All the cases I've cracked, the mysteries I've solved, yet I never thought to question the single death that defined my life.

Did the Comandante have doubts? He never shared them. Did he perhaps conduct a discreet investigation?

Of course he did.

Sat back at the desk, I call him.

'Anna Guerra,' I say.

Silence. Or a silence filled by the noise of cicadas. He's in the garden in Cesenatico. It's the afternoon, so he's probably reading the final volume of Scurati's novelised biography of Mussolini – Giovanni's choice of a light holiday read – in the shade of the pomegranate tree, a jug of iced tea on the table beside him. 'What about her?' he says finally.

'I want to talk to her.'

A further silence. The chatter of a child – I can recognise Little Lucia.

'She passed away.'

Naturally, he kept a track on her.

'When?'

'Some years ago. Six,' he adds, as he knows I will press him. 'Cancer. She was seventy-two.'

'Two years later,' I say. He says nothing. 'I have new information.' Silence. 'You looked into the circumstances.'

'Thoroughly. I devoted the agency's resources to it.'

'And you didn't find anything . . . suspicious.'

'Had I done so,' he says tetchily, 'you would know.'

'Would I?'

'If there had been anything worth sharing, yes.'

'Anna Guerra was speeding, hit her, panicked, reversed. Everything that we know from the court case.'

'As she confessed, yes.'

'Was there any conflicting witness testimony?'

'No.' He sighed. 'Tell me, then.'

'I met a credible witness who claims it wasn't Anna Guerra in the car, it was a man.'

The rustle of newspaper in the seaside breeze. I imagine his morning *Corriere della Sera* weighed down by a coffee tray or the book. 'We spoke to everyone in the surrounding blocks. We visited the apartments of anyone who had a view of the scene. Everyone.'

'Including the squatters?'

'Including them, yes.'

'I saw one of the squatters. Well at least someone who joined them later on, riding Lucia's bike. I'm trying to track him down. To get the bike back.'

'I didn't know it had gone missing,' Giovanni says. I stop myself from saying – not every stone was left unturned, then.

'I met a woman who was at the squat,' I continue. 'She

told me she was stood by the window and when she heard the impact she looked out. She is adamant that she saw a man behind the wheel, and I believe her.'

Silence. Cicadas, the animated chat of the little girl. Finally, the Comandante's hoarse voice: 'She gave you a description.'

'In his thirties, shaved head and a beard.'

Anyone else might have denied that this was possible, that an error had been made all those years ago; that I was thinking wishfully, wasting my time, but not the Comandante. He barely misses a beat.

'The car wouldn't restart, after . . . the incident,' says the Comandante. 'If it had— *They would have gotten away.*' He says this last part as if it is a revelation.

'We . . . *I*,' he continues, 'committed the cardinal sin . . . of fitting the evidence to the crime. I took it at face value, but of course – had the car not stalled, then the driver would have escaped and, as you say, the driver may not have been her. I will need to talk to the witness.'

'She will be at her farm now,' I say. 'And I don't think you'll get any more out of her.'

'I will arrive tonight.'

The phone goes dead.

Il vento della sera comes as little relief. The late afternoon breeze fans the heat as if just around the corner the city is engulfed by flames.

I should be in shorts, sandals, a T-shirt, but again I'm overdressed in chinos and a navy-blue shirt, way too formal for an *aperitivo*, but I chose my clothes like armour. Against what, I'm not sure, but then I'm not too sure about anything right now.

The call came out of the blue – Cristina, of all people. She and Rocco are passing through before leaving for Finland. After their usual Floridian sojourn, they're planning to take a train up to Rovaniemi on the Artic Circle, and beyond.

'We'll hire a car,' says Cristina, 'see how far we can get.'

'She expects we'll fall off the end of the world,' says Rocco.

'He exaggerates, as usual,' she pokes her husband fondly, 'but at least we'll see some reindeer and seals.'

'And Stefania?' I mean her daughter, and Rose's best friend. 'Is she rescuing plenty of turtles?'

Rocco rolls his eyes. Along with his teeth, they are his only white bits – the rest is a profound, and largely permanent, tan he tops up skiing in the winter. 'She's certainly spending plenty of time on the beach,' he says. He glances at Cristina. 'Together with "Bob".'

Cristina smiles. 'He's just a *friend*.'

'Big Aussie lug. Surfer dude. Probably takes his pick of the interns.'

'As I tell Rocco, if that's the case, then we don't need to worry about an Australian son-in-law. Anyway, she'll be back for our trip north, and then she'll have to focus on her studies.'

They are a handsome couple, similarly dressed in flowing 'natural' cottons, with expensively curated long hair, in his case, a lustrous combed-back tawny brown, flecked grey. They exude a different sort of quality to the Contessa or freemasons. Non-conformity is their conformity. They are classic 'Bobos' – bourgeois bohemians – who have come from money and continue to accumulate it via their respective legal practices. They have been my bulwark ever since Lucia died,

Cristina unquestioningly including Rose in all her daughter's activities and frequently having her over for sleepovers. The two only children have grown as close as sisters, and miraculously never had any (major) fallings out.

'Is she still going to the Academy?'

Cristina means Rose. 'It seems so.' My daughter has her heart set on becoming an artist.

'I suppose if it doesn't work out,' says Cristina, 'she's always got the family business.'

'And a doctor,' Rocco adds approvingly.

'Hold on,' I say. 'She's eighteen. I hardly expect her to end up with Antonio any more than your Stefania will become a beachcomber with "Bob".'

'You should be encouraging them,' Rocco shoots back. 'A doctor's just what every family needs!'

'You're welcome to him, the dunderhead.'

'He's a nerd,' says Rocco. 'And nerds are good. They earn the money. I can't see Bruce making anything from turtles, unless it's soup!'

'Bob,' says Cristina, 'short for "Robert", right?' I nod. 'But what about you? Surely the Comandante can't be making you stay here the whole summer.'

'I—' I haven't given it much thought. My ambitions haven't stretched further than a sun bed in Cesenatico, despite it being my first summer wholly without Rose. I realise, slightly startled again by the obvious truth – I am on my own.

'What?' says Cristina.

'Nothing. Anyway, it's been a pretty crazy summer so far.'

Rocco frowns. 'What's happened?'

I tell them about the bike, and our gory discovery. 'My

God!' says Cristina. They open their phones and scroll. 'Yes, it's here – body found in squat. It doesn't say anything else.'

'It's only a matter of time before it comes out.'

'But that's dreadful. Even for you it must have come as a shock. And Dolores was there too? How's she handling it?'

'Surprisingly well.' I sip my beer. 'But coming back to the bike, it occurred to me that I never properly asked you at the time – what was Lucia actually doing at the ex-Fabrica? Nuovo Bentovoglio, I mean. I knew she had gone there for work, but I realised that I never asked you why she was there.'

Cristina blinks. 'Well, I . . .' She rifles in her raffia Fendi bag, producing a pack of cigarettes. Rocco reaches across to steady her hand. 'I'm sorry.' She blows the smoke away from me. 'It's the . . . you understand.'

'I apologise for bringing it up. It's just that the bike—'

'No problem. Honestly, I wish I could tell you more . . . I didn't think to ask at the time, either. I know she was close to Ludovica and had told me she was worried about her, you know, afterwards.'

'You mean after the meeting?'

'That's it. She wasn't doing her shopping, eating properly, that kind of thing. Anyway, that's where I thought she had gone, then . . .' She waves the cigarette. '*Poof!* Sorry. I'm so sorry, that sounded crass. What I mean is, it just happened so out of the blue. It changed our lives. Yours of course. *Rose.* Everyone.' Her eyes well up. 'Everyone,' she echoes. Rocco takes her free hand. It's true – it wasn't just me and my daughter. Cristina had resigned from the charity shortly afterwards. She said it reminded her too much of Lucia.

'And no one said anything to you about what happened?

Anything we might not know?' She looks blank. I tell her about meeting Sofia.

They're dumbfounded. 'But have you gone to the police?' Rocco asks.

'Not yet. To be honest, I'm still trying to process it. And really – after all this time, the word of one witness – even if she is prepared to talk?'

Cristina's toffee tan has paled. 'Excuse me,' she's on her feet, heading for the bathroom.

'She doesn't look too good.'

'It hit her really hard,' sighs Rocco. 'Honestly, Dan, I'd never seen her so distraught, not even when her dad died. In the end we had to go to the doctor. I got her tranquillisers. That was why she left the charity in the end. Couldn't go on.' He arches his sun-blond eyebrows. 'I admit, I thought it was a little crazy. I mean no offence old friend, but it was as if *she* had been hit by that fucking car.' He thumps his chest. 'The shrink reckoned it was down to something inside. Unconscious, I mean – not just losing a friend, but another mother, a mum like her, gone in the blink of an eye, some kind of existential crisis.'

Cristina finally reappears looking breathless. She reaches for her Prosecco. 'I'm sorry, I thought I was about to faint!'

'Rocco told me how upset you were. I apologise, I should have been more sensitive.'

'Don't be silly – it's me.' She takes another gulp of wine. 'A man.' She levels watery brown eyes on mine.

'That's what Sofia said – she was adamant. Bald or shaven-headed with a beard. He couldn't have been the woman, Anna Guerra.'

'But then *how* . . . *Why*?'

'Did you know Anna Guerra?'

'I had never heard of her until it happened.'

'Then this man doesn't ring any bells?'

'None.'

'Cristina,' I say. 'Please – I know you were good friends as well as colleagues. Do you have any idea why someone might have done this to Lucia on purpose? Any reason at all, anything – please, tell me, I can take it.'

She leans forward to clutch my hands, looks straight at me. 'There is no reason I know, Dan. I understand what you're implying, but you should know – Lucia really loved you. She loved you with all her heart.'

'Okay, let's go through the form.' This time I wasn't upon the other side of Plexiglass, but I was sitting at a desk, and determined to treat 'my' clients better than I had been.

Lucia was on a site visit but had double-booked interviews in English with a family of asylum seekers who were waiting to hear the verdict of their application, and in the meantime were supposed to be accommodated by the comune because they had children. Except that the comune had not found them anywhere and they were currently being sheltered by a local church.

'So you come from Pakistan?' The father looked at his daughter.

'Yes. Balochistan,' she said.

'Okay, can you spell that?' I couldn't actually write, given my right wrist, but we were recording it so Lucia could input the information upon an Italian form later. 'And what was the date you claimed asylum?' She told me. 'Where?'

'Greece.' If I had had a pen, I would have held it suspended in the air.

'You came from Turkey?' She nodded.

'But you also claimed asylum here, in Italy?' She nodded. I looked at them, and they at me. I didn't know who had said what to whom, and who their daughter had spoken to, and I certainly didn't want to get her into trouble, but I was beginning to understand where the problem might lie, especially if they had been confronted by the kind of unhelpful (or, in the strictest, Italian-sense, *inflessibile*) official as I had been at AUSL.

'Excuse me.' I was on my way to the main office to have a word with Cristina when I noticed Alfonso in the small reception. In fact, what caught my attention was signor Molino in a sky-blue suit a size too small, his flushed face drained a powdery white, with a pile of folders balanced on his lap.

He stood up as Cristina came in from outside. Balancing the bundle upon one arm, he reached a beefy hand out to her with the other. She caught hold of a handful of folders before they toppled off the top, and the pair proceeded past me. It was only then that I spotted the felt boots of Alfonso poking out from around the corner.

'What are you doing here?' I hadn't told him that Lucia had warned me off of him, but I didn't think she would be happy if she discovered we were still in touch, worse – he was visiting me at 'work'.

'You're not at the canteen any more, and I tried you at home, so I assumed you must be here. Is that blonde lady the lawyer?'

'Cristina, yes. Although I'm not sure she's going to be able to deal with your case,' I didn't want to say her priority probably wasn't owners of *palazzi*. 'She has a lot of . . . large-scale issues on her hands at the moment.'

This didn't seem to discourage him. 'Perhaps she takes private cases. I will leave her my card.' He dug deep into an inner pocket and handed me one, gold-bordered, which read Cav. Dott. Alfonso Umberto Emanuele Lambertini, Worshipful Master, Mixed Lodge of Italy's Right and Acknowledged Masons, Bologna.

'Fine,' I said. 'I'll pass it on.' And she'll have a huge laugh, I thought.

'But that's not why I'm here, Daniel – news! I have news! The laboratory results came back, and you were right – we were poisoned!'

'What?'

'If you could call it that. The figure in black was *not* an hallucination, but everything that came afterwards may well have been. The tests came back positive for Lysergic Acid Diethylamide.'

'LSD?'

'Don't you see? It explains everything! Certainly my "episodes" – clearly, they were hoping to trigger another psychotic break. It's all become clear now, what they're trying to do. Which is why I need a lawyer.'

'Hold on,' I said. 'You're suggesting your family has been slipping LSD into your water to have you committed?' I considered this – the figure's robes morphing into raven's wings, the walls of the tunnel warping around me, the all-seeing eye – 'But how would they know about the tunnels? Wouldn't they have to be a mason? Have the kit? The cloak, I mean?'

'The cloak is probably easiest to answer,' he said. 'You can even buy them off the internet. It's never been the same since that Spielberg film.'

'Really? Which one?'

'With the Scientologist . . .'

I could only think of Tom Cruise. 'You mean – Kubrick. *Eyes Wide Shut*.'

'If you say so, but you see – if I happened to come across the poisoner, then I would claim I had seen a mason and it would have all been a part of my mad visions!

'The tunnels are more troubling. I told you that my cousin's father had been a mason, so it is possible they might know how to gain access to the temple.'

'And there's Olga.'

He shook his head dismissively. 'She would never betray me.' I might not yet have been a battle-hardened private investigator, but even then this seemed a dubious proposition.

'You forget the tunnels,' he said as if reading my mind. 'One is only invested into this secret when one reaches the grade of Master Mason.'

'And how many people have reached this grade?'

'Seven. The entrances were used in more difficult times, when masons did not want to be seen even coming and going from the *palazzo* in case they were arrested for plotting revolution. One also leads to the canal. Of course, it is possible that someone may have come across an entrance and broken in, but the doors are locked.'

'From what you're saying it is more likely that one of your rite – a Master Mason – is in cahoots with your family.'

Alfonso looked pained. 'It may well be,' he sighed.

XXI

The small, red-brick church looks out of place in Bologna where grandiosity is the rule. Size certainly mattered to the Papal State when Bologna was its second city, and huge classical facades loom along many a narrow street. Whenever the papal authorities had a bit of extra cash, they seemed to think – municipal building? Hospital? Park?

No, what we really need is another enormous church.

But the Oratorio dello Spirito Santo in Via val d'Aposa is the exception to this rule. Were it not for its Romanesque facade decorated with the terracotta 'medallion' portraits of anguished saints, it might be a Welsh chapel. The plaque of a red cross against a white background indicates, in fact, that it belongs to the Knights of Malta.

Everything seems peaceful in the sunset-red side street, although the sun set some time ago, leaving the rusty brick to cool. From nearby Piazza Maggiore, *Apocalypse Now* is audible. The screening begins around ten, so I imagine Martin Sheen and his crew are reaching the end of their river journey, approaching the Montagnard base where natives wait among decapitated heads while Marlon Brando lurks in the heart of darkness. I meanwhile linger in the shadow of the portico, figures drifting past like dreamers. We are drunk on the heat, although for all but the most devoted drinkers it is too hot to actually consume alcohol.

It is midnight, and although nothing begins on time here, apparently the Maltese Knights they do things differently. The wooden door opens just enough for it not to be a trick of the light, and a figure emerges from the dark side of the church, flitting inside. The door closes.

I step on to the road and slip across into the shadows on the other side, where the street branches into the even narrower *vicolo* Spirito Santo.

I press my back against the warm brick of the church, edging up to the corner so I can see anyone else who arrives. It is five minutes past the hour. I pull my pick wrap from my back pocket. I'm not going to try to break the lock – that's a noisy process – but I'm betting they've kept the door on the latch, so I produce a strip of white plastic a little larger and more flexible than a credit card that I should be able to slot in and open the door with relatively quietly.

I'm about to make my move when I hear the turn of spokes. I draw back into the shadows.

I hear them get off the bike. As they unravel the chain and begin to attach it to the railings, I take a look. It isn't Lucia's, but it *is* Quinto.

This means there must be at least three of them inside.

I've reached the point, I think, when I should contact the *commissario.* If these kids have anything to do with the body in the bathtub, or even if they don't, Rita Miranda would say it was my duty to call, and I'll get in hot water if I don't. Certainly, Quinto's in the frame for the killing. It forms a definite pattern: all that masonic graffiti, and now an actual dead mason in his bath. Add that to the so-called 'terrorism' of Reclaim Bologna, and he and his friends have clearly got a lot of explaining to do.

On the other hand, if the cops get hold of them, my chances of finding out what's really going on will be severely curtailed. The police are not entirely cynical – they generally want to catch wrongdoers – but their daily experience has led them to understand that the most obvious solution is correct nine times out of ten. The majority of crimes are relatively easy to solve. Criminals are not, on the whole, geniuses – they tend to find themselves on the wrong side of the law due to recklessness, or because they can't find an honest route to advancement, so they're likely to be impetuous, greedy, lazy or stupid, all of which lead them to fuck up one way or another. And as for that tenth time? It's a numbers game – if the authorities pursued every wrong doing as if it was Agatha Christie, the other nine villains would run free. Reclaim Bologna are firmly in the frame for the masonic murder, whether they're involved or not.

Quinto raps on the door twice, then once again. I can see where this is going. With a silence that surprises me, I manage to slip up behind him as the door opens. Inside, the church flickers with candlelight. The kid – Otto, from his lime mullet and fluffy moustache – is clearly startled to see me there, but Quinto hasn't yet cottoned on, and I shove him forward. As he stumbles into the church, I shut the door behind me. The pair fall back. I raise my hands, although there's certainly not much to see except my phone and the lock wrap in my back pockets.

'I just want to talk,' I say quickly.

The other one's at the back. Of course, it should have been obvious – the kid who was sitting with Lorenzo at the bar – only in this company he doesn't seem quite so kiddish. A muscular torso shapes his black T-shirt, and although his dark hair is swept back into a ponytail, there's something military about his bearing. His steady, unsurprised black eyes settle coolly upon me.

He walks between the stubby pews of the bare church, its only apparent concession to Catholicism a cream stucco ceiling. The walls are whitewashed as if they have been scrubbed clean.

'He's a private detective,' he says. 'An "agent of the bourgeoisie", apparently.' The other two look puzzled. 'Just some shit Lorenzo was saying.' He stands in front of me, legs apart, hands on hips.

'I come in peace.'

'You just want to get your bike back?' He sniggers. 'It's your bike he wants, by the way, Otto.'

'Mine?' Otto looks affronted. 'It's not mine, it's the squat's.' His juvenile moustache wriggles like a restless caterpillar. 'Although I suppose it's mine more than anyone's. I mean, I repaired it. If he wants—'

The kid raises a hand. 'I'm guessing it was you that called the police.'

'You mean who found the body in Quinto's bathtub?'

Quinto, brushing a lick of hair from his eyes, looks at me agog. 'I didn't have anything to do with that.'

'I guessed. Any idea what it was doing there?'

'*None.* None whatsoever. I got home and as soon as I opened the door there was water on the floor and I was "oh fuck there must be some leak" and then . . . and then . . .' His jaw drops open and he looks wildly between his friends.

'It was pretty gruesome,' I say. 'A *mason*. Cut in two.'

'Wait,' says Otto. 'You mean . . . chopped? In half?'

'That's it.' They begin to back away from Quinto.

'I swear,' Quinto says desperately. 'I couldn't have, it's not possible.'

'And why's that?' I ask.

'Because . . . Well, *because*. I just *couldn't*.'

'You know what? I believe you, but I doubt it will satisfy the police.'

'I . . .' He looks helplessly at the soldier. 'Secondo?'

'You're the second?' I say. 'What's all this with numbers? And masons, while we're at it. You don't look much like masons to me.'

'Secondo' leans back against a pew. For the leader of a group wanted by the police for terrorism and possible murder, he seems remarkably relaxed.

'Just a joke. Quinto's stupid joke.' He frowns. 'Which has apparently got a bit out of—' There are two knocks at the door, followed by another.

They look at each other. 'Third?' he says.

'Arrested – in the house.'

'Fifth and Sixth, then? But aren't they in Alban—'

There it was again.

'Seventh?' Otto mutters as he warily opens the door a crack.

He steps back as the snout of a Beretta is shoved in his face.

The man's camouflage hoodie is pulled tight around his head while the bottom half is concealed by a black muffler. Only determined grey eyes and matching eyebrows are visible. But it's those blue plastic shoe covers and surgical gloves that worry me.

He's got only one thought in mind – to kill.

I make my move before he's fully through the door, grabbing his wrists and forcing them upwards. Whether he lets off a shot by instinct or design is beside the point. It deafens by proximity, but it's aimed high, above the head of Otto, who cowers back.

Another. This bullet explodes the stucco, raining clumps of plaster as we continue to struggle.

'Help me, then!' I call, but no one comes.

He's twisting, he's kicking. Another shot, lower this time as he tries to pull the weapon down to me.

I swing his arms sideways and try to butt him, but he sees it coming, dodges. I try again, but only manage to shave his forehead.

He's pulling back the gun, and he's going to succeed this time. I can't say he's stronger, but it's easier for him – he's going to pull back his arms and pull the trigger.

A couple of bullets in the belly or chest. They'll maybe even go straight through at this range.

I harness all my strength. Wrench his hands back up and

lean forward. Bite hard into his left hand – he yells, lets go – then the right – another scream even as I feel his free fist hammer the back of my head.

The gun clatters on to the floor. I fall straight after it; whatever he might do, I'm already on top of it as a kick arrives in my ribs. I fumble for the gun beneath me, grab hold of it, roll on to my back, ready to pull the trigger . . .

He's gone.

The church door hangs open.

The trembling barrel of the pistol still aimed at the doorway, I begin to shift back across the tiles, so I am propped against a pew. Only now do I realise – through my ringing ears, the fine patina of white dust, my dog-like panting – that there's no other sound.

I get to my feet, gun still trained on the doorway. 'Anybody?' I risk a look around. No one. Are they crouched behind the pews?

But first things first. The door remains half-open. I'm not going to do the Hollywood thing and venture into the dark only for him to jump me.

I sidle around the door, keeping the gun trained on the opening, and kick it shut. It closes with a satisfying *thunk*.

I take in the church again.

'Hello?' Nothing. Candles flicker. Dust settles. I walk along the aisle but the pews are empty.

It's to the side of the altar I see it – a small, open doorway, so low that I have to duck down on to *vicolo* Spirito Santo, the lane that descends to Palazzo D'Accursio and the *piazza*.

I train the gun left and right along the blood-red alley on this blood-red night, but there is no sign of the assailant. No sign of anyone, until I spot a syrupy trail leading down the lane.

I begin to make my way along the *vicolo*. From the *piazza*, I can hear Marlon Brando asking Martin Sheen where he's from.

Ohio.

Did they say why they sent you?

That is classified, sir, Sheen replies, although we, he, and Brando know what he has come to do. Who he has come to terminate.

With extreme prejudice.

I glance down at the trail, turn to check I'm not being sneaked up on. Menace lurks in each pool of shadow.

A cough. I halt, straining to hear.

Scuffling, scratching ahead. I shine the phone light. The emerald eyes of a huge black rat glint up at me over a pool of blood. It turns its head incuriously back down.

I step around it and carry on.

Inside the church had been Secondo, Quinto, and Ottavo, I'm thinking – and one of them is injured.

Brando asks why they want to terminate his command.

Sheen tells him that is classified, sir.

They thought it might be 'Seventh' at the door, whoever he is, and where there's a 'Second' there has to be a 'First'.

It is no longer classified, says Brando.

Sheen tells him that he has gone insane.

I'm running out of lane, I'm running out of shadows. The

bright windows of a boutique hotel illuminate the end of the lane, a couple appear around the corner and begin to make their way towards me.

I stuff the gun in my belt and shine my phone at the trail of blood apparently leading all the way to the square, packed with hundreds, thousands.

I join the hundreds, the thousands, while I try to keep track of the trail, looking hopelessly around as Sheen sits battered and thirsty in a tiger cage, and the photographer, played by Dennis Hopper, offers him a cigarette and asks him why he wants to kill a genius.

Balanced between gruesome fantasy and sweaty reality, the gun against my coccyx nudges me toward the inevitable.

I send Commissario Miranda a text. To my surprise she calls me straight back.

'There will be a car along in a minute,' she says.

'Do you ever sleep?' I ask.

'With one eye open.'

XXII

I was already asleep when I received the text, but the vibration woke me. The clock read 12:07. Shifting warily away from Lucia, snoring daintily, I checked it – Alfonso. I leaned further away so Lucia couldn't see.

I need your help, it read. *Can you call me?* I gazed at the message glowing in the dark. I considered shutting off my phone and turning back over, but instead found myself slipping out from under the duvet and sneaking from the room. I trod softly along the corridor, ducking my head into Rose's room to find her blissfully asleep, before entering the living room and closing the door behind me. I pressed the telephone icon.

'What is it?' I said softly.

'I need to go,' he moaned without any apology for the hour.

'What do you mean, "you need to go". Go where?'

'Get out. They're coming for me tomorrow morning. I received a tip-off.'

'Who are coming for you?'

'The police, or whoever it is that takes mad people, which I apparently am. A judge has given a provisional ruling – I am a risk to the public and myself. I need to be detained in order for an official assessment to be made, which the court will then consider in due course. Do you have any idea what "in due course" means in this country? It's akin to a life sentence! And of course, once you're in, the onus is on you to persuade them you're sane, and the more you protest you are, the more they're convinced you're a lunatic!'

'But what about these tests you had done that prove they were lacing your water?'

'Don't you see? That's precisely why they're doing this now – they know we're on to them and want to get me locked up before I can make a move. And in any case,' he wailed, 'they could claim the LSD doesn't mean anything – they could say I planted it there myself.'

'I'm a witness,' I said. 'I saw everything.'

'One witness,' he said glumly. 'A foreigner talking about someone dressed in a masonic robe and chasing them along tunnels until he collapsed himself. You'll be lucky if they don't lock you up, too.'

'I thought you said they liked the English – they were "tremendous Anglophiles" you said.'

'You were supposed to testify to me being sane, not acting mad yourself!'

'What, then?'

'That's precisely why I have to go.'

'And what am I supposed to do?'

'Why,' he said as if I was stupid. '*Drive* of course.'

I looked down at my busted wrist. 'Look, you can borrow our car if you have to.'

'But I need you to drive me.'

'What? You need a chauffeur?'

'I don't drive,' he yowled.

'Who are you offering to lend our car to?' I twisted around. Lucia was standing there.

'No one,' I said. 'Alfonso,' I admitted. 'The authorities are coming to arrest him, apparently.'

Her eyes widened. *'And you've offered him our car*?'

I held up my wrist. 'It was only because I can't drive.' Lucia muttered something in Italian that sounded very much like: *I wish they would take them both away.* She snatched the phone from me and launched into a tirade in her own language too quick for me to follow. She paused, waiting for a response, then grunted, expelled another outburst, and ended the call. She handed the phone back to me.

'Now,' she said, turning away. 'Come back to bed.'

'But Lucia, they're going to pick him up.'

'If only they'd done it sooner, we wouldn't have this bullshit.' She glanced at the clock. 'Come on, we've only got five hours. I told him we'll go and get him before I'm due at work.'

XXIII

Commissario Miranda snaps on a pair of black latex gloves and takes the barrel of the Beretta between her fingers. 'I could have done without you stuffing it down your arse crack.'

'I'm sorry,' I say. 'That wasn't a priority at the time.'

'What should have been a priority,' she takes a transparent green evidence bag from her desk drawer, 'is telling us where you were going in the first place.'

'Well,' I say, 'it was just a hunch.'

'And when you saw Quinto enter the church, what?'

'I wasn't thinking,' I say.

The office windows are open and the *commissario* spins on her chair, plucking a pack of Marlboro Lights off the sill. She turns back to me. 'You know we kid about your citizenship application, but we can not only lose it, signor Leicester, we can also oppose it on the grounds that you're an undesirable alien, and frankly, you're looking pretty undesirable right now.'

'I told you, didn't I? I brought you evidence, and a description.'

'You brought us,' she waggles the cigarette dismissively before lighting it, lets out a grey-blue cloud of contempt, '*stuff*. If you had shared your "hunch" with us, we could have had three in the cells.'

I nod at the bagged-up gun pointed towards me on the desk. '*Decisive* evidence – clearly, this was the true culprit, the one that carved up that mason.' The *commissario* narrows her eyes.

'Excuse me, have you been to police school? Have an inspector's qualification, do you? I'm sorry, I may have missed that.'

'This guy came there to kill. Quinto said he had nothing to do with it, and I believe him. These guys aren't killers,' I hesitated – well, apart from 'Secondo', possibly – 'they're kids, protestors. There's no way they're going to chop up a mason like that.'

'And yet they fled.'

'Of course they did! Someone was coming after them with a gun.'

'So what's your theory, *sleuth*? What the hell was Michele Manfredi doing in Quinto's bathtub?'

'It totally freaked Quinto out, I swear. Look – this chap,' I eyed the gun, 'definitely came to kill, and leave no trace. But maybe he did, maybe there's DNA.'

The *commissario* didn't even glance at the gun. 'I doubt it. I immediately noticed the serial number had been filed off, so they clearly know what they're doing. The only DNA we're likely to find will be from your sweaty arse.'

'The make then,' I say coldly.

'Standard Beretta 92. Have you any idea how many of these are in the system? They're issued to everyone from the bag check at Marconi to special ops. It's probably the most anonymous gun in Italy. What you've essentially given me here, *detective*, is a piece of scrap metal.'

'Do I get marks for effort?'

'You'll be lucky if I don't throw you in the cells. So – who told you?'

'About what?' She cocks her head. How much do I have to tell her? The masons is one thing, talking about the driver of the car that killed Lucia quite another. The police mislaying Lucia's bike might well have been 'cock up over conspiracy,' but as for the rest? Until I know, that's need to know, and the *commissario* currently doesn't.

'One of the people in Quinto's squat,' I say. 'But that's it, I mean – that was all she knew, about their emergency rendezvous.'

'Her details?' I confess, I don't have them. She looks like she's really about to throw me in the cells so I call Dolores, who, albeit reluctantly, passes them on.

'Bugger off, then,' says the *commissario*. 'Out of my sight.'

I get up. When I look back, she's already turned to the computer, a fresh, unlit Marlboro Light hanging from her lips.

The relief I feel as I push through the Questura doors has left me by the time I begin to make my way along Via D'Azeglio. I had been a little concerned Miranda might decide to keep me overnight just for the hell of it – she can be as capricious as the old gods – but I feel myself rapidly running out of steam as I drag myself past the Bastardini and across to Via Paglietta. Weary, bruised, and miserable by the time the gates of the *La Residenza Faidate* part like open arms, I step in as if I have come a thousand miles.

Claudio's ground floor light is off, but on the *piano nobile* I can see the Comandante has arrived home. I decide to slip past his floor and catch up with him in the morning.

'She let you go then?' Out of the darkness, it is the man himself, sat at the table beneath the tree. I can smell it now – the mosquito coil. There's his iced tea and box of cigarettes beside the ashtray.

'You're a psychic now,' I say as the gates close behind me. I come to sit beside him, immediately feeling a mosquito settle upon my forehead. I try, futilely, to splat it.

'Dolores wrote to me. She was concerned they might not release you.'

'Oh.' I pick up his carton of cigarettes as if I might have one myself, what harm could it do? But put it back down again.

'I can handle the *commissario*.'

The Comandante, pointedly, does not respond. All I can hear is a mosquito buzzing near my ear.

'But you didn't mention anything about the driver of the car,' he says.

'Do you take me for a total fool?' The Comandante picks up the carton himself and lights one up.

'Not at all,' he says kindly. 'Only sometimes a little impatient. You have done well to bring us to this point – you have done better than me.'

'You did your best.'

'You did better,' he says firmly. His face is cloaked by the dark, but I can tell by his voice he's torn up inside.

'Whatever we find out,' I say, 'it won't bring her back.'

'You look tired,' he replies, sounding exhausted himself. 'I would like to leave first thing tomorrow.'

I get up. 'Don't stay out too long,' I say. 'The *zanzare* will eat you alive.'

'I'll come up shortly.'

I leave him there, with his cigarette and mosquito smoke.

XXIV

Jacopo surveyed me quizzically and I him. It was a rarely seen sighting of Lucia's kid brother before lunchtime. He was technically at the university, where he was taking business, but seemed most devoted to the study of video games. He was thirteen years younger than Lucia, and I had idly wondered whether he had been a mistake or the result of a lot of effort. Probably the latter, as the Comandante was a strict Catholic and one of the few to, for the most part, actually take the teachings of the church seriously.

But despite being something of a *mammone* – a mummy's boy, albeit without an actual mother – he was a good kid, remarkably reliable despite his habitual look of baffled amusement, especially now as he scratched his mop of unruly black hair, a family trait, wearing a Bologna FC tracksuit and flip-flops. He might have been a handsome Stan Laurel.

'Sis says you've got to help a crazy man get away?' He

suppressed a yawn and began filling the Moka.

'Something like that.'

Another yawn. 'Can't you get in trouble for that?'

'Only if you get caught.'

He began going through the cupboards. 'Rose likes porridge,' I said.

'What?'

'Don't worry. Cereal will do.' He took out some bread and Nutella.

'What time's school?'

'Eight.'

He winced. 'Yeah, I remember that.'

Lucia emerged in a parka with gloves and a woolly hat. She looked as if she was heading off on an Arctic mission.

'All set?' she asked.

'Set.'

As we went out, Jacopo called: 'Don't get caught.'

We took the Punto, disdaining the Comandante's black Lancia limo which was not likely to be much good if we had to make a swift getaway down tight medieval streets.

Alfonso had been tipped off that the authorities ('the men in white coats', he called them) would turn up at eight-thirty. It was now six-thirty, dark and dead in the sodium lamplight. A ridge of grey snow was piled along the portico as we rumbled along the gritted Via Barberia. Above, ranks of shuttered *palazzi* stood crimson as crusted blood.

Lucia's profile was set straight ahead, her pretty nose red with the cold. We had barely spoken since she had announced we would be going for Alfonso, and I wasn't sure what to say.

I had broken our compact by being caught in touch with him and I had no idea where this left me. In the doghouse again, I supposed. But she had to understand it wasn't that simple – I couldn't just cut him off. She might be angry with me now, but would she want to be married to a man who would abandon a friend in need?

She slammed on the brakes halfway down San Felice, the car juddering to a halt in a spray of flying grit.

'What?'

'Look.' A police van was parked up ahead, its blue light revolving. 'That's where your friend lives, right?'

'Just about. I'll check.' It was impossible to be sure from the road so I got out and, digging my heel into the impacted snow, stepped up to the portico. About thirty metres along, I could see a pair of cops hanging around outside Alfonso's *palazzo*, smoking. I climbed back over the snow and went back to the car.

'We're too late then,' said Lucia. She sighed. 'He wanted you to come last night but I told him not to be silly.'

'I'll give him a call,' I said. 'There still might be a chance.'

'Ah, yes,' Alfonso said when he picked up, sounding remarkably calm. 'I was afraid something like this might happen. Can you make it around the side, where you emerged the other evening?'

'Won't they see you in the car as we come out?'

'Not if I keep my head down!'

We drove past the police van and were just about to turn into the *vicolo* when I saw it: 'Stop!'

An ambulance was parked right outside the exit with a pair of men, literally in white coats, sat inside. We carried on along the road. I called him back.

'Ah. They appear to have it all worked out then.'

'I'm very sorry, Alfonso.'

'I'm sorry, too,' called Lucia.

'Never fear,' he said. 'All is not lost. However, it may be a somewhat more awkward getaway . . .'

'Tell me.'

'I can't believe it will be unlocked,' said Lucia.

'It's a squat,' I said.

Sure enough, the entrance to the building beneath a portico on Via Pratello, which ran parallel to Felice, swung open with a push. There should probably have been someone on the door, if only to alert against potential eviction, but these were mostly kids like the squatters in the ex-Fabrica, and it would have been freezing guarding that doorway. Squats tend to only have a skeleton crew in winter. Spring is the time for, literally, fair-weather squatters. As such, the site of the former kindergarten seemed lifeless, almost abandoned.

We trod softly down the corridor, emerging into a small porticoed courtyard decorated with political graffiti and limp banners. The remaining squatters would presumably be snuggled up in the rooms off the courtyard, so as long as we didn't bump into any en route to the bathroom or using the old refectory, we might get away with it.

Of course, it hadn't always been an ex-kindergarten. It had presumably been many, many things over the centuries, most likely to do with the legion of cottage industries the city had required, from tanning works to cartwheel repairs to printing presses. In any case, in the grey outlines of a snow-crusted winter morning, it was bleak, whatever it had been.

We continued along the portico to the refectory, which would perhaps seat twenty. We crossed it, opening a door on to a small allotment. Alfonso had called it a garden, which may have been its original purpose. A life-size statue of Garibaldi, who even the most modern revolutionaries would struggle to make cause against, was sat upon a rock in 'confederate' cap and beard, hand supporting his chin, face turned thoughtfully towards a brick wall – presumably a relatively new addition – separating the garden from the neighbour's. I followed his gaze as instructed to the bottom of the wall where, sure enough, I found a loose brick. I pulled it out and removed an iron key.

A tar-black door was set in the wall. I couldn't manage to turn the key with my left hand, but Lucia tried with both and it clunked open.

One might have expected to find another garden, but the door opened on to a chamber, red brick like the wall, with a low ceiling reinforced by iron beams which grazed the top of my head. A rust-speckled sign read: *RIFUGIOI ANTIAEREO* – Air Raid Shelter. A finger pointed downwards. Our phone lights revealed a set of concrete steps descending into darkness. Cold rose to greet us.

'You stay here,' I told Lucia.

'Are you kidding me?' Taking hold of the grimy iron banister, she began to make her way down.

The steps lasted longer than I would have expected. We finally arrived at the bottom, where we faced a pair of open blast doors. Beyond: a long, arched brick tunnel, the bricks not the usual Bologna red, but cream, like a Victorian asylum. Another rust-pocked sign read: *STATE CALMI*

SIETE GIA AL RIPARO – Stay calm, you are in the shelter. Another – *SILENZIO QUI, L'ARIA E PREZIOSA*, Silence, air is precious.

We made our way past the cobwebbed cadavers of wooden cots still chained to the walls. Between every half-dozen or so was set a small table and couple of cane chairs, their latticed seats largely disintegrated. Grime-coated cups and utensils remained where they had been left; newspapers curled and blackened, an empty tan *Nazionale* cigarette pack.

'I can't believe it,' Lucia whispered, her breath trailing before her. 'It's like it was just left.'

We passed a black contraption with a flue that looked like a stove but had a crank, presumably for ventilation. Another rank of cots, then a brick wall. I moved my light across and saw a door marked *USCITA DI EMERGENZA*, emergency exit. Another iron door, locked apparently from the inside.

We drew back stiff bolts and it groaned open. Darkness, rushing water. Our lights darted around. Lucia grabbed me: directly below was fast-moving water.

To our side was a ledge that broadened out to a set of steps leading down to a paved bankside where further along stood an ancient stone bridge.

We walked along the bankside as Lucia's light played over the shells of structures set back into the walls. She pulled me up. 'I can hardly . . . Do you see that?'

'What?' Her light travelled across the dark mouth of a doorway and a solid stone counter.

'That.' A smatter of maroon mosaic along the rear wall, like an archipelago. 'You know I think these may be *Roman*.'

'That can't be possible,' I said. 'Can it?'

'*I've* never heard of this place.' We continued on towards the bridge, her light lingering over the handful of other 'shops' we passed, each little more than an empty shell. 'Maybe they're kept secret by the comune, but,' now her light inspected the bridge where a time-worn VI was still inscribed upon a marble block at the opening and wheel grooves ran across the stone, 'I find it hard to believe. This must have all been covered up in the olden times. They probably stripped all the precious stuff, then forgot about it. But don't you realise? This is a bloody Roman street.'

'*Someone* must have known about it,' I said. 'Otherwise, why would the emergency exit lead here? Alfonso obviously did.'

Her eyes widened. I almost saw a light bulb come on above her head. '*Masons.*' She nodded as if this explained everything.

As if to prove her point, the first thing our lights picked out as we crossed the bridge was the symbol of an hourglass carved into the lintel stone above a dark oak door.

XXV

It is eight in the morning and I can already feel the sharp edge of another scalding day on the back of my neck as I open the automatic garage doors.

Mina's 'Se Telefonando' belts out on the radio as I climb into the Alfa. I switch her off and back the SUV out, swinging around to where the Comandante stands in his cream linen suit and matching trilby. He is wearing tortoiseshell blue-lensed sunglasses and already smoking a cigarette. A tie might have completed the picture of the Marlowe-esque cop, but he is not 'esque' anything, rather, a grey-bearded former Carabinieri out to find the truth about his daughter.

We swing by Pratello where Dolores is stood waiting by the Orthodox Church in a green cotton trouser suit with straps across her bony, bronzed shoulder blades. It must have come from a charity shop, but with her cropped hair and big shades, she looks as if she's modelling it. She jumps into the back, leans forward and kisses the Comandante on the cheek. I'm about to say, 'you never greet me like that', but think better of it.

The farm is about thirty kilometres outside Bologna, at the heart of the Valley of Argenta. Part of the Po Delta, it is an expanse of wetlands caused by sediment rising from the mighty river to create a vast lagoon, the most famous part of which faces Venice and is known for its pink flamingos. This, on the other hand, is the most obscure part of the Emilian countryside – neither truffle-rich hills, nor art-rich cities. A place of silence and high reeds, isolated farmhouses and mosquitoes. Almost no one comes out here except birdwatchers, especially this time of the year when the wetlands broil.

A woman in a tatty wide-brimmed straw hat, transparent white cotton dress, and well-worn Birkenstocks approaches unselfconsciously across the courtyard. She would probably wander around naked if the weather permitted, and certainly has the body-shape of most nudists – better left covered up.

A pair of Marella sheep dogs, similar to golden retrievers only larger, white, and bred by herders to fend off wolves or bandits, dutifully slouch behind. Any Italian would know what they were, but they might take the hand off an unwary tourist.

She squints at us. 'Are you lost?'

'We'd like to speak to Sofia,' says Dolores.

'And you are?' Dolores removes her glasses.

'Well, this is a turn-up for the books.' She takes another look at me and the Comandante. I'm afraid she's about to give us the usual anti-establishment spiel. Instead, she steps up to me, her slopping-out expression turning tender as if she has chosen to view us a little more like people than pigs. She wipes her hands down the side of her dress and reaches out to shake my hand.

'I knew Lucia,' she says.

'She would often call in at the squat to see how we were doing,' she explains as she leads us through the courtyard. 'We'd studied housing together on our sociology degree, so I knew her from way back, but while I stayed on to fight the good fight, she buggered off to England, where she met you.' A wistful frown. 'I'd have loved her to have seen what we've achieved here – we often talked about organic farming, setting up a sustainable farming community.' I suppress my surprise – she had never discussed it with me.

The farm seems ramshackle, half-derelict, but I have learned to read the signs – the patchwork of reclaimed corrugated iron on the roofs of the barns and sheds running to gutters cut from old tyres for rainfall. The windmills of wood and metal, ubiquitous solar panels. The farmhouse with its odd doors and shutters, patched together with fragments of tile and brick, those green, bottle-base windows, hand water pump, chickens and pigs roaming between yet more creatively employed tractor tyres. It may resemble a rubbish dump, but this is actually an efficient hippy farm, and I am infinitely grateful not to be living here. I begin to understand why Lucia never bothered mentioning it. Now Rose has grown up, would she have run away to here, venturing out at dawn to feed the chickens and clean out the pigs? Perish the thought.

'Sofia mentioned she had met you,' she says. 'And Dee.

How about you, Dolores? We've still got room on the farm, and with your knowledge of dairy . . .'

'Maybe one day,' she says. 'When I've saved up enough money.'

'You should pay her more, then,' the woman mock-scolds me.

'Or possibly not. I wouldn't want to lose her.'

We follow the woman into the farmhouse. 'Sofia!' she calls. There's no answer. 'I'll check upstairs.'

Here the reclaimed theme has continued, and been done very well – an entire kitchen engineered from recycled materials and constructed with a great deal of skill. An old granite sink that looks like it has been rescued from a canteen. A wood-burning stove with an open-cast iron door revealing a one-eyed russet and black-spotted cat nestling on a bed of straw, weaning a troupe of kittens (Dolores gasps and crouches down before them; I'm wondering how on earth anyone manages to cook).

A huge table running the length of the room is topped by what looks like blue and white church tiles from down south, while the chairs running along both sides have clearly been sourced from a variety of settings, but are all sufficiently trendy to give it the feel of a 'shabby chic' café. The stone walls are whitewashed and the floor has – perhaps the sole original feature – typical hexagonal red tiles.

'She's not there,' she says, coming down the stone steps. 'Maybe she's over at the barn.'

We follow her back through the courtyard to one of those sheds as chickens scatter. 'Sofia!' she calls. 'People!'

The sun has risen sufficiently for the surrounding wetland

to emit a sulphurous stink. Flies busy themselves around our heads, and even the Comandante has taken to fanning his hand rhythmically in front of his face.

One of the Marella pads ahead, indifferent to the hens as they are to her. She stretches across the trench designed to dissuade hogs from entering and slips into the darkness of the shed. I hesitate, worrying the pong might bowl me over. But then the dog begins to howl.

We cross the planks. From bleached light to that musty, dusty gloom. The thickness of the flies, stench of hen crap. Pigs – you wouldn't want them in here as your eyes adjust and you spot the woman stretched out on her back on a bench of bales wearing only a pair of silky black shorts.

Her head is tilted back over the edge, face cherry-red as blood drips from her hair on to the ground among a busy bustle of hens.

The woman shrieks; Dolores swears. The Comandante brushes past me, hatless. Using his trilby to fan away the flies, he bends down to inspect a gory splodge between her breasts.

XXVI

'You managed then,' Alfonso Lambertini shouted above the rush of water, ghoulish in our phone light. 'Always pays to have one up your sleeve.' He pushed the door closed behind him and locked it.

'But won't they know about it, too?'

He picked up a hefty haversack. 'I take them down for a tour when I invest them in the secret of the Master Mason, but I always tell them this tunnel has fallen in. I was saving it for my successor, the final mystery!' He gurned thoughtfully. 'But you're right, you never know. Better not idle, then!'

We followed him back across the bridge and along the bankside.

'So you're saying no one knows about any of this?' asked Lucia.

'Any of what?'

'The bridge, these stores – they're Roman, aren't they?'

'Hm? Yes, apparently.'

'Then does anyone know?'

'Technically, yes. They were discovered during a survey a couple of centuries ago. Although it's true,' he said as we arrived at the steps to the shelter, 'great-grandfather might have arranged for that particular section of the report to be "misfiled" when he began his building project.'

'And this?' said Lucia, meaning the shelter.

'The printing works belonged to a member in the nineteen thirties, so . . .'

We made our way back through. Mid-way up the steps to the exit, Alfonso set the sack down and hung to the rail, breathing heavily. 'Here, let me take it,' I said. After some resistance, he let me pick it up with my good hand. It weighed a ton.

'My God, what have you got in here?'

'Oh, just some pants and socks. And a few books.'

'More than a bloody few.'

I carried it to the top. Lucia pushed open the door and we crossed the garden. Alfonso, I noted, delivered Garibaldi a respectful salute before we re-entered the refectory.

'What the fuck?'

The fellow stood there like an upright centipede, holes cut in the top and bottom of his zipped-up sleeping bag for his arms and legs. Long blond dreadlocks trailed down his back. His face seemed skull-like in the moonlight.

'Nothing to worry about,' I said. We faced off across the canteen counter, where he was standing holding a jug of water.

'What the fuck?'

'We'll just be on our way.' I gave Alfonso a little shove.

'What the fuck are you doing here?' He slammed the jug on the counter. I saw a light come on in the portico.

'Let's just get out of here.' I began to hurry us towards the exit when another guy emerged from the shadows on the other side of the refectory wielding a police baton.

'Paolo?' He blocked our path.

'Tito – this lot have just come from the garden.'

'What?' He looked at us. 'How's that possible?'

'Long story,' I said. 'Could you just let us through?'

'What are you doing here?'

'Like I said – just passing through. Now, if you'll let us—'

'Police spies?'

'Do we look like police spies?'

'What's in the pack? Are you thieves, then? We don't tolerate thieves.'

'We are not *criminals* here,' spat the centipede. 'Whatever the pigs might say.'

'Neither are we,' said Lucia. 'We came through a tunnel in the garden—' Alfonso squeaked. She elbowed him. 'Don't be ridiculous. There's a door in the wall – an old air raid shelter linked to the underground canals.'

'I've always wondered where that went,' said the centipede.

'Never could open it,' sniffed Tito. 'Why?'

'Why what?' asked Lucia.

'Why are you coming up from the canals through a secret tunnel and mysterious doorway at five in the morning?'

'Actually,' said Lucia, 'it's coming on for seven.'

'Whatever. While it's dark.'

I noticed more lights coming on. It seemed the entire squat was waking up.

'Look. I promise we're not thieves,' I said quickly. 'This was simply the only way to—'

A woman dashed in. 'Tito. Paolo. Police outside.'

'What?' He raised the baton again. 'What the fuck have you gotten us in to?'

'*Nothing*,' I insisted. 'Truth is, we're helping him escape because his family want to have him committed so they can steal his property. *Now* do you get it?'

'Do what? Come again?'

'We're . . .'

There were raised voices outside.

Tito scowled, grabbed the haversack. 'Let me check that.' He hefted it on to the table and undid the straps. Lifted the flap. 'Books,' he said. 'Fucking books.' He stared at Alfonso. 'Are these worth anything?'

'Nothing,' Alfonso replied glumly. 'They're just precious to me.'

The woman called: 'They're coming in!'

He slapped the flap back and pushed the bag across to Alfonso. 'You'd better come with me.'

We followed him across the refectory. I glimpsed the sky blue of Polizia uniforms in the portico. Tito opened a door and shoved us inside, raised a finger to his lips. Everything went dark.

There was an earthy smell to this confined space and the trample of police boots outside.

Voices – the weary, clipped tone of cops who didn't want any trouble. Tito's gruff, monosyllabic replies. An upper-crust woman, all apologies.

The boots moving on. The scrape of the outside door.

Silence. I switched on my phone light to take in our surroundings – a larder. Sacks of vegetables, grains, flour. Large tins of tomatoes.

The centipede's low murmur to Tito. A tap running. A chair pulled. The whiff of marijuana smoke – doubtless a deliberate provocation. A door scrapes, the boots return. Manly grunts and womanly apologies. The boots recede.

We wait, wait.

The door opens. Now the refectory is full – of its skeleton crew, at least. Half a dozen drowsy-looking squatters dressed as if for a medieval winter.

'They've gone,' said Tito. 'So you can bugger off, too.'

'The woman,' Alfonso pipes up behind us.

'What about her?'

'She was blonde? Pale? Elegant?'

'That's about it,' Tito nods.

As we made our way back through the complex, I ask him: 'You know her.'

'My cousin,' he mumbled.

Lucia peered outside to check there wasn't anyone lurking in wait, then went for the car. She pulled up in front of the squat so we could climb swiftly inside.

It was getting light, bars were beginning to open, residents emerge.

'You haven't said where you actually want to go,' she said. 'It can't be far, I've got to get to work.'

'It's not,' said Alfonso.

XXVII

Predictably, Commissario Miranda arrives in a cloud of Bottega Veneta and ill will. The sight of the Comandante, however, appears to soften her, as if something has been added to her water. The formal *lei*, which she has certainly never used with me, materialises, and as they stand alone beside the corpse, he appears to do most of the talking. In fact, as they walk back, ripping off their surgical gloves and the uniformed cops beside us extinguish their cigarettes, she's wearing that rarest of expressions: a smile. Albeit a somewhat sardonic one.

'Do you think someone's trying to tell us something?' she says.

'Honestly,' I spread my hands. 'I have no idea.'

'First that chap cut in two – obviously I looked into it – the punishment reserved for the Master Mason who transgresses. It seems they didn't quite finish the job, however – their bowels are meant to be burned to ashes, and those ashes "scattered over the face of the earth and wafted by the four winds of heaven". At least that's what it says in the books.

'Now this one with her throat cut and tongue torn out, which is apparently just for the apprentices, although from what I can understand, she had nothing to do with it. Or did she? What secrets did she let slip, eh?'

I glance at the Comandante. 'Beats me.'

'As I explained, Commissario,' he said. 'She merely shared with Daniel what she had seen the day my daughter died.'

'And suggested it wasn't a woman driving, but a man.'

'That's right,' I say cautiously.

'And you didn't consider that worth telling me about when we spoke?'

'You asked me how I came to know about the rendezvous at the church. I told you.' I gaze into the barn. 'I had no idea this would occur.'

'Then do you think she was killed because she was linked to the masons, or at least these weirdos who are going around spraying masonic graffiti and leaving dead bodies as well as smashed-up houses in their wake.' She takes out her cigarettes and offers them to the Comandante and Dolores. 'Fucking flies. Maybe smoking will help.' She lights the three up. 'Or because she was associated with you, signor Leicester, and it had something to do with what she had told you about your wife's death?'

'That hadn't even occurred to me,' I confess. 'Why would it have anything to do with Lucia?'

'You tell me. It just seems like a remarkable coincidence that you should stumble across *two* masonic murders. Okay, one dead mason – I'll give you that – but a pair?'

'She wasn't a mason,' I say. 'At least not as far as I know.'

'What we do suspect,' says the Comandante, 'is that the same person or people behind the *first* murder are most likely to be behind the second. There is clearly some connection with Reclaim Bologna, who we can link this unfortunate young lady to, as well. Then there is the man who turned up at the church with the apparent intention of murder. These are the salient facts. But I do struggle to see how her information about the driver of the car that killed my daughter can be related to this, Commissario.

'What I *do* see is a pair of murders also explicitly linked to the freemasons, in addition to this group of troublemakers who may, or may not, consider themselves "masonic". The appearance of their would-be assassin at the church suggests that someone wishes to either implicate them in the murders, or actually eliminate them altogether.

'The principal questions I am asking myself are – if these killings really were the work of masons, would they be so explicit about it? Would they, as an institution, conduct such grotesque acts that point directly to them? I find that hard to believe, especially in this modern age. *Insomma*,' in short, 'this seems more like the work of a mad man.'

'Ah, madness,' nods the *commissario*, 'there are many forms, however, are there not? The violent undercurrent of terrorism has an edge of madness to it, don't you think? Each act of Reclaim Bologna cranks up the drama, becomes more extreme. You know the signs, Comandante – they are pushing themselves, daring themselves to conduct ever greater outrages.

'And then – violence begats violence. Now – let's consider

your proposition of the lone perp. Could they be someone these anarchists may have crossed? Someone whose property they have *already* defiled?' She looks at the uniformed cops. 'I want to see a list of all the victims.' She turns back to us. 'They have already destroyed people's lives with their juvenile antics. Maybe someone has a vendetta, and is using their dalliance with things masonic to deflect attention.'

I recall the municipal policeman and his request to be kept informed – *they think they can treat us Municipale however the hell they like, but only the once, if you get my drift.*

That gun had been standard Municipal Police issue, too.

'Still,' says the Comandante, 'this is, as you point out, Commissario, a remarkable coincidence. 'Could you be being followed, Daniel?' Both he and the *commissario* look at me inquisitorially.

'I don't,' I glance instinctively over my shoulder, '*think* so.'

'Otherwise, it is difficult to understand how they would come to target this lady.' He grunts, turns to the *commissario.* 'Never mind the masons,' he remarks. 'It's also as if they are trying to set up my son-in-law.'

'Or me,' Dolores pipes up. 'Well, I mean – I was there when we discovered the one in the bath, and now, this time.'

'And you had links with these folk,' says the *commissario.* She takes a final puff, drops the cigarette. 'As usual there's no shortage of possibilities, but it is precisely when there are so many, one begins to suspect conspiracy – "*è stato insabbiato.*" It's being covered with sand. A very Italian expression which implies a deliberate effort to obscure a crime. "When the obvious answer is staring you in the face."'

She stares in my face, then breaks into that unsettling

smile. 'I think you may have a point about the masons, Comandante.' She shrugs. 'Although I still wouldn't put it past them – perhaps committing acts so outrageous precisely so no one would actually believe it was them?'

A thin smile: 'That would be *very* sandy.'

'But a vendetta or lunatic seems most likely. Balls!' Then we all notice it – the splutter of a Vespa. 'You know who that is.'

'Maurizio,' I say.

'Who tipped him off?' She scowls at the pair of uniforms. 'Find out, or it'll be your asses on the line.'

The *Carlino*'s Maurizio Estiva pulls up in the courtyard as the uniformed cops approach, holding out their arms.

'Another one?' Maurizio cries.

'Fuck off,' shouts the *commissario*.

'Hey, English Detective! What are you doing here? Is this connected to Reclaim, too?'

The *commissario* sighs. 'He's already writing his story. Take my advice – say nothing.'

'Absolutely,' I say. 'This is definitely the type of publicity we can do without.'

XXVIII

Alfonso was right, it technically wasn't far, but it was deep enough into the hills abutting the south of Bologna to encounter roads only partially cleared of snow that our poor Punto wasn't equipped for. Lucia navigated each curve as if the car was a sled, complete with 'oohs' and 'aahs' from her passengers. We risked sliding into the sides of the road, or even tipping over the edge, far more times than was comfortable for any of us.

We finally crawled into a tree-sheltered, gritted drive that led up to an old church.

'It was the home of the Aelia Laelia Crispis,' Alfonso explained cheerfully, as if the morning's getaway was already forgotten. 'A memorial with a mysterious, metaphysical inscription about the identity of said Aelia Laelia Crispis.'

He recited in Latin: '*Aelia Laelia Crispis, Nec vir nec mulier nec androgyna, Nec puella nec iuvenis nec anus, Nec casta nec meretrix nec pudica, sed omnia*. In English: Neither man, nor woman, nor androgynous nor child, nor young, nor old, nor chaste, nor harlot, nor demure, but all this together.' He took a breath.

'Killed neither from hunger, nor from iron, nor from poison, but from all these things together. Neither in heaven, nor in water, nor on earth, but wherever it lies, etcetera, etcetera.

'It has been the subject of endless discussion and study, and no shortage of mystery authors have taken inspiration from it.

'Of course, many have linked it to freemasonry, I mean the riddle pointing to the Holy Grail or some such. Personally, I suspect it was just some Renaissance jokers having a little fun – people forget they had a sense of humour in the olden days, too.'

Lucia had stopped the car, and we sat looking up at the seemingly deserted old church on the crest of the hill. Through a break in the trees, medieval Bologna was laid out below, terracotta rooftops and red brick nestled within the bounds of the lost walls, the old city wreathed by wood smoke or boiler fumes, the peripheral tower blocks obscured by the morning haze.

'Well then,' said Alfonso.

I turned around. 'This is it?'

'Yes, you can leave me here.'

'There isn't anyone.'

'Don't worry,' he smiled with certainty. 'There will be.'

We got out and I helped him lift his haversack on to his back.

'Are you sure you'll be okay?' I felt unexpectedly emotional. I realised why – he was my first and only friend here.

'I'm sure,' he said. He gave me a hug. He smelled of pipe tobacco.

'We'll see each other again, though,' I said as he began to make his way up the track.

'Indubitably,' he called. 'In this life, or the next.'

I watched him go until he disappeared around the tower.

I got back in. 'All set?' asked Lucia, looking straight ahead.

'All set.'

She put the car into gear and with three icy lurches, we had turned back around.

We finally made it on to properly gritted roads, and then the Viale.

'I can drop you at the office, if you want,' said Lucia.

'It's all right. I can get out here, I could do with a walk.'

Lucia pulled up the car. She took my good hand and kissed it. I looked at her in surprise. I still remember those tender eyes, peach lips. The red tip of her nose.

'Thank you,' she said.

'What for?'

'For being you. Reminding me.'

'What?'

She tilted her head. 'That you're not so bad, after all. And I can be a fucking bitch.'

'*Come on.* That's not fair – you're great!'

'Oh I don't think so.'

'Oh I *do* think so.'

'Oh I don't.'

The traffic rushed past and we kissed, we kept kissing.

XXIX

SLAUGHTERED LIKE A PIG, OR A MASON?
By Maurizio Estiva

'We found her in the barn,' said a police insider. 'Lying on the hay half naked with her throat cut like a pig. Her tongue had been ripped out and placed on her chest.'

Another outrage – now in the Bolognese countryside at a commune in the fraction of Fiorana with all the hallmarks of a further twisted masonic rite.

The body of Sofia Duranotte, 42, was discovered yesterday morning by other members of the commune alongside investigators who believed she might have had information about the preceding murder – of Michele Manfredi, 68, who was found cut in two in a bathtub in Bolognina. Manfredi was also discovered at a property linked to the commune.

The Polizia di Stato was called at 10:20 to the scene in the wilds of the Po Delta together with the ambulance service. The investigation is being led by Commissario Rita Miranda. A crack forensic squad under the leadership of Commissario Paolo Beneficienza had the scene quickly sealed off.

The commune is run by former squatters with links to urban terrorists Reclaim Bologna, currently on the run, not just under suspicion for the murder of Manfredi, but a long list of outrages, ranging from destruction of property and hijacking to bombing.

When asked about the Masonic link, Commissario Miranda refused to comment. Meanwhile, known freemasons have been called to the Questura for interrogation.

The questions on everybody's lips are – what is the link between Reclaim Bologna and the masons? Why was Sofia Duranotte savagely assassinated? Could it have been revenge for the murder of Michele Manfredi? Have the terrorist activities of the anarcho-squatters stirred a secret society from its slumber? Or is a twisted serial killer stalking the porticoes of *La Rossa*?

The only response Commissario Miranda can give is: 'No comment.'

I put the paper down. I suspect the *commissario*'s response to the article will be somewhat more colourful than that. The Comandante harrumphs.

'This Commissario Beneficienza probably had something to do with the leak,' he says. 'Or perhaps the "insider" requested to the reporter to mention him to put the signora off the trail.'

'More sand,' I say. 'It gets everywhere.'

'It does indeed.'

We are having breakfast at the bar around the corner, a cornetto impregnated with cream for the Comandante, another cannolo for me. It seems Giovanni is also content to escape the eagle eye of his granddaughter.

'The reporter, however,' he says, 'asks legitimate questions, and I especially admire the suggestion that the killings of Michele Manfredi and Sofia Duranotte could have effectively been a sort of "tit for tat", albeit it seems rather too reminiscent of the bad old days when the communists and fascists used to get up to the same thing. Is this what we are reduced to, Daniel? One group of oddballs battling another?'

'I'm not sure your communists and fascists were much better.'

He frowns. '*No no no* – that was the sharp end of an undeclared war – the Cold War – this . . .' He shakes his head bemusedly.

'There is one thing that's been bothering me,' I say.

'Just one?'

The buzz of my phone. Dolores.

'I've followed Nancy Bonelli and a man to an address.'

'I admit,' I respond, 'with everything else, that had slipped my mind.'

'Well at least someone's still doing their job.'

'True.'

'What do you want me to do?'

'Where is this address?' I ask.

She tells me. I get to my feet.

'There was something that was bothering you,' says the Comandante, flakes of pastry suspended from his beard.

'It can wait,' I say. 'In fact, it may not be bothering me for much longer.'

I try the front door, but this time it is locked.

'Do you want to try out your skills on this one?' I ask Dolores.

'We're going to break in, is what you're saying? Don't you think that's a bit extreme?'

'Not at all,' I say. I take a step back. 'Go on, then.'

She gives me a questioning look but pulls out her wrap. The Ghetto is especially somnolent as the sun warms the cobbled road between the porticoes. My partner crouches in the shadow, grumbling as she twists and teases the lock.

'No pressure,' I say. 'Except we might get arrested.'

'Thanks.'

'Well, you might get arrested; I'll just say I was passing by.'

'I'm sure you will.'

'Can I help?'

'I'm doing fine, thanks.'

'Of course, that's why they test you on time at the lock school. You did pass that module, didn't you?'

'Yes. I. Fucking. Did.' There's a crack and Dolores tumbles through the doorway.

'Seven out of ten for execution,' I say. 'Three and a half for style.'

She scowls up at me. I help her to her feet. 'Are you going to tell me what we are doing, Dan? Wasn't our brief just to follow Nancy and get the details on who she was with?'

'That *was* the plan,' I say. 'But things have moved on a little since then.' I begin to make my way along the lurid green corridor. The glass door at the end appears to be hanging open, but with the CCTV I presume she will see us coming. Well, it can't be helped.

I prod the door wider and look around for the camera. Sure enough, there it is, bolted to a tree. Its red light blinks obediently.

I duck back in. 'This man Nancy Bonelli was with,' I say. 'Was he tubby?'

'Not especially.'

'He had curly hair, probably rather grey by now?'

'Hard to tell. He was wearing a hat, one of those brimmed ones like the Comandante, but I think his hair was black. He was very smart, in a double-breasted blue suit and dark glasses. Oh, and he had a big moustache.'

'A big black moustache?'

'Yup.'

I hesitate, I might be about to make a huge mistake, but it's too late now – I'll have probably been spotted. I push decisively through the door and begin to march along the path.

'Age?'

'Hard to tell, but old enough. Sixty?'

'But black hair?'

'It might have been dyed.'

The path curves through hedgerows to the fountain, and it is here we come across the following tableau: Nancy Bonelli sat at a table in the shade, Marta Finzi stood, mobile phone in hand, having presumably just been alerted to our arrival, and beside her the gentleman in a navy suit, who it would be hard to place if my assumptions didn't fill in the gaps – he might have been a visiting uncle, circa 1910, his cream Panama hat with its maroon ribbon placed upon the seat, his wavy black brillantined hair matched by a 'Zapata'-style moustache drooping down either side of his tanned face.

Alfonso Lambertini's suit fits him snugly and, despite the heat, a purple floral tie with a gold clip is knotted to the collar, but Dolores is right – one could not say he was tubby. If anything, he looks perhaps a decade younger, albeit like a time traveller from the previous century. But I suppose that is nothing new.

'Discussing your South American trip?' I ask. 'Would this be your agent from Thomas Cook?' I bow to Alfonso. 'Have you been explaining the steamer rates?' His eyes twinkle and, as he smiles, the sides of his moustache withdraw like stage curtains. He removes the hat from the chair and pulls out a pipe from his inside pocket as he sits back down.

'Your Italian has improved, old pal.' He gestures at an empty seat. 'Come, join us.'

'I never asked you about your Spanish,' I say, sitting down as Dolores positions herself behind me on the edge of the fountain. 'I guess you must have needed it for all the travelling,' I look at Marta and Nancy, 'Peru, Bolivia, Chile . . .'

'You were listening to us?' says Nancy. 'But—'

'Trouble?' Secondo appears around the corner. Footsteps behind him – Quinto and Otto skid to a halt on the gravel.

'Great,' I say. 'Full house.' I look at Otto, his forearm bandaged. 'Now can I have my fucking bike back?'

Alfonso lets out an amused puff of pipe smoke. 'I heard about that. The Great Architect surely does move in the most mysterious ways, but move he does, although I would have probably looked you up at some point anyway. Discreetly.'

'Or perhaps I would have come visit you in gaol when they lock you up for what you did to Michele and Sofia,' I say, 'although I honestly struggle to see the link.'

'That's because there isn't one, prick,' says Secondo. Alfonso raises a hand.

'Actually there must be,' he says. 'But do you *really* think I could have been behind, let alone committed, those crimes, Daniel?'

I look at him evenly. 'If you were to ask me when we had first met, I would have said no, you're just a harmless eccentric. But by now I've seen a lot more of human nature, and I would say,' I gaze into his earnest eyes, 'I don't think one can ever truly know what someone is capable of.

'And you do have a history of psychosis, Alfonso. Who knows how what lasting damage that "medication" they slipped into your fridge might have done.'

'Have I ever lied to you, then?'

I smile. 'Not . . . knowingly.'

'Then if I told you that I – that we – had nothing to do with the murders, would you believe me? At least give me the benefit of the doubt?'

I glance at the lads. 'Well I suppose I've already given it to them. Although you lot could have helped me out in the church. He came to kill you, not me.'

'We didn't know who you were,' says Secondo. 'We didn't know who to trust.'

I turn back to Alfonso. 'So who is behind all this, then? And why Michele?'

Alfonso nods appreciatively. 'The choice of Michele was clever,' he says. 'It perhaps reveals more about them than they may realise. Yet it also, of course, incriminates me.'

'How so?'

'A Master Mason, who receives the prescribed punishment.'

'For what?'

'I would never have guessed until now, but I would presume Michele was somehow involved in my betrayal, and the story would, of course, be that I was out for revenge.'

'And Sofia?'

'That,' he raises a finger, 'is a real mystery.' He twists around to the boys. 'If placing Michele in your tub was not enough, perhaps this is to unambiguously link us all?'

'But how the hell *are* you all linked?' I took them in – the two fine ladies, the eccentric mason, and the trio of *punkebestia*.

'Oh, a very good question, old pal, a very good one indeed. And I have you to thank!'

'In what way?'

'If you hadn't helped me escape that night, I would never have come across this group, and over my long years of lonely exile, their provision of shelter often came back to me. I thought how, despite the differences in our appearance, wealth, status, our values were not so very dissimilar.

'Of course, there has always been a struggle within freemasonry that could best be defined as "internal" versus "external" – that is, to improve the person within, or the world without? As you know, I was in the latter camp, believing our cause was best expressed by the revolutionaries of bygone eras, and that the more modern tendency towards "improving oneself to improve the world" was simply shorthand for self-enrichment and self-satisfaction. Unfortunately, despite my best efforts, this appeared to have become the prevailing view!

'Meanwhile, naturally, I kept abreast of events at home.'

'How did you manage to get out of Italy?'

Alfonso smiles at Nancy and Marta. 'I was in possession of that rarest of artifacts – a passport issued by the Knights of Malta under a name of convenience.'

'You mean a false name.'

'As you please, and assisted by the Honourable Order of Women Masons.'

'Why didn't you use your own lodge?'

'What with all the carryings on, I simply wasn't sure who I could trust, but Nancy here had been a member before leaving to establish her own branch.'

'And you, Marta? I thought you were a Marxist.'

'In the past tense,' she says. 'After everything that happened with the world, I began to lose what little faith in the cause I had. I knew Nancy anyway, and through her I came to appreciate that freemasonry had weathered everything centuries of competing faiths and ideologies could throw at it, yet still somehow managed to preserve something.' She shrugs. 'Pure. As Alfonso says – the desire to change the world, but also the pragmatism to acknowledge you won't get there through a *platform*, speeches, elections, I mean. People are easily manipulated to vote against their best interests. Democracy's a dead duck. It's naïve to think otherwise.'

'That still sounds a bit Marxist to me,' I say. 'Which is presumably what appeals to you lot.' I meant Reclaim Bologna.

Secondo smirks. 'He showed up with cash, lots of it, and a plan. What's not to like?'

'And what *is* your plan, Alfonso?'

He smiles sadly. 'A lot has changed in Bologna since we first met.'

'I lost my wife, for one,' I say.

'Yes, your lovely Lucia. I was so sorry to hear that.' Silence, or at least the silence of the Finzi garden with its cicada drone, the lethargic trickle of the fountain. 'Of course,' he continues, 'the process had already begun when I was still here, but back then, it was more like the old battle over the choice between converting unused properties into homes or hotels – about housing, in short. Now it has become much more serious – homes themselves are being converted into hotels and Bologna is becoming unaffordable for the Bolognese, a process which, I might add, many people, including my fellow masons, have been profiting from.

'It is the modern world, we are told, it is "inevitable". But this is a lie – it is always about choice. As Marta says, the politicians have many interests and, to be honest, I think they are quite happy to see Bologna hollowed out. Keep the money train flowing, no? Airbnbs contain no voters! No more complaints and inconveniences. And what do we have left? A "showcase" for visitors, businesses, other politicians. A shop window, a city without a soul.

'No – the only way to stop it is to put a spanner in the works, a sleeper on the tracks, a brick through that shop window. To undermine confidence in the system as a whole. It is not enough to "put tourists off", we must persuade those that profit it is not worth the risk.'

'Smash rentier capitalism,' grins Secondo.

'Still sounds pretty Marxist to me.' I glance at Marta.

The cicadas furiously rub their wings, the fountain splashes. 'It's a funny thing,' I say to Alfonso, 'but wasn't one of your tunnels called Omega?' Alfonso nods.

'I am the Alpha and Omega,' says Dolores. 'The beginning and the end.'

'And wasn't that the name of your husband Carlo's illicit company, Marta? Omega – the Omega Group, Omega Holdings?'

She shrugs. 'It's a common enough name, which is presumably why he chose it.'

'Which specialised in property development. When we first met, it was out to convert the old maternity hospital – as you mentioned, Alfonso – into an hotel.' Afonso's pipe goes out and he produces a silver lighter. He stuffs some more tobacco into the end before lighting it. I look at Secondo.

'How do you lot decide which short lets to target?'

'We don't,' says Quinto. 'We—' Secondo scowls at him to shut up.

'You get your instructions from these three.'

Secondo shrugs. 'They're paying.'

'Which is what you were doing in Strada Maggiore, Otto. You'd gone there for instructions from her.' I nod at Nancy Bonelli.

Secondo holds up his hand, Otto keeps schtum.

I look back at Alfonso. 'So you decide who they target. You are, after all, paying. This isn't about some form of hybrid communism, is it. This is about revenge. I'm guessing the properties you choose are somehow linked to the investments of Carlo Manzi, who was a mason.'

Marta scoffs, Alfonso lowers his pipe. 'He most definitely

was not,' he says. 'The man was a leftist.'

'Well, we've seen that's no bar to entry. And is it a coincidence, given the law on inheritance, that the fruits of his investments will not be going to you, Marta, but to "that bitch in Rome"?'

Marta sighs. '*Michele* was the mason,' she says. 'A business partner of my husband.' She looks at Alfonso. 'And not only Michele.'

'It may be *seen* as a vendetta, I grant you,' Alfonso says. 'I prefer to view it more as a righting of wrongs. Do you know what became of *my palazzo*, Daniel?'

'I've no idea.'

'Converted into "VIP apartments" by my family, in association with Mr Manzi's Omega Holdings SpA. Marta is wrong to infer my cousins are masons, although I suppose they know the territory well enough. But they are, or at least were, a "masonic family".' His mouth twists with distaste. 'Which went on to invest in Mr Manzi's other enterprises.'

'Carlo got the idea from your Mrs Thatcher,' spits Marta. 'At least that was what he said – "doesn't everyone want to own their own home?" Only in his case, it was to provide the funding to enable people to buy a *second* home to rent out. It's cheaper than buying and servicing them themselves – they top up the savings of the "owners", who they get to do all the work, and just take a slice of the profits. They part-own hundreds of properties.'

'And these are the ones you're both targeting,' I say. 'Do you think they know it's you who's been putting these guys,' I nodded at the *punkebestia*, 'up to it?'

'Apparently so,' says Alfonso.

I frown. 'But – *murder*? I can see why they might have wanted to get you out of the way, but would they— Hold on. This woman – the woman who was with the police that day when we were hiding at the squat. You said it was your cousin?'

He snorts. 'I certainly did – Ginny. Such a cow – she manages the family's holdings.'

'And she looks like?'

'A classic beauty, although I suppose she can afford it. She's a contessa, you know.'

I feel sick. 'Ginny,' I say. 'For Ginevra?'

'That's right.'

'I think we may have a problem.'

XXX

We kept kissing, the door closed, the clock at the early hours – before, during, after.

Side-to-side, I could have looked into those eyes forever. I certainly thought that I would, the sure weight of that certainty drawing down my lids like a mother's feather kiss, or the touch of a soldier-companion upon a corpse.

I started, wide awake again.

'What?' asked Lucia.

'Nothing,' I frowned. 'Really, nothing.'

'You gasped, as if you'd had a shock or remembered something.'

'I don't know what.' She reached out, pressed her hand against my chest.

'Your heart is racing.'

'It always does when I'm close to you.'

She chuckled. 'After all these years?'

'Now more than ever.' I took her hand in mine. 'I'm sorry.'

'We're past that.'

'About not making more of an effort, I mean – to integrate, study, commit to our life here. I think part of me couldn't quite believe it was real.'

'I think quite a few Italians have that problem, too.' She sat up and reached for a glass of water. 'We dress up the ugliness of the world to somehow distance ourselves from it, but it's the same old bricks and mortar: like Alfonso's family betrayed him to get hold of his fortune. And it turns out the builders of Nuovo Bentivoglio "recycled" the old masonry from the factory to build their new development, and in their effort to cut costs, managed to poison the residents.'

'How do you know this?'

'From the horse's mouth – Molino, the builder, as much as admitted it. He asked me to meet him for a coffee and spilled the beans, or some of them at least. I think he's pretty desperate to cover his arse, cut some kind of deal, before the official survey results come through. I'm not sure.'

'He looked pretty uncomfortable at the meeting. Now we know why.'

'But I'm proud of you.' She lay back down and kissed me on the nose.

'How so?'

'You're changing – you don't even see it.'

'Changing? How?'

'For a start – your Italian is *much* better.'

'It doesn't feel like it.'

'Even the Comandante remarked on it.'

'Praise indeed.'

'He likes you, you know.'

'Now I know you're having me on.'

'When you get to know him better, you'll understand.'

I wasn't convinced, but reached out to brush her cheek, with the wrong hand. I winced.

'How's it feeling?'

'Still hurts,' I said.

'Don't worry, my love. It'll get better in time. Time heels everything.'

'No shortage of that, at least,' I murmured, before finally falling asleep.

XXXI

'That's outrageous,' says Nancy Bonelli. She turns to Marta. 'I will sue her.'

'But what do you think is more likely, signora,' I wonder out loud, 'that the Contessa di Castiglione engaged us to follow you because she thought you might be involved with someone, or because she already knew who that someone was and instead was seeking to discover his whereabouts?'

'Most certainly the latter,' says Alfonso. 'That's precisely the sort of trick she might play. But do you think my cousin knew that we were acquainted, Daniel?'

I thought hard. 'I don't see how, but . . . *Michele*. Michele Manfredi – we sat at his table, remember? If he was in cahoots with her . . .' I let out a long sigh. 'She gave me all this flimflam about being ignorant about freemasonry, when her father had been one. When I told her about Nancy being a member, she acted shocked.'

'If she did know you were familiar with the masons,' says Dolores, 'she knew you would pick up on the clues, which would lead you to the murder scenes and incriminate this lot – and Alfonso.'

'But still – would she really go as far as murder?'

'If she was worried he might take his money back.'

'If I was to pop up again,' Alfonso says. 'Although admittedly, I might have a struggle to prove my sanity.'

'Even more so if you have a string of grisly murders to your name.' Something twists in my stomach. I look at Otto. 'The bike. How long have you had it?'

He shrugged. 'Not long. Honest, if it's really such a big deal—'

'Where did you get it?'

'It was just there. Against the railings of our squat in Bolognina. I thought – well, someone obviously doesn't want it, so I brought it inside.'

'And you'd never seen it before then? No one had?' He shook his head. 'No one,' I repeat. 'It just appeared.'

'Like I said.'

The whop-whop of a helicopter. It is not an uncommon sound during the summer – the police or fire service swooping low above the old city to check for fires or, perhaps more likely, a bit of fun.

The noise usually crescendos before retreating in the direction of the hills. Only this time it builds and builds.

Branches bend, foliage swirls. Alfonso's hat flies into the fountain where the spray arches away from the descending rota blades.

Dust in our mouths, eyes, but I spot Alfonso and the lads

on the move. They're making towards the house, while across the lawn black-clad figures begin to clamber over the wall.

Dolores in my ear: 'What shall we do?'

I shake my head. 'Nothing. There's nothing we can do.'

Nancy's hands are holding down her dress while Marta looks angrily up at the helicopter. Lines drop and more black-clad figures abseil into the garden.

The helicopter begins to ascend. I can hear Marta shouting: 'Disgrace! Fucking disgrace!'

A stormtrooper, only his upraised visor indicating he is human, bursts through the bushes. He raises his carbine. We raise our hands.

Rita Miranda is wearing a tight-fitting cotton khaki boiler-suit secured with a thick belt which is definitely not combat issue. Neither, I suspect, are her tan, high-heeled, Gucci sandals or those squared blue-glass Dior sunglasses. She sets her camouflage-pattern Dolce & Gabbana Tote Bag on to the table with a clunk as the helicopter moves away.

'You can lower your hands,' she says.

'What the hell do you think you're doing?' yells Marta Finzi. 'This is private property. Do you have a warrant?'

'Signora,' the *commissario* says tartly. 'You think I would be able to order a full-scale *action* without one? Have you any idea of the bureaucracy involved in something like this?'

'Then what the hell do you think you're doing?'

'Well, I expect to arrest a group of masonic terrorists who have been murdering their way across Bologna.' She looked vaguely in the direction of the house as the cops began to converge.

'What are you talking about? What nonsense!'

'You deny you are involved with them, then?'

'I have no idea what you are talking about!'

'And you, signora Bonelli, do you deny you have been assisting Alfonso Lambertini in his murderous designs? As I said, you can lower your arms now, signora.'

Nancy Bonelli does as she is told but otherwise appears struck dumb.

'This is a very serious business, signora.' Rita Miranda permits herself a smirk. 'You may not be invited to any more openings.'

Marta Finzi rests a protective hand on Nancy's shoulder. 'This is all to intimidate us. Don't say a word.' Signora Bonelli does not look as if she is about to.

'I wonder what you will look like in a prison smock,' continues the *commissario*. 'Of course, it is better for when you are cleaning the toilets.' Now Nancy lets out a little sob.

'You won't see a moment inside,' Marta assures her. 'I promise.'

'Oh yes,' chuckles the *commissario*, 'take the word of a communist, with no little experience of terrorism herself. See where that gets you.'

'What are you actually doing here?' I ask. 'I mean – how did you find us?'

The *commissario* shrugs. 'Intelligence.'

'The Contessa di Castiglione? Things aren't as they seem – this is a set-up.'

She gives me a pitying look. 'Didn't I warn you about getting sand in your eyes? People are being butchered masonic-style across Bologna at the same time as a mad

Grand Wizard who went on the run re-emerges, out for revenge, some might suggest. He's been lying low thanks first to a masonic network – represented by these fine ladies – and latterly the usual suspects who, unfortunately for him, have been spellbound by his bullshit and given to leaving clues all over the shop. From where I'm looking, it's a great deal – two for one.'

'That's not how it is,' I say. 'The Contessa is behind the murders – precisely to stop Alfonso reclaiming his fortune.'

'Sounds like a tall order to me,' says the *commissario*, 'if that's the defence case. Still, let them persuade the judges.' She smiles. 'Ah, here they come.'

A pair of cops emerge from the front door of the *palazzo*, carrying a figure between them like an insect in the mandibles of a beetle. As they come closer, I can see Quinto suspended between them, his legs dangling in the air.

'The others?' she asks.

One of the cops shakes his head. 'We found this one at the bottom of the cellar steps. He must have slipped and hurt his ankle. The others, we couldn't find a trace – we believe they got away into the underground canal system.'

The *commissario* puckers her lips and, as if realising they are missing something, pulls out her cigarettes. 'You know about this, I presume, signora? Access to the canals.'

Marta shrugs. 'I'm saying nothing more to you without the presence of a lawyer.'

'And you will need one, believe me.' She glares through the cigarette smoke at Quinto. 'Take him away.' She picks up her bag. 'In the meantime, we will see quite how deep into this you really are.'

She sets off toward the house.

It turns out, however, that although the police manage to discover the room where Alfonso was staying and bag up everything from aged volumes on esoterica to his toothbrush, and locate the concealed door through which the trio apparently escaped, the *commissario*'s warrant, presumably secured in a rush, does not extend to the arrest of either Nancy Bonelli or Marta Finzi, although, before she leaves, she instructs them to appear at the Questura the following morning, unless they require a court order to do so.

We see the back of the final cop and Nancy Bonelli bursts into tears. Marta tries to comfort her, but it's no good: 'What have you got me into?' she moans. 'You said he just needed the money for expenses. No one said anything about involving these,' she spat the word, 'delinquents who are wrecking people's homes. Clearly, the *commissario* is right – Alfonso *is* barking mad. Who knows what he's been getting up to. Anything is possible!'

'I can assure you,' Marta says dryly. 'Alfonso is perfectly sane.'

'And you knew about him working with these people to do all this damage?'

'I . . . had my suspicions,' she admits.

Nancy's face turns into a sneer. 'You were in cahoots! I genuinely thought you had left Karl Marx behind – I argued strongly on your behalf with the sisterhood. You let me down!'

'That's not true, Nancy,' she says. 'I still feel the same way – as does Alfonso, and his masonic credentials are beyond dispute.'

'To smash up Airbnbs? To bomb stores? I think his sanity – and yours – are definitely in question. And what was it the *commissario* meant by your former involvement in terrorism? You never mentioned that.'

Marta glances at me. 'Because I never was,' she says. 'It was just to do with a boy I knew, back in the eighties, who got in with the wrong crowd. I never had anything to do with it,' she presses her hand to her chest. 'I promise you.'

'What a mess! What will Tancredi say?'

'I'm sure your husband will understand.'

'You know my husband, do you? This could mean the end of my marriage!'

'I'm sure it won't come to that.'

Signora Bonelli gets to her feet. 'I've had enough of your assurances, Marta. I will report, as requested, to the Questura first thing tomorrow morning, and tell the *commissario* everything. Every little thing.' She crosses herself. 'And hope God will be merciful.'

'That will be a first,' I hear Dolores mutter behind me.

'And you will do well to do the same.' She points a trembling finger at Marta. 'If you really are as innocent as you make out.' She walks away. '*Dio mio*,' we hear her exclaim beyond the bushes. 'What a scandal!'

'She's got a point,' I say, as we accompany Marta Finzi back to the *palazzo*.

'And what point would that be, precisely?'

'That you're in trouble. You're up to your neck in it.'

'What tangled webs we weave, huh? I'm not especially concerned, Daniel. You can look at this story from any angle.

From mine it will be that Alfonso came to stay, and I was happy to accommodate him. I had no idea of what he was involved in, or who those young men were. That's it.'

'And their escape through the cellar?'

'So? He found it when he was snooping about. In fact, that was how he came and went without my knowledge.'

'And what if Nancy Bonelli tells the whole story as she threatens, implicating you – after all, you both apparently knew all about his travels.'

'Nancy can say what she likes, if she's foolish enough to do so, which I doubt her husband will permit, incidentally. I will just say she's playing the police game which is constructed upon fantasy. It's all just a story – one story after another. Where's the proof?'

'How about the bodies?'

We are inside the hallway now. The police have done their usual job – throwing the contents out of the kitchen cabinets on to the floor, now a mess of pots and pans, packets and cans. A torn-open carton of muesli has been shaken over the lot to make their point – that you are on the wrong end of the law, and no longer worthy of respect. Dolores expels a string of expletives and crouches down to extract an expensive-looking wok.

'I prefer your version,' says Marta, gazing upon the chaos, unmoved. 'That the Contessa was behind it.' I follow her into the large, open-plan living room with its huge sofa (cushions detached and thrown around) and suspended, globular fireplace.

'You wouldn't happen to have any evidence of her involvement?'

She gazes out of the picture window toward the trees. 'I haven't bothered to clear Carlo's office yet,' she says without turning around. 'Second floor.'

The first thing I do is open the widows. It's not much cooler outside than in, but at least it feels a little less like a pressure-cooker. The cops have already visited, but not done a great deal of damage. It is a sterile, unloved place – shelves of unopened hardbacks on law. Certificates of graduation. A large, framed photo of Berlinguer, the famous communist leader. A full-size election poster featuring a youthful Carlo Manzi, presumably marking his first mayoral win. It wouldn't have been so much an election, of course, as coronation – to stand for the Partito Democratico in these parts is like running as Tory MP for Chelsea.

The row of filing cabinets is locked, the venerable oak desk looking out over the garden is largely clear, except for a silver framed black-and-white of Carlo in his doctoral robes, and another of him, his new girlfriend – 'the bitch' – and their ten-year-old boy sat on his lap. He wasn't being subtle. A modern pine desk facing the wall has a PC monitor attached to a tower below, both gathering dust. The rest of the space beneath the desk is filled with cardboard boxes that seem to contain papers taken from his senate office.

But I have one thing the cops lacked – a key. I go back to the filing cabinets and unlock the first. I pull out the top drawer. It seems full of political stuff – old reports, flyers, that kind of thing. I close it and try the one below – more of the same.

Those three cabinets turn out to be full of party material

except for the final, bottom drawer, which is only half full and appears to cover Manzi's senatorial career. I try to pull it out the whole way but it gets stuck. I push the files back and reach in, thinking that some paper has become stuck in the mechanism, but instead take hold of a metal spigot. I crouch down and peer inside. It is a large, black tap-shaped handle. I turn it clockwise, then anti-clockwise.

A metal, yawning sound.

A bang.

The entire cabinet jolts an inch towards me.

I get up and peer behind. Cool, stale air. I brace myself to pull the cabinets further from the wall, but when I try, they shift forward surprisingly easy – I realise they are on rollers.

A low opening. I have to duck down to get inside, fumble for a light switch. Finally, I turn on my phone light, pick out a desk lamp.

I switch it on.

It is more walk-in wardrobe than room, one side devoted entirely to shelves stuffed from floor to ceiling with brown and green folders ragged with old papers. On the other is a battered desk with an old-style computer bordered by a pair of filing cabinets.

The upper part of the cream, cracked wall abutting the desk is covered with Carlo Manzi's greatest hits – a framed newspaper front page of that first mayoral victory, photos of his graduation, his doctoral *viva voce*; black-and-white photos of him leading student protests behind a communist banner, looking serious as he debates on television, cigarette in hand as he pontificates at a 'section' meeting surrounded by young acolytes.

Beneath this march of triumph, his trophies. Perhaps twenty black-and-white and colour snapshots, all hung in the same cheap black tubular plastic frames – naked young women. Some look relaxed, cheerful, almost joyous as they pose for him – perhaps they believe what he tells them, perhaps they are simply drunk or high – others more reserved with severe, studious looks on their faces, because these are almost certainly his students. A few cover their breasts with an arm, others both nipples and private parts. Yet all of them, even the supposedly cheery ones, look into the camera with a flicker of apprehension as if at that moment, deep down, they wonder if anything he says is true, if one day they will be hung on a wall like this.

I lean closer.

That beautiful young blonde, her eyes accusing even though she is too proud to show her shame, to cover her pink nipples and fair triangle.

I press my palms to the desk.

It is definitely Cristina.

A sound escapes from somewhere deep inside.

Not Cristina.

But – why *not* Cristina?

She was politically active, which is how she had come to head up *Bologna dei Popoli*, a role that had once been in the gift of the Partito Comunista, which became the Partito Democratico della Sinistra, which became the Partito Democratico, and the NGO had been nominally independent, but . . .

I spin around, pull out a file at random. A bunch of planning applications to restructure various properties by Omega

Holdings SpA. Another – more planning applications, this time to build an industrial unit on a brownfield site.

I move along – more Omega business. Accounts, properties. Real estate agencies.

But I already know all this.

I turn to the filing cabinets.

Better – the one on the left, fittingly, covers Manzi's early career and is full of flyers for marches, membership lists, and – more pertinently – a letter signed and witnessed stating that he was an informant for the security services while he had been busy stirring up trouble. His get-out-of-gaol card – after all these years, he had kept it safe.

Now a passport, packed with stamps – France, Germany, Bulgaria, the Czech Republic – under another name, Carlo Buonafede.

And in the right cabinet, the true fruits of that labour. After all, Manzi was not the type to give something for nothing. In the top drawer, receipts for payments made by the Carabinieri along with a blue, hardback accountancy book scribbled in his fastidious hand across grey columns tracking how he reinvested in various enterprises, including, I note, a notorious right-wing publisher.

In the middle drawer we can see he is becoming more serious. Certificates of incorporation of companies with the blandest of names, the sole director, one signor Buonafede. Another book of payments, only this with many more columns – larger sums, both from his own (Buonafede) bank account and (via that) from other sources simply labelled with the Greek alphabet, into other businesses.

This is what true corruption looks like – a shadow world

of code, of shell companies funnelling money through bank accounts into legitimate (or seemingly legitimate) enterprises. Who knows whether these sums come from supposedly straight sources, are siphoned-off public or political funds, or even from organised crime, which is precisely the point: money is money is money, indivisible once absorbed into investments, and like Manzi's death itself, does anyone care enough to investigate?

Here. Here it is – Oslo Homes received funds from seven sources, including as far as I can tell, €1,173,000 from one Buonafede, as director of Italia Developments.

Yet Manzi had not hesitated in throwing Molino to the wolves.

I look again at Cristina's photo.

Lucia had been investigating Oslo, had pressed hard for an enquiry. I hadn't sensed any resistance from Cristina, in fact – enthusiasm. She had seemed as devoted to the cause as Lucia and met with Molino himself.

'But does that mean anything?' I ask. I look hard into Cristina's eyes. 'Does that mean anything at all?'

I lean further forward, whisper: 'What did you do?'

Marta Finzi is busy putting the *soggiorno* back in place when I come down the stairs. 'Did you find what you were looking for?'

'Perhaps more than I wanted.'

'Ah,' she says, beating a cushion. 'Isn't that always the way?'

'It was you, wasn't it?'

'Me?'

'Who did it.'

'What?'

'Pushed Carlo out of the window.'

She bends to pick some magazines off the floor. Sets them down on the coffee table, but then takes the top one, flicks through it.

She finds a photo of a rustic Mediterranean-style kitchen and holds it up to me.

'What do you think?'

'Very nice.'

'Not for here – but I'm thinking of restructuring the place in Sardinia.'

'That's in your name then?'

'It was my great-grandmother's. Lovely location, the sea is just over the hill.'

'Sounds idyllic.'

She sighs. 'It is. At least I have a little spare cash to my name now – divorce was always going to be expensive.'

'You knew all about his secret office.'

She looks at me pityingly.

'You certainly took your time,' I say. 'Getting rid of him, I mean.'

She tosses the magazine down. 'You act as if it was planned! We were smoking, he went to open the window. I wasn't really thinking, or if I did, I thought "just one little push" and,' her eyebrows arched, 'whoops, he was gone.'

'And no one noticed you?'

'Oh, most people work from home these days. I took the stairs down and left via the emergency exit. No one saw a thing. To be honest, I don't think they even bothered to look into it. Accident? Suicide? It could have been anything. And, as I told the police, I had no reason to believe anyone was out to get him.'

'Which is why you so easily bought my theory,' I say, 'that the Contessa is behind the murders. It's not really about the money, is it – the Contessa di Castiglione thinks Alfonso Lambertini killed your husband, and that she will be next.'

'Give her some credit, Daniel – I believe the old crow is genuinely afraid for her life.'

'And prepared to have others killed to protect it. But how? Who is she using?'

'That,' she says, 'I'm afraid I can't help you with. Carlo might have been able to but—' She shrugs.

XXXII

Without a doubt Italy always represented a form of escape for me, not just from the threats, real or imagined, conjured by Inspector Bull, but from reality itself. Home, wherever it is, can always seem just a little too real. But I didn't realise, I think as I drift beneath the porticoes in the noon heat after leaving Marta Finzi's home, that instead of escaping from reality to this fantastic city, this city of phantoms, I was rushing toward it – hard fate awaited me in the soupy shade of a place I had never once thought of until I turned up at that London café, chosen at random from the dozen in the chain, and met Lucia. How romantic that would sound if it had not culminated in her death; a grief that stalks me like my shadow.

Ginevra, Contessa di Castiglione, has played me like a *burattino*, a marionette, very much deprived of agency. But isn't that another characteristic of true conspiracy – to have others do your bidding without their knowledge? And isn't that also precisely the intention of the masons, at least according to the interpretation of Alfonso and Marta? To manipulate events behind the scenes, albeit for the common good (although I'm not sure how 'good' one could say Marta Finzi actually is)? Carlo Manzi, meanwhile, might not have been a mason, but he was a consummate politician who could have taught them a thing or two – it seems that even Cristina was playing a part.

When I finally arrive at *La Residenza* I notice a letter from the comune in the box, requesting my presence to confirm my Italian citizenship, *although it will not be official until twenty-four hours after the signing ceremony*, I am informed.

'Bad news?' asks Claudio, slouched on a recliner in only his underpants (well, it is just us men).

'Why do you ask?'

'The look on your face.'

'They're going to make me Italian,' I say.

'It's not a mistake?'

'After all this time, it could be,' I say. 'Have you seen the Comandante?'

'He went out. Here,' he pats the lounger beside him, 'pull up a pew, fellow citizen.'

I frown. 'I'm working.'

'You don't sound convinced.'

'I'm not sure I am,' I admit.

'Do you even know what day it is?'

'A Wednesday?'

'August fifteenth. Ferragosto, a public holiday. As an Italian, you should know that.' He pats the lounger again, and I give in.

'Shouldn't you be heading to the beach?'

'You're kidding. Today? It would be three hours there, three hours back on the Autostrada. Here,' he gets up, his big, hairy belly wobbling. 'Stay there. Chill out. I'll get a beer, we'll have a barbie.'

'I'm not sure—' But he is waving away my objections over his shoulder, and you know what? He may have a point.

I take off my shoes. Recline in the shade of the elm. Claudio returns with a bottle of Menabrea.

'Saluti.'

'Saluti.'

'So,' he says, 'tell me – what's been going on since we caught that chap bombing the estate agents?'

I tell him.

'Hold that thought!' He goes for a pee and returns with an icebox full of beer. 'You were saying?'

I continue up to the point where I discover Carlo Manzi's secret office. Claudio variously nods, swears and grins at the tangled web that has been woven. He finishes his beer and sighs.

'And you're sure you want to be Italian?'

'What choice do I have?' He slaps my leg and gets back up.

'I'm hungry.' He pads across the grass to the garage. I open another bottle of beer and strip off my own shirt and trousers, although I am comforted that my boxer shorts appear more like swimming trunks than his red briefs which are, frankly, largely obscured by his girth.

'That's the spirit,' he says, returning with the barbecue and a sack of coal. Vasco Rossi's *Vita Spericolata* begins to boom out of the open window. 'The meat is in the fridge.'

I go inside and grab it. When I return, smoke is already rising as Claudio prods the coal with one hand and studies my mobile phone with the other.

'What's your passcode?'

'Why do you want to know?'

'Now don't be like that. Hold on. What was Lucia's birthday?' I tell him.

'There we go.'

'What are you doing?'

'I was just thinking,' he says, swiping through the apps, 'it seemed pretty odd, the way they were following you. You haven't downloaded any suspect software, have you?'

'You mean links? Apps?' He nods. 'Not as far as I know.'

'I can't see anything but software, that's more Jaco than me, and he's . . . Well, god knows where he is. What do you think of his Celeste, by the way? *Mamma mia*, a bit of a ballbreaker that one, do you think Jaco knows what he's got himself into?'

'I suspect it's too late now,' I say. 'Do you think they've hacked my phone? But how would that be possible?'

'Anything's possible these days, Dan. Anyway, I can't see a problem, but I'll tell you what I'll do: if it's okay with you, I can hook it up to a programme that will grab the raw data, and I'll bung it over to Jaco, wherever he might be.'

'It's okay with me.'

'*Bene.* Keep an eye on this then.' He heads to the house while I turn the burgers.

It is dark when I wake up, which does not exactly come as a surprise – the afternoon stretched into a Claudio-led deep dive into the back-catalogue of the 'Rocker from Zocca' and other lesser-known Italian icons as we exhausted the beer and moved on to wine, ordering pizzas at some point, and more beer.

Claudio is turned to his side, snoring. I tip on to the grass amid the beer bottles and paper plates and have made it half-way to the stairs before I realise I don't have my keys.

I fumble through my discarded clothes to dig out the keys. I drop the trousers on to the grass and make my way back, absently scratching at the mosquito bites. I grasp hold of the rail to pull myself up, stone steps still warm beneath my bare feet.

I slot the key surprisingly smoothly into the lock. The apartment is fuggy with heat – this time, I apparently remembered to turn the air-conditioner off before leaving – and I'm about to open the windows when I remember the mozzies, so switch the air-con on. I open the fridge and pull out some cold filtered tap water, pouring myself a pint glass and carrying it through to the bathroom, where I turn on the shower.

I down almost the entire pint of water before stepping under the cold tap – predictably lukewarm – and remain there, insect bites beginning to smart.

I finally step out of the shower, and after drying off, try and reach most of the bites with ZanzAway balm before returning to the fridge and pouring myself another pint of water. I head to the bedroom. It is three am.

I lie there, waiting for sleep. But of course, the waiting room is full of unprocessed thoughts: the death of Carlo Manzi, the murderous designs of the Contessa. My own bit part – as puppet. But what seems like the deepest betrayal of all: Cristina. If betrayal it was, or am I just seeing conspiracies everywhere? Have I fallen victim to *behind-ology* myself? I begin to appreciate why Italians are so fascinated with the science – so many of their hypotheses turn out to be true.

I silently reply to Claudio – it seems a suitable time to become a citizen.

I must have fallen asleep, because I certainly wake up and it is light. It could be any time, but the clock informs me it is 05:47, so I probably only had an hour, give or take the time I was passed out.

I wonder what time it is in Finland. I pick up my phone and check – it would be coming on for five in the morning, although probably just as light. I sit up. I don't have the hangover I anticipated, although perhaps it hasn't arrived yet. But I didn't escape entirely unscathed – I am covered in bites.

I robotically swing my legs off the bed and go to the bathroom, where I take another shower and slap on more ZanzAway. I slip on some shorts and a T-Shirt and head down to the courtyard, which Claudio has also vacated, the pair of us leaving enough trash around the recliners for a small party. I open the garage with the intention of getting some plastic bags to begin the tidy up, but instead press the car fob. The Alfa unlocks, I get in. I look in the mirror. Am I really going to do this?

Apparently, I am.

I back the car out, swing it around. Drive past the mess and through the opening gates.

Rocco and Cristina have a lovely villa up one of the hills off

Via Saragozza, outside the walls. This was where the well-to-do, but not the very rich, who had country estates and could maintain their *palazzi* in the centre, relocated in the late nineteeth century, and like most Italians who know they are on to a good thing, the family kept hold of it. These ample walled grounds, also include a sizeable swimming pool that the girls take full advantage of during spring, summer and autumn.

I have parked the car in a space just outside the decorative iron gates, in front of a pair of recycling bins. I'm not sure what my intention is, exactly, but what puppet does?

I open the car door. Even the air is better here – fresher, pungent with garden herbs and perennials; pomegranate, fig and olive trees.

I place a bare foot on the tarmac, then another. I cross the road and begin to climb that gate. Its swirling ironwork is, by design, fiendishly difficult to scale, but I make some progress before they automatically begin to part.

Coming down the path, Rocco, baseball bat in hand.

He lowers it.

'Dan?'

I drop on to the gravel and fall on to my backside. 'Is everything all right?' He helps me to my feet,

'What are you doing here?' I ask. 'I thought you were in Finland.'

'We were – we are. We're literally leaving now.'

I look up the driveway. Cristina and Stefania are stood by their huge silver Mercedes SUV. 'What are *you* doing here?' asks Rocco. 'Dan – you're not even wearing shoes. Are you okay?'

'I'm okay,' I brush the gravel off my elbows and knees.

'You're covered in bites. Have you been drinking?'

'I have,' I admit, beginning to make my way towards the two women. 'I may even still be a little drunk.'

'What's this about?'

I stare at Cristina, stood behind the open passenger side-door as if it might protect her from gunfire.

'Uncle Dan,' says Stefania, already in her hoody and big boots ready for the north. 'Is everything all right? Has something happened to Rose?'

'Rose is fine.' I try to smile, although I sense it comes out wrong – Steffie doesn't appear reassured. 'Maybe you should go inside, darling.'

She frowns. 'Why? What's going on?'

I look back at Cristina. 'He's right,' she says. 'This is private.'

'Really?' Stefania replies. 'I'm not a kid you know.'

'Go,' I hear Rocco say behind me. Stefania looks at the three of us and shrugs. *Che palle*, she mutters and heads off. 'Our flight's due in three hours and we've got to check in,' she adds, before slamming the door.

'What is this, Dan?' Rocco asks softly. He is still, I note, holding the bat, but I don't think he means to use it.

'Do you want to tell him?' I ask Cristina.

She closes the door, but remains stood beside it, her arms hanging forlornly by her sides.

'Tell me what?' I hear Rocco say.

'I had nothing to do with it,' she says hollowly. 'I promise you.'

'Do with what?' asks Rocco.

'Nothing?'

She shakes her head. 'It's true, I knew Carlo – from when I was at university. He was my lecturer, and then,' she shrugs, 'my *mentor*, I suppose.'

'Did you fuck that son-of-a-bitch?' asks Rocco.

'I . . .' She looks down.

'Son of a bitch,' Rocco spits, and throws down the bat.

'It was him who got you the job at *Bologna dei Popoli*, right?' She nods. 'So you owed him.'

She looks up. 'I had no idea he was . . .' She struggles to find the word.

'Corrupt?'

'That's it – I believed him. I believed *in* him. We had a cause. When I was young, a girl . . .'

'You mean when you were fucking him,' says Rocco.

'He had founded the organisation. I didn't even realise I was—'

'Working for him?' I say. 'When you told him about what was happening with Oslo Homes, with the builder, Molino?'

'He said he was supporting me, he wanted to help. Our . . . affair.' She looks at Rocco. *'Amore*, it ended years before we met. It never occurred—'

'It's not as if I imagined you were a virgin,' Rocco says. 'It's just a creep like that!'

'I was young, naïve. Don't tell me you never had a story with someone you didn't regret.'

'You're saying you kept him informed about Oslo Homes,' I say. 'Not knowing that he had a stake in the project.'

'I didn't know, I swear – not at that point. I mean, I never knew – *for sure*. But . . .' She holds her arms out beseechingly towards me. 'Daniel, I swear to you I didn't realise. I didn't realise when I told Carlo that Molino wanted to come clean it would in any way implicate him. I didn't know.' Her voice breaks. 'When I told him about the meeting between Lucia . . .' She swallows.

'Hold on,' I say. 'What meeting?'

She sinks to her haunches, covering her face with her hands.

'That day – that's who she was meeting. Molino. He said he had some more information . . . I couldn't imagine that anything would happen. I didn't realise – I honestly didn't realise. It wasn't until Molino, too . . .'

'That you suspected Manzi?'

'I still couldn't quite believe it. Everyone was talking about Lucia's death as an accident – they had that woman who had confessed – even the Comandante. Even the Comandante, Daniel, seemed to believe . . . Only *I* knew something nobody else did – that he knew, that Carlo had known – and something didn't sit well with me. I kept telling myself it was nothing but a tragic coincidence, but I think deep down I began to realise . . .'

'That you had been used.'

'I was afraid of that, yes.'

'Another puppet,' I mutter. 'And you didn't think of going to the police?'

'What could I say? That I had told Carlo Manzi and these people had died? One an accident, the other a suicide? They would say – so what? And in the meantime, he would find out, and he was the mayor, you know.'

'You could have told the Comandante, me.'

'I could have, but what would it have achieved? *Lucia was dead*. It was an accident, everyone said so – I had no *proof*. All it would do was open a wound when what we were doing, what everyone was doing, was trying to heal.'

I can see Stefania looking through the window. How she's grown, I think, a young woman now.

The cicadas start up – the morning call.

'Some of us never healed,' I say, and walk away.

I lower the car window. 'Where have you been?' The Comandante is stood in a short-sleeved shirt beneath the shade of the tree. The loungers and trash have disappeared, and the garage door beside ours is open where Claudio has just wheeled the barbecue, a black T-Shirt advertising Ducati in yellow script now covering his belly. 'You weren't answering your telephone,' he adds testily.

'That's because he didn't have it, chief.' Claudio says. 'In fact, that must be what woke me up.'

'Went for a drive,' I say.

'At this time in the morning? I came across the pair of you when I returned home yesterday evening lying passed out like a pair of down and outs.'

'We were relaxing at home,' says Claudio.

'We have a second one for that,' he says. 'Although your wife might have appreciated the company yesterday.'

'I'm sure Alba sees enough of me as it is, Comandante,' Claudio replies jauntily. 'Here,' he hands me the phone. 'Although if I was you, I would bin it.'

'What do you mean?'

He produces his own. 'Jaco took a look at the data, says

he thinks its infected by Pegasus, the spyware – it's taken over your entire device, has access to your messages, email, phone calls, GPS, you name it. The operator basically has your phone in their pocket, if you get my meaning. May even be able to track you when it's turned off.'

'But how could that happen?'

'You click on a link or maybe through an app. It's top-drawer stuff, used by military, governments, big corporations and the like.'

'But I can't imagine I would—' I remember the photo of Nancy the Contessa sent me, and the trouble it had to download. 'Could it be contained in a photo, for example?'

'Oh yeah, sure.'

Pixies. How we'd laughed.

'I don't understand,' says the Comandante.

'That's how she did it – knew my every move.'

'Who is *she*?' asked the Comandante.

'The Contessa di Castiglione. She's been behind it all.' Giovanni does not react. 'You're not surprised?'

'You can surprise me on the way,' he says, 'after you have put some proper clothes on. In the meantime, I would like you to drive me to the home of the man who killed my daughter.'

XXIII

It is a large, modern house out Casaleccio way, set back from the main road with an ample front garden, big enough for the German Shepherd pictured on the front gate with the warning *ATTENTA IL CANE* – BEWARE OF THE DOG – to have a fine time playing catch. There is a climbing frame and a swing, and, above the double garage, a basketball hoop.

'Not bad for a security guard,' says the Comandante.

'Is that what he is? Who is he?'

'Filippo Cardinale, the son of Anna Guerra. He was living with the mother at the time of the . . . incident. My hypothesis is that the mother witnessed the crime, possibly from her window which overlooked the scene, and as the son struggled to get the car restarted and thereby make his escape, she took over. Alternatively, she may have been nearby. In any case, he got away, possibly on Lucia's bicycle, and the mother took responsibility for his actions.'

'It was deliberate, you know,' I say. 'Murder. Molino had almost certainly spilled the beans about Carlo Manzi's involvement in the scheme and he ordered the hit.'

The Comandante remains expressionless, not taking his eyes off the house.

'The description fits,' he says. 'Apparently he shaved off his beard for a year or so afterwards, but eventually let it grow back, albeit that it now appears to be grey.'

'The guy who came for us at the church had a muffler beneath his hoodie that could have concealed a beard. And grey eyebrows . . . But how do you know all this?'

'Re-examining witnesses, old contacts. I have no reason to believe signora Guerra understood that her son was involved in a criminal conspiracy. I believe she thought it was simply a case of reckless driving and he might lose his job. She did what any mother might do.'

'Well, not any mother.'

'There,' says the Comandante. One of the garage doors begins to open. A gleaming black BMW 3 Series emerges and begins to head towards us.

'Not bad for a security guard,' I say.

'Block the driveway, Daniel.' But that is easier said than done – traffic is coming from both directions, and we've parked on the other side. By the time I'm being let out, Filippo Cardinale, dressed in his black uniform, has already pulled in front of us. At least he's going our way.

'And what did you plan to do, exactly,' I ask irritably. 'He's presumably armed.' I frown. 'Are you?'

The Comandante shakes his head. 'But you're right,' he says, staring ahead. 'I should have been. I was not thinking clearly.'

I glance at him. Beneath that icy facade, I realise the man's a mess.

'He's heading to the centre,' I say. 'Dressed for work. I wonder how he explains the house, the car.'

'Inheritance, probably,' says the Comandante.

'Having seen the mother, that seems unlikely. Still, I suppose not too many questions asked.'

'Not if you don't want to hear the answer.'

We keep two or three cars behind in the slow-moving traffic. Another relentlessly sunny day, the low morning light bouncing off the chrome and forcing down visors. We put on our sunglasses.

Giovanni lowers the window. A hit of cool air and exhaust fumes. I might have asked him to put it back up and turned on the air-con, but I get it – we are tracking prey and there's something about being connected to the world around you.

The Comandante explains Cardinale is based at the company headquarters in the centre, part of a 'rapid reaction squad' sent to check home alarms, so he should be making for the underground car park in Piazza Otto Agosto. Only as we turn off the Viale down Via San Felice, he pulls up in a space near Alfonso's former *palazzo*.

'Stop,' says the Comandante.

'Easier said than done.'

'Drop me, then.'

I hesitate, but let him out. 'Don't do anything stupid,' I caution him, but he has already gone.

It takes me a further five minutes to find a space to park the car – and then in a Disabled slot. I barrel back up the portico to find the Comandante stood outside the *palazzo*, smoking.

'Well then?'

'He went inside.' He contemplates the polished brass bells. 'He had a key.'

'The first time I came here,' I say, 'there was just the one bell. Now – six.' Five of them simply have the inscription *Appartamento*, running from one to five. Only one has a name – *Lambertini*.

'Of course,' I say, 'before she was a Castiglione, she would have been a Lambertini.' Just then, the front door opens and a tall Japanese woman emerges with a European man. They both look, and are dressed, like models.

'Excuse me,' the man says with an American accent. We step aside, but I stop the door.

I look at the Comandante. 'Shall we?'

He considers the dark entrance and nods grimly. I follow him inside.

Palazzo Lambertini has clearly been cleaned up since I last visited. A polished plaque beside the staircase indicates Apt. 1 and Lambertini, while another pointing towards the tidy inner courtyard, Apartments 2–5.

The sweeping stairway is no longer splattered with birds' mess. Cheap lanterns do not balance upon the heads of the now gently backlit statues. The Comandante declines my offer of a supportive arm as we make our way up, relying instead on the freshly painted handrail.

There is a scent of patchouli as we make our way up, and even the huge frescoes of fierce, thunderous deities have been restored to their former glory, providing a vivid impression of what *palazzo* living must once have been like, and evidently still is, for those who can afford it.

As we arrive at the top, the plaque reads *Lambertini*.

'Cardinale will recognise me from the church,' I say. 'He'll know we're on to him.'

'You hang back,' says the Comandante. 'I am calling on the Contessa to provide her with an update on our investigation, to explain that there were some unforeseen circumstances, and it appears the man she was concerned about was not, in fact, having an affair with signora Bonelli but was actually involved with a criminal gang.

'But I am an old man,' he continues. 'My bladder is not what it was, so if I decide that your services are required, I will return and let you in.'

I retreat back down the stairs, and crouch by the curve of the banister.

Where the doors once rested off their hinges, now the apartments are closed with proper *porta blindata*. The Comandante rings the brass bell, smoothing his thin hair as he waits.

He rings again.

A third time, and he keeps his finger there.

The door opens. A man's voice. Peering around the banister it is difficult to make him out, but it seems familiar.

As the Comandante begins to explain, I snake around the stairs to get a better view. The man is repeating that the Contessa is not at home, that he is her grandson, that he does not know when she will be back.

By now he has opened the door wider, relaxed merely to find this elderly gentleman caller, and by the time he hears me dash up the final steps it is too late, I have pushed Otto back through the doorway and have a hand firmly across his mouth, my other arm squeezed around his throat. As he wriggles, I squeeze tighter.

'Who was it?' A call from the next room. It sounds like Secondo.

I consider the kid, my fingers digging into his moustache, then the Comandante, who raises his eyebrows.

'Are you sure you're not armed?' I whisper. He shakes his head.

'Friends,' I call. Silence, then Secondo emerges, holding a pistol.

'Let him go.' I glance at the Comandante. *'Let him go.'* I do as he says. 'You brought the cops with you this time, too?'

I shake my head.

'How do we know?'

'Because the lady here hasn't got access to my telephone.' Secondo snorts.

'She's a clever one, that's for sure.' He considers us a little longer, then stuffs the gun down the back of his jeans.

We follow him into the ballroom, only now it has been restored to its former glory, velvet upholstered seats lining the walls, the mirrors, although still tainted with age, gleaming. The stucco has been restored and a trio of chandeliers blaze.

The shutters are closed, but it is air-con cool. A tripod holding a telephone is turned to face the pair sat in two of those seats placed in the centre of the room: Filippo Cardinale, his wrists and ankles secured by plastic cuffs, and the Contessa, in a gold silk dressing gown and raffia sandals, with her hair in a snake-green turban. She appears painfully thin like this, and white as snow.

'Not in the Dolomites?' I ask. She does not deign to respond. She only has eyes – of sheer loathing – for the man sat across from her.

Alfonso Lambertini, in a black cloak, peels his hood back and smiles.

'For all our talk of freemasonry, old friend, you never saw me in my finery. Only Michele – well, I think it must have been Michele raiding my fridge, Ginny here hasn't said. But I'm glad you could make it, although I promise, I would have in any case sent you a copy of our little film.'

I look at Cardinale, the killer of my wife. He glances back at me with disinterest.

'He's mad, you know.' It's the Contessa. She nods at Alfonso. 'Look at him, mad as a fruit bat.'

'But harmless,' I say. 'Well, mostly. You, on the other hand . . .'

'Harmless? Do you know what he's planning to do when he has our "confessions"? He's going to blow this place up! Blow it to smithereens, and us in it.'

I look at Alfonso.

'Not madness,' he says calmly. 'Judgement. Do you know what Faustian bargain Michele and the others struck when I was out of the way? They sold off the *palazzo* on condition that they could retain the temple. They sold out *one of their own* – their Worshipful Master, no less – for pecuniary advantage. Oh yes, they pocketed a pretty sum, don't you doubt it. Money, you see, corrupts everything it touches.'

'You and that communist make a perfect couple,' says the Contessa. 'No wonder you've made such mischief with this rabble.'

'Then you simply picked up where Carlo Manzi left off,' I say. 'Using his man for your own ends. And you,' I turn to Cardinale, 'what did you get out of it?'

He looks dully at me. That, of course, is the worst thing – the motiveless killer, the killer who is prepared to destroy not one life but many simply for a pay cheque. No remorse, guilt, shame. I stare into the abyss that is Filippo Cardinale, and the abyss stares back.

I turn to face the mirrors. My hands open and close. Open and close. Ready to topple him off that chair, press him to the ground, close my fingers around his throat until it's done. I picture the life splutter, spit out of him. Eyes bulge then dull, feel the texture of his flesh as it becomes lifeless, like dough.

I see it all in that speckled reflection. This is where it will end, where I will erase him, as he erased you, Lucia, this killer to whom you were nothing more than another job. Let him experience your suffering, your panic as he loses everything. Let him reach out in depthless sorrow for all the pain he will leave behind. Let my hateful face be the last thing he sees.

But I am startled to find you looking into my eyes, Lucia, and to know you have always been there, that you always will be. And you would not want this.

The shot slams around the room, the old mirrors sing.

I turn to see the Comandante stood over Cardinale, who has been knocked sideways onto the floor. His limbs are still twitching, attached to that chair, even as the blood glugs out of the side of his skull.

The rest of us are still as mannequins.

Giovanni turns to Secondo. Asks gruffly: 'Can you find some scissors?'

Secondo hesitates, then digs into his pocket. 'Here,' he hands him a pocket knife. The Comandante lays the gun down and cuts off the plastic still attaching Cardinale to the chair. He wipes the gun with his handkerchief and places it in Cardinale's hand.

I help Giovanni up. He looks wryly at Alfonso and then the camera.

'Perhaps you should cut that bit out,' he says.

'I thought you said you didn't have a gun.'

'I didn't – it was his.' He nods at Secondo.

'He moves fast for an old boy,' says Secondo. 'Although actually,' he nods at Cardinale, 'it was his. Grabbed it when we jumped him.'

'And so the circle is complete,' remarks Alfonso. 'Well,' he pulls his hood back over his head. 'Almost.'

The Contessa tears her eyes away from Cardinale. 'But he's dead,' she says.

'Suicide,' I say. 'What's the problem? You're good enough at giving orders. Surely, you can't be squeamish. Now we know what to look for,' I say to Alfonso. 'I'm sure we'll find her investments in Italia Developments and other transfers to "signor Buonafede".'

'Not nearly enough,' says Alfonso. 'I want you to admit it, Ginny. That you were behind the murders, and sought to blacken my name from the beginning.'

The Contessa looks back at Cardinale, then straight into the camera. 'Fine,' she says. 'I was afraid of what you did to Carlo and thought you were coming for me. As I couldn't locate you, I thought I'd do the next best thing – set a dog on your scent and, through him,' she glances at me, 'and him,' she nods at the corpse, 'a whole pack. Satisfied?'

'Except I didn't touch Carlo Manzi,' says Alfonso. 'That was nothing to do with me.'

She barely misses a beat. 'You're a lunatic,' she says. 'Always were, always will be.' She looks at me. 'It's congenital, you know – runs in the family.'

'That,' I say, 'I can believe.'

Alfonso nods to Secondo and Otto and they move either side of the Contessa.

'What are you doing?' I ask.

They pull her to her feet and begin to drag her down the ballroom. 'No,' she pleads. 'I told you. What more do you want?'

His face swallowed by the depths of the hood, I hear Alfonso say: 'Why cousin Ginny, that is just the first part.'

I look to the Comandante, but he is stood contemplating the corpse.

'You've got your confession,' I say to Alfonso. 'She will clear your name.'

Alfonso shakes his head. 'She will do no such thing. She will claim it was under duress. I'm "a terrorist", after all.'

'Not yet you're not.'

'If you want to make real change,' he says, 'you have to make real sacrifices. Solomon's Temple became infinitely stronger after it was torn down.' He begins to follow the two men manhandling the struggling Contessa down the ballroom.

'You're going to let him?' I ask Giovanni. He looks dumbly at me. I grab his arm. 'Then for God's sake just get out of here.' I push him towards the exit.

*

By the time I catch up with them, they're almost at the library.

I try and pull Secondo away from the Contessa, but he twists quickly, throws a sharp jab which connects with my chin. I fall back against a wall. By the time I have picked myself up, they've reached the library. The bookcase is open, the temple lit up inside.

This time I don't play nice. I wallop Secondo on the back of the head.

He falls forward, letting go of the Contessa and stumbling inside.

Otto screams, clutching his cheek. The Contessa has clearly made use of those manicured nails. And she's off, whipping past me like a sprinter a quarter her age.

Secondo picks himself up, rubbing the back of his head. 'Motherfucker!' He's about to come at me, but Alfonso shouts – 'Leave him!' He's stood at the entrance, still in his cloak but I can see his face now, deep inside the hood but cast golden in the lamplight. He begins to pull the bookcase closed.

'Alfonso,' I call. He gives me a fleeting, wistful smile and is gone.

I'm trying to pull the case back open when there's a hand on my shoulder. I turn, expecting to find the Comandante, but it's Otto.

'You won't be able to open it, English. It's locked on the inside. Come on – we've gotta go.'

'Is he really going to blow the place up?'

'Oh yeah,' he says. 'Secondo's ex-army. They've stockpiled chemicals and fertiliser. It's all in there.'

'Alfonso!' I hammer on the bookcase. 'Don't do it!'

'It's too late for that,' says Otto.

I follow him through the *palazzo*, Cardinale a shape on the ballroom floor in an expanding lake of blood. As Otto begins to descend the staircase I say: 'What about everyone else?'

He looks at me bemusedly.

'*The people in the apartments* – the tourists.' His eyes widen. 'See if you can find a fire alarm.'

I press the bell across the balcony. Press and keep pressing. Finally, a paunchy middle-aged man in shorts and sandals opens up, looking irritated.

'*Ja?*'

'You must get out,' I say. 'There's going to be an explosion.'

'A what?'

'A . . . a gas leak,' I say. 'There's going to be a big explosion in the building. You have to get out now.'

He looks at me as if this might be some kind of scam. I raise my hands. 'I promise you – no joke. There's going to be an explosion – you have to get out.' I back away.

'Seriously?'

'Seriously.'

'But I've got two families here.'

'Then get them out – now.'

I've done my best. I dash down the stairs and across the courtyard. I can hear Otto having the same problem upstairs. I take the steps two at a time. Another good-looking young couple. At least this pair is British.

'It's true,' I say. 'No bullshit. Gas leak. Just get the hell out now – you can lock up, wait outside, I don't give a damn.'

Leaving them looking uncertain, I drag Otto down to the other apartment. General scepticism greets us here, too, but by the time I am standing in the courtyard shouting 'Evacuate! Evacuate!' we appear to be making some progress. The German families, parents scowling sceptically, have begun to file down the stairs. Watching from their windows, this appears to have had an effect on everyone else. Beyond the gates I hear sirens.

'Come on, you need to get on to the street.' I begin to herd them through the wicket door.

A crowd is gathered beneath the portico – guests who have already made it out, and curious passers-by. The road running between the porticoes is clear of traffic – on either side, I can see the sky blue of Polizia di Stato Alfas parked cross-ways, lights revolving.

A troop of cops jog down the portico towards us while a lone woman struts along the middle of the road in a sand-coloured trouser suit, flak jacket and Aviator sunglasses, her mobile pressed to her ear. I take the steps down on to the street to meet her.

'There's going to be an explosion.'

Commissario Rita Miranda signals for me to wait.

'Right,' she says. 'Yes, ha-ha.' She puts the phone down. 'That was your pal, Ispettore Alessandro. He's supposed to be taking over from me. He thinks it's funny, this nightmare week I'm having.'

'Alfonso's got a bomb – he claims he's going to blow the *palazzo* up. I believe him.'

'And now do you see what I was saying about terrorism?' She tilts her sunglasses down and gazes at the portico. 'That's one of them,' she screams, pointing at Otto trying to move people away from the entrance. 'Grab him!'

'He's been trying to get people out,' I say.

'Oh, very good, Daniel,' she nods. 'So glad you could be of help.' She marches towards the portico. 'Cuff him,' she calls. 'And clear the area!'

The Contessa di Castiglione is stood haughtily outside a bar on the other side of the road, her gold dressing gown wrapped around her as if she is an Egyptian deity.

'I told you he was mad,' she says. 'And here's the proof.'

'We also have proof that you were behind the murders. That you tried to frame him.'

'Do you think any of that will matter once he's blown the place to pieces? I was absolutely right to do what I did.'

I look at her aghast. 'How can you possibly say that?'

'There's a reason people like me pull the strings,' she says. 'You saved me, and you don't even know why.'

'You're wrong. I know precisely why – so you can face justice. There's your confession, and we can back it up with the facts.'

She lets out a shrill giggle. 'You're worth every penny.'

'I'm really not so naïve,' I say. 'I know how things stand. Lucia understood, too, but she still fought for what was right. True – maybe you'll get away with it, but no matter how much gold you wrap up in, you'll never disguise the stink.'

XXIV

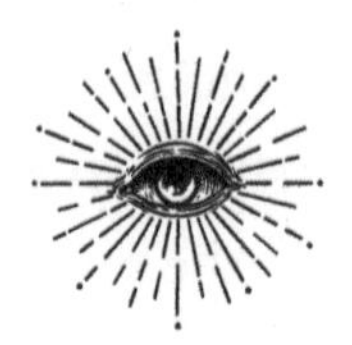

I'm walking away when I spot it – the bicycle propped up against the alley wall. I hesitate, but no one can see me, they're too busy clearing the street.

I approach it as one might a herd of deer, but it's not going to spook, and I can't see anyone about to jump on it.

It's not chained, just resting there.

I lay my hand upon the saddle, already warm from the sun.

The tunnel door that leads to the temple is slightly ajar. I'm tempted to peek inside but decide – no, I'm done with that. I climb on the Raleigh. It's set for Otto, so my feet rest either side, but it's not too low to ride.

I set off down the alley.

Arriving at Via Pratello, I turn east, steering on to the smooth section running between the cobbles and the old, wood-beamed porticoes on either side. I pass the high walls of the kids' prison plastered with flyers and posters, then turn right, across Piazza San Francesco, before cycling up Marconi to Via Nossadella.

I'm riding high on the bike, the warm air against my skin, sun upon my crown, the back of my neck, when I hear it – like a clap of thunder on this otherwise cloudless day. Windows rattle, dogs bark. The distant sound of car alarms.

But I carry on, turning in to Via Urbana, as empty as any August morning, pass the red-brick walls of the Collegio di Spagna, then the red-brick walls of the Monastero di Santa Caterina De' Vigri. I'm going the wrong way, but we cyclists don't give a damn.

I'm swerving on to little Via Paglia, then crossing Via Solferino, as pretty as a box of chocolates, before ducking back into the shade of Paglietta, where on the corner an old painting of the Madonna marks her fantastic appearance in 1738.

I come to a halt on Via Mirasole, resting my feet upon the ground. I open the gates of the Residence and ride slowly in. Dismount, lean the bicycle against the tree.

'You got it back, then?' Claudio behind me.

'I'm sorry?'

'That bike.' I nod. 'Cool,' he sniffs. 'You don't see many Raleighs. Here.' He hands me the square parcel. 'Courier delivered it.'

It doesn't seem like a courier-delivered parcel – it is flat, in brown paper secured by string, with just my name hand-written in swirling italics. I place it beneath my arm and wheel the bike to the garage. Tomorrow, I think, I will buy a chain.

I take the parcel off the car bonnet and close the garage door. I head up to the apartment where I place the package on the kitchen table, using a carving knife to cut the string and pull the paper open.

I look down at a pair of oil-painted lovers, who only have eyes for each other.

'What's that?' asks Lucia.

'Oh,' I say, 'something somebody left for me – a gift.'

'It's lovely,' she says. 'We could put it in our room, above the bed.'

'That would be nice.' I frown. 'You're all wrapped up.' She has got her big old black duffel on, and a roll neck beneath that.

'Things to do, people to see.' She looks warily outside. The residue of snow still clings to the balcony wall. 'In fact,' she checks her watch. 'I'd better be going.' She hugs me and I breathe in wool and peaches. I kiss her neck, her lips, so soft. She breaks away.

'Stay,' I say.

'I'm already late,' she smiles.

'Thank you.'

'What for?'

'Just . . . everything.'

She goes on tiptoes and kisses my nose.

I listen to her descend the gritted stairs, the scrape of the workshop door. With some difficulty I manage to open up our terrace and step cautiously on to the ice in time to watch her walk the bike along the cleared path.

'Lucia!' I call.

She turns, smiles, waves.

Lifts her bike through the wicket door, which closes behind her.

Across the ferrous rooftops, black smoke rises against the ever-blue sky.

AUTHOR'S NOTE

BOLOGNA

Eri grassa, eri dotta, eri
bella rossa: che cazzo
t'è successo?
Come ti sei ridotta!
Sono finiti la crapula,
il comunismo, la dottrina: c'è la piaga
e il formicaio impazzito.
C'è stata una strage: fra due secoli,
sarà dimenticata.

BOLOGNA

You were fat, you were learned, you were
a beautiful redhead: how the fuck
did this happen?
How you have reduced yourself!
The orgy is over,
communism, the doctrine: there's the plague
and a crazy anthill.
There was a massacre: in two centuries,
it will be forgotten.

Nicola Muschitiello

While Bologna herself could be said to be a brooding, but (mostly) silent character throughout my Daniel Leicester series, there has always been another who, while playing a significant role in the stories, has also had little to say – Daniel's late wife, Lucia. With her appearance in this sixth outing, I am pleased she has finally been granted a voice.

I have also found myself returning to a theme I touched upon when I first introduced *'La Famiglia Faidate'* and which has only grown in prominence as time has moved on.

When I began my debut, Bologna still seemed largely unknown outside Italy – it lacked the unprompted associations of Rome, Florence, Venice or even Siena – and I realised I would need to 'world build' in the manner of a fantasy or science fiction author. Familiarising readers with the smouldering 'red city' where life pulsed through the porticoes became a priority.

To encourage a sense of consistency, we also moved forward chronologically – illustrated most obviously by Rose's development from precocious thirteen-year-old to, I think we can agree, an appealing eighteen – and watched her father evolve from naïve Briton to one who may see the world through English eyes, 'but interprets it like an Italian'.

However, I have cheated on one account: I have telescoped 'real' time. The contemporary setting of my 2020 debut was actually rooted more than a decade earlier.

When we arrived at our first home 'inside the walls' in 2008, there were squatters in our street, squatters around the corner, squatter banners everywhere. In Via Paglietta, coincidentally close to *La Residenza Faidate* in nearby Mirasole, we found ourselves on the front-line of one of the final battles between the forces of 'old' Bologna and 'new', although I'm not sure either side realised that at the time: we still had a final sleep before the arrival of the iPhone, Ryanair and Airbnb.

In the notes to *A Quiet Death* I mention how I was inspired to write about Bologna after reading the wartime diaries of Norman Lewis in his *Naples '44*. Yet I had no idea my novels would not only come to describe the city I was living in, but inadvertently chronicle its transition from a place that appeared to have largely avoided the homogenising forces of the twenty-first century, to one about to be exposed to them in full.

I have marked this transformation in all my books, but especially in the food-themed *The Hunting Season*, which effectively jumps from the 2010 Bologna of *A Quiet Death* to a decade later when 'faux' aged signs have appeared above *osterias* occupying the sites of former ironmongers or grocers, and of course leads to the roof being blown off of Palazzo Lambertini in *The Bologna Vendetta*.

Yet according to Professor Maurizio Bergamaschi, director of the Centre for the Study of City and Land Problems of the Department of Sociology and Economic Law at the University of Bologna, it would be wrong to imagine this is a recent phenomenon. The professor explained to me that during the sixties and seventies, while many other Italian councils permitted the 'commercialisation' of their city centres to run its course, Bologna's Communist-controlled comune made a concerted effort to maintain a viable population together with the services it required. But this commitment began to 'run out of steam from the eighties onwards,' he said. The decade that also saw the Italian Communist Party's *'Svolta di Bolognina'* coincided with a 'loss of will' to maintain the liveability of the city centre.

This was echoed by Pier Luigi Cervellati, 'father' of modern Bologna, who as assessor between 1964 and 1980 developed the polices that preserved a liveable city. In an interview with *Il Corriere della sera* in 2023, signor Cervellati observed that 'unfortunately the historic centre is dying . . . Bologna: it has no truly shared vision of its future; it has favoured tourism, allowing homes to be turned into B&Bs; it has abdicated planning. It has thrown itself into dominant neo-liberalism.'

Still, even writing in 2024, I can recall that a decade ago the city appeared to balance 'liveability' and 'visibility' – it was still overwhelmingly a place for locals, where foreigners came to study Italian precisely because few people spoke English. Admission to most sights was free and their attendants (if there were any) were surprised enough when roused from their slumber to ask you where you were from.

Until something happened.

First turnstiles and admission fees. Then tour groups and travel bloggers. The comune had begun a concerted effort to attract tourism, something which in itself is no bad thing – Bologna, as I hope I have conveyed alongside the grit and graffiti, is one of Italy's treasures. Like many of us, I am an enthusiastic traveller and tourist and am not going to pretend my own modest efforts have not benefitted from the increase of interest. I write about Bologna precisely because I want to share my fascination with the city. I can also appreciate the comune's broader strategy – to generate not only cash but raise Bologna's profile among European cities competing fiercely for investment. While (according to 2022 figures) 70,000 might live 'inside the walls', there are 400,000 within the city boundaries and almost a million in the wider metropolitan area.

Nevertheless, the sudden uptick in visitors has not come without a cost.

While Professor Bergamaschi is undoubtedly correct to identify a drift that began in the 1980s, I think today's problems spring from the confluence of the comune's publicity campaign with the triad I mention above – affordable flights, online tourist lets, and the technology that makes everything so easy.

As a consequence, recent years have seen the city centre lose a third of its available housing stock to short-term tourist lets (as Maurizio Estivo mentions, a higher proportion than Florence), traditional markets like the Quadrilatero become crowded with eateries and tour groups, homeless students setting up tent cities in the piazzas and, recently, a report in *La Repubblica* that Bologna is among one of the most expensive places to live in Europe.

Bologna's ruling parties side-step direct action, calling upon the national government to curb short lets while rejecting moves like neighbouring Florence to ban them (which Professor Bergamaschi may correctly observe is 'closing the stable door after the horse has bolted'). They do, however, promise ten thousand new homes (outside the centre) over the next decade, but even if this turns out to be true, it seems unlikely to meet the city's requirements.

Writers have mourned the passing of Bologna since Muschitiello penned his poem in 1983 and, no doubt, before.

His 'redhead' presumably reinvents herself for every generation, but I can only speak for mine, and over the course of a theme traversing six books, we have seen the city change in real, if fictional, time – a place that evolved to accommodate university students now at threat of losing them; a city once famous for maintaining a local population now at risk of being priced out. In what seems almost like a fit of absent-mindedness, a way of life that endured for nearly a thousand years is poised to vanish within the historical blink of an eye.

At the end of most major thoroughfares in Bologna stand gate houses, often flanked by ragged brickwork marking where the imposing walls that had ringed the city since the thirteenth century were torn down in 1903. The authorities argued that it was a necessary economic measure, although few would now disagree with the great poet Carducci who lamented a short-sighted act of municipal vandalism. Even now, although they have been gone for more than a hundred years, the Bolognese still talk of being 'inside' or 'outside' the walls.

Bologna persists in its psychogeography and the stories we tell. The walls may truly be irreplaceable, but while the heart of the city remains intact, there endures the hope of preserving its character. After all, as Cervellati observes: 'History teaches us that the city is a combination of urbs (the physical structure) and civitas (the social body, the community). The former does not exist without the latter.'

I began to take an interest in freemasonry, which had always seemed to me like an eccentric hobby and handy foil for 'pulp authors', as 'Michele' might put it, when I learned about the membership of some of Italy's founding fathers. European masonry, it turned out, played a significant role in the revolutions of 1848 and went on to be persecuted by competing creeds – religious, sectarian, political – thereafter.

Many European nations lacked any real semblance of democracy or self-determination well into the nineteenth century, being either colonised or under monarchical rule, thereby excluding the burgeoning middle-class from government. So while British freemasonry largely abjured revolution, presumably because its members were already absorbed into the ruling class through (limited) suffrage, in Europe, freemasonry provided an association through which the ambitious, educated and wealthy could channel their occult efforts to overthrow the established order.

As well as meeting local freemasons, I read widely around the history and practice of masonry, drawing upon everything from Andreas Önnerfors' *Freemasonry: A Very Short Introduction* to Albert G. Mackey's exhaustive manuals on freemasonry penned in the 19th Century and recent papers by professors Anna Sergi and Alberto Vannucci of Essex and Pisa universities on the links between freemasonry and criminality. But my most influential source was Lilith Mahmud's *The Brotherhood of Freemason Sisters: Gender, Secrecy, and Fraternity in Italian Masonic Lodges*, which provided a superb insight not only into female freemasonry but Italian freemasonry in general, and is written in an accessible narrative style that transports the reader into the day-to-day practice of freemasonry and the perspective of its members. I have not come across a book that presents a more convincing portrait of modern Italian masonic practice, which should not come as a surprise as the author is a professor of anthropology at the University of California. The Comandante's observation that masonry was 'more like the *Da Vinci Code*' was taken directly from a comment by a freemason in *The Brotherhood of Freemason Sisters*. And yes, they do sometimes conceal temples behind bookcases.

I would like to thank Nicola Muschitiello for granting me permission to use his poem. It is taken from *Lo Strazio* (Poesie 1980–1986), Calamaro Edizioni, Bologna 2024.

I would also like to express my gratitude to Professor Bergamaschi for taking time to see me. Seeking out his office beneath the louring frescoes of Palazzo Hercolani felt very much like being in a Daniel Leicester novel.

I am sometimes asked – *are you Daniel Leicester?* While it may be true that 'the later Leicester' may bear me some resemblance as he becomes increasingly 'Italian' in his outlook, I have always regarded Daniel as very much a different 'person'. There are too many dissimilarities to go into here but, having said that, this is probably my most 'autobiographical' novel to date. Daniel's path to (semi) fluency via language school and as a doorman at a canteen for the poor was certainly my own, along with his early encounters with bureaucracy. Things certainly became simpler when I, like Daniel, was finally granted Italian citizenship.

A huge thank you to Beta readers Mike Bailey, Prue Crane, Bernadette Williams, and Mehmet Denis Oz for taking the time to read my draft manuscript and providing helpful suggestions.

I am tremendously grateful to both my agent Bill Goodall and editor Krystyna Green for their enthusiastic support. *La Famiglia Faidate* has come to life in their 'fortress in a city street' thanks to you.

I would also like to express my gratitude to my fellow authors in the D20 group for their support throughout the year, especially Trevor Wood, Catherine Cooper, Philippa East, Victoria Dowd, Frances Quinn, Louise Hare, Nikki Smith and Louise Fein, who were kind enough to read my previous novel, *Last Testament in Bologna*, at proof stage, and authors Ian Moore and Harriet Tyce for their continuing support.

Thank you to ever-patient Amanda Keats for steering me through the production process, along with copyeditor Colin Murray, proofreader Rebecca Lee, and of course publicist Clara Diaz for garnering those all-important reviews.

Finally, a huge thank you to my wife Lea, who ensures that my observations about Italy (as well as my spellings) are on the ball, and is my editor of first resort.

Tom Benjamin
Bologna, 2024

Available now

When the body of a radical protestor is found floating in one of Bologna's underground canals, it seems that most of the city is ready to blame the usual suspects: the police.

But when private investigator Daniel Leicester, son-in-law to the former chief of police, receives a call from the dead man's lover, he follows a trail that begins in the 1970s and leads all the way to the rotten heart of the present-day political establishment.

Beneath the beauty of the city, Bologna has a dark underside, and English detective Daniel must unravel a web of secrets, deceit and corruption – before he is caught in it himself.

Tom Benjamin's gripping debut transports you to the ancient and mysterious Italian city less travelled: Bologna.

Available now

It's truffle season and in the hills around Bologna the hunt is on for the legendary Boscuri White, worth more than its weight in gold. But when an American truffle 'supertaster' goes missing, English detective Daniel Leicester discovers not all truffles are created equal. Did the missing supertaster bite off more than he could chew?

As he goes on the hunt for Ryan Lee, Daniel discovers the secrets behind 'Food City', from the immigrant kitchen staff to the full scale of a multi-million Euro business. After a key witness is found dead at the foot of one of Bologna's famous towers, the stakes could not be higher. Daniel teams up with a glamorous TV reporter, but the deeper he goes into the disappearance of the supertaster the darker things become. Murder is once again on the menu, but this time Daniel himself stands accused. And the only way he can clear his name is by finding Ryan Lee . . .

Discover Bologna through the eyes of English detective Daniel Leicester as he walks the shadowy porticoes in search of the truth and, perhaps, even gets a little nearer to solving the mystery of Italy itself.

Available now

In the sweltering heat of a Bologna summer, a murderer plans their pièce de résistance . . .

'Only in Bologna' reads the headline in the Carlino after a professor of music is apparently murdered leaving the opera. But what looks like an open-and-shut case begins to fall apart when English detective Daniel Leicester is tasked with getting the accused man off, and a trail that begins among Bologna's close-knit classical music community leads him to suspect there may be a serial killer at large in the oldest university in the world.

And as Bologna trembles with aftershocks following a recent earthquake, the city begins to give up her secrets.

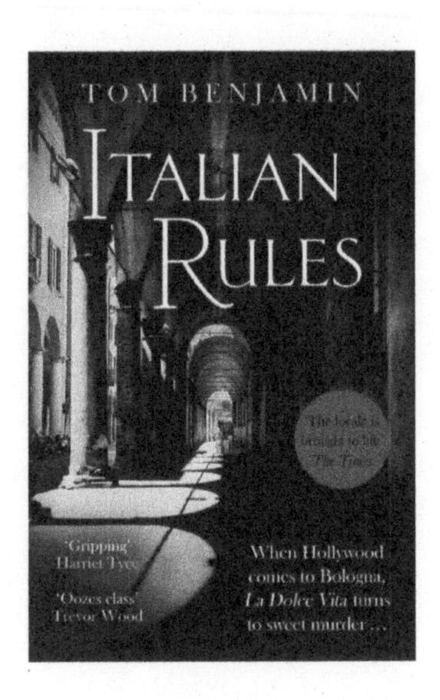

Available now

When Hollywood comes to Bologna, La Dolce Vita turns sweet murder . . .

A famous Hollywood director arrives in Bologna to remake a cult film and the city's renown cinema archive decides to mark the occasion with a screening of the original, only to discover it has disappeared. After English detective Daniel Leicester follows the trail of Love on a Razorblade to an apparent murder-suicide, he begins to suspect there may be more at stake than missing negatives – could the film contain a clue to one of the city's most enduring mysteries?

Together with a star from the forthcoming remake, Daniel moves from the glamour of Venice Lido to the depths of Bologna's secret tunnel system as a sinister network closes in and he learns some people are ready to kill for the ultimate director's cut.

Available now

Discover the world of Bologna's English detective in this critically-acclaimed series that transports you beneath the blood-red porticoes of one of Italy's most venerable and mysterious cities.

When an old man makes a bequest to investigate the mysterious death of his son, English detective Daniel Leicester follows a trail to one of Bologna's wealthiest families – makers of some of the world's most coveted supercars – and discovers that beneath the glamour of the Formula One circuit lurk sinister interests that may be prepared to kill to keep their secrets.